Inner Line

Inner Line

The Zubaan Book of Stories
by Indian Women

Edited by
Urvashi Butalia

An Imprint of Kali for Women

Inner Line: The Zubaan Books of Stories by Indian Women
Edited by Urvashi Butalia

Published (2006) by
Zubaan, an Imprint of Kali for Women
K-92, First Floor,
Hauz Khas Enclave,
New Delhi – 10016, INDIA
Email: zubaanwbooks@vsnl.net and contact@zubaanbooks.com
Website: www.zubaanbooks.com

Zubaan is an independent feminist publishing house based in New Delhi, India, with a strong academic and general list. It was set up as an imprint of the well known feminist house Kali for Women, and carries forward Kali's tradition of publishing world quality books to high editorial and production standards. "Zubaan" means tongue, voice, language, speech in Hindustani. Zubaan is a non-profit publisher, working in the areas of the humanities, social sciences, as well as in fiction, general non-fiction, and books for young adults that celebrate difference, diversity and equality, especially for and about the children of India and South Asia under its imprint - Young Zubaan.

ISBN (10)   81 89013 77 7
ISBN (13)   978 81 89013 77 7

Typeset at Sanchauli Image Composers, New Delhi – 110059
Printed at Raj Press, R-3, Inderpuri, New Delhi – 110012

Contents

෴ ෴

Acknowledgements

ৡৡ

We would like to thank the following for permission to use their stories.

1. Anjana Appachana for Incantations from *Incantations and Other Stories*, Rutgers University Press, 1992 and Penguin India, 1991.
2. Mahasweta Devi for 'The Wet-Nurse' from *Truth Tales*, Kali for Women, 1986.
3. Ambai (C.S. Lakshmi) for 'A Kitchen in the Corner of the House' from *A Purple Sea*, 1992.
4. Vandana Singh for 'Thirst'.
5. Indira Goswami for 'The Offspring' from *The Slate of Life: An Anthology of Stories by Indian Women*, Kali for Women, 1990.
6. Temsula Ao for 'The Last Song' from *These Hills Called Home*, Zubaan, 2006.
7. Manjula Padmanabhan for 'Stains' from *Hot Death, Cold Soup*, Kali for Women, 1996.
8. Shashi Deshpande and Penguin Books, India for 'The Valley in Shadow' from *Best Loved Indian Stories of the Century Volume 1*, 1999.
9. Mridula Garg for 'The Tree of the Century'.
10. Bulbul Sharma for 'Mayadevi's London Yatra' from *My Sainted Aunts*, Indus, 1992.

11. Javed Chowdhry for 'Portrait of a Childhood' by Shama Futehally from *In Other Words*, Kali for Women, 1995.
12. Anita Agnihotri for 'Life Sublime' from *Forest Interludes*, Kali for Women, 2001.
13. Nayantara Sehgal and Penguin Books, India for 'Martand' from *Best Loved Indian Stories of the Century Volume I*, 1992.
14. Githa Hariharan and Penguin Books, India for 'The Rainmaker' from *The Art of Dying*, 1993.
15. Priya Sarukkai Chabria for 'Menaka Tells Her Story'.
16. Chandrika B. for 'The Story of a Poem'.

Introduction

Long years ago when Kali for Women, India's first feminist publishing house, set out to publish a volume of short stories by Indian women writers, the task of locating authors was not easy. Existing anthologies had little to offer, most women writing in their own languages in India were not known outside the language group or area. Many saw their own writing as somehow inferior, and preferred to keep it in the background in deference to the work of their writer husbands, or other writers. Thus it was not surprising that the first two anthologies put together by Kali, *Truth Tales* and *The Slate of Life*, passed virtually unnoticed. A larger project, begun some years later and covering many different genres of writing, excavated other writers, other work and brought to public attention the wealth of writing by women that lay in obscure libraries or that had been written but not published for lack of attention and importance on the part of the publishing world.[1] Together, the work of feminist scholars and feminist publishers represented the first steps towards the remaking

---

[1] *Truth Tales: Stories by Indian Women*, Kali for Women, New Delhi, 1986; *The Slate of Life: An Anthology of Stories by Indian Women*, Kali for Women, New Delhi, 1994; *Women Writing in India From 600 BC to the Present, Volumes I and II*, Susie Tharu and K. Lalitha (eds), Oxford University Press, New Delhi, 1991.

of the canons of writing, and questioned how these canons were made, and indeed who made them.

The kinds of silences that had, for long, surrounded women and women's writing are perhaps best represented by a moving story in this volume. The protagonist of 'The Story of a Poem' by Chandrika B. is a housewife and also secretly a poet. It is this that provides the oxygen in her life. Whenever the urge to write takes her, she struggles to find time in the little moments of freedom she has between household work, between her daily tasks of sweeping and swabbing and washing and cleaning. One day, her husband and children leave the house, he to go to work and the children to go to school. She quickly finishes her morning chores and goes in for a shower. While there, the first few lines of a new poem come to her. She runs out to pen them down before they go out of her head. Standing naked and dripping by the dining table, she writes her lines. Later, involved in housework, she thinks of another few lines, rushes to where her piece of paper lies, and writes them down. Then, between this and that, other lines are added. As evening falls and the light begins to fade she writes the last few lines and just then, hears her family returning. Immediately, she picks up the paper with the by-now-complete-poem and shreds it to bits, throwing it into the bin. The author now tells the reader that if she wishes to read the whole poem, the only way to do so is to piece it together from the story!

While Chandrika's story reflects one kind of silence, there are many others, for example of language, of region, of subjects – for some subjects were considered 'permissible' for women and others not – that meant that women's voices remained unheard. Indeed, a long history of writing on a wide variety of subjects did not, for long, ensure for women the kind of space in the literary scene that their writing so richly deserves. Not only has it been difficult, sometimes almost impossible for women to get published, but even today what they write continues to be seen as marginal, the issues they write about as peripheral. Faced with the difficulty of being taken seriously, many women like Chandrika's protagonist, choose to destroy their writings, or keep them secret. Others hide their gender, assuming a male persona, and still others choose to write on the'safe' areas, those that remain within the realm of the 'private' and do not encroach on the 'public' – the one being seen as female and the other male.

The general truth that women's writing is, by and large, given a subordinate status to men's writing still holds across the world. The time-honoured division of labour ensures that women occupy the domestic space while men monopolize the public, and the hierarchies that attach to this, ensure that women's roles are generally seen as subordinate. Different histories and environments, however, contextualize these histories differently. India's ancient civilization, its rich history of women's writing on a vast variety of subjects, have come down to us through its many languages that have long and well established literary traditions, and literally hundreds of dialects. And writing is only one part of it, for as important as its many writing traditions are India's oral cultures, and its traditions of storytelling in which women play a major role. Add to this a multiplicity of cultures, peoples, lands, histories and traditions, and you have a writing environment that is rich with possibility. And yet, as many women writers have asked, how many actually have access to everything the environment offers? How many have been able to benefit from it in the same measure as men have? 'A woman's writing,' says Bengali writer Nabaneeta Dev Sen, 'is her gesture, and like all gestures, is subject to social codes.' Social codes, moral sanctions, attitudinal biases, political manoeuvring have all ensured that women have for long remained at the margins of the literary world.

As everywhere else, however, women have not taken this without protest. They have resisted, confronted and negotiated with the world of patriarchal writing. As early as

1940, the Andhra writer, Unnava Lakshmi Bai, walked out of a literary gathering where only male writers had the floor, saying, 'In a thousand years of Andhra literary history, couldn't you even find a single woman ? I cannot sit in a meeting which dishonours women thus.' In the 1930s Urdu writer Ismat Chugtai chose her own form of protest by writing what is by now a well-known story, 'Lihaaf' (The Quilt) about a relationship between two women. For this she was arrested and pilloried, but she remained steadfast and went on to become one of India's best-known writers. Or take the work of Ruth Vanita, Maya Sharma and other younger writers who have dared to speak of same sex love, rescuing many unknown and invisible writers from the past and present, questioning how canons are made and established. Or that of Mridula Garg, a Hindi writer, who was castigated by the literary establishment for writing on the taboo subject of sexuality.

More recently, a strong and dynamic women's movement and its confrontation with the many aspects of women's oppression, has helped to create a hospitable environment within which women's writings are received. Many writers have testified that they felt encouraged to know that there was at least the beginnings of a constituency of readers 'out there' who were interested in their writings. The growth of feminist presses, for whom the project of searching, excavating, presenting and disseminating women's writing, has been both a passion and a single point agenda, has been another major factor in bringing these hidden voices into the public arena. Indeed, it would not be wrong to say that the market for women's writing and women's books in India has, in many ways, been created by feminist publishers. As well, a flourishing publishing industry, growing numbers of bookshops, and the success of a few women authors in both the national and international marketplaces, have meant that publishers are now much more open to publishing women's voices, and indeed, many publishers will agree that these are the books that sell the most out of their entire lists.

In response to the interest in the marketplace, more and more women are writing and getting published. Subjects such as humour, satire, sex, earlier often taboo for women writers, are now being addressed boldly and imaginatively. While there is plenty of writing in the classical mould, a new generation of younger writers is experimenting with language, genre, structure and subject. All this makes for a vibrant writing environment in which the woman writer now occupies an important place.

The Indian literary tradition is not only rich and varied in content and tone but also multi-lingual. However, in the way that these histories unfold in countries that have been colonized, the language of the colonizers, in this case English, becomes the language of privilege and social mobility. So also in India: while writing takes place in all languages, and some languages such as Hindi and Bengali are spoken by millions of people, they still remain, in the terminology of literature, 'regional' languages, at some sort of disadvantage in terms of hierarchy while English, which is spoken by only 5 per cent of the population, remains the language of privilege. The stories in this volume come from some – not all – of India's many languages, and a relatively larger number come from English. The reality is that these latter make for an easier transition into international translations. But whether Indian languages or English, which is also now another Indian language, they represent a sensibility that is deeply gendered.

The writers who feature here are among some of India's best known women writers. India, as the cliché goes, but like all clichés, this too has some degree of truth in it, is a country of contrasts and contradictions. So the 'truth' of some of the darker stories in this volume is as authentic as the truth of the lighter ones. Each story testifies to women's many concerns, whether with a way of life, or with being caught inside the four walls of the home, or in a relationship with someone other than the husband, or being caught at the intersection of many forces within a situation of political violence and armed conflict. In one way or another the woman's body becomes a site upon which many battles take place: for control, for power, for progeny, but there is seldom a resolution in which the woman remains a mere victim, or more acted upon than acting. Whether she is in the palace of the gods, or caught in the body of snake, or speaking through the spirit of the countryside which witnessed her rape, the woman's voice is unique, singular and in each story, different. While this gives substance to the cliché that India is a country where many and varied realities exist simultaneously, it gives the lie to the cliché that all women speak with a sameness and a commonality of experience.

Incantations

Anjana Appachana

One hot summer night, when I was twelve and tear-deep in Victorian fiction, dreaming in bed beside my sister that I was Jane Eyre and Agnes wooed by Rochester and David, I felt my sister shuddering. It was the eve of her wedding, and I, with all the wisdom of my twelve years, turned to her, and putting my arm around her heaving body, assured her that there was no need for pre-wedding nerves, for wasn't Nikhil, her husband-to-be, kind and tender and handsome, and she, beautiful to boot? Turning to me then she held my hand in a painful grip and said that two days ago she had been raped by Nikhil's brother, Abhinay. As she put the back of her hand to her mouth to stifle a moan, I moved over to her bed, lay beside her and held her. But the sounds from her throat could not be controlled. Our parents would hear. I helped Sangeeta out of bed to the bathroom, pulled the flush, turned on both taps and shut the bathroom door. She sat on the pot, I on the damp floor, and after ten uncontrolled minutes, she laid her head against the wall, and, turning away from me, spoke.

Nikhil's mother had taken her shopping for sarees two days ago and Abhinay, his younger brother, decided to join

them. 'You'll make someone a good husband,' his mother
had teased, 'if you have so much patience with women
shopping.' And patient he had been. After the shopping he
had told his mother that he would drop her, then Sangeeta,
home. He dropped his mother and then asked Sangeeta if
they could stop briefly at the barsati where he lived, as he had
to pick up something. He insisted she didn't stay alone in the
car, so she went up with him. Once inside, he locked the door.

My sister, who had been staring at the wall as she spoke,
now looked at me. I try now to imagine how I looked to her
then, pyjama-clad, thin, hair in a tight plait, my face like the
photograph she once took of me, guileless, adoring. My sister
turned away from me and said, 'Then he raped me.' I put my
hands around her bare feet and held them tightly, leaning
my face against her thighs. 'I didn't fight,' she said. 'He said
he'd deny it and tell everyone I wanted it. He said no one
would believe me. And he took so long over it, so long.' She
turned to me and felt my cheek. 'Do you know what rape is?'
I made a sound of assent and felt my cheeks wet against her
nightie. Yes, I knew what rape was. I wasn't supposed to know,
I wasn't even supposed to know what sex is. Relentlessly my
friend and I had proceeded to find out, our only source being
the books we were not supposed to read. The *Reader's Digest*,
though not forbidden, gave us a vague idea, for there was
always something about the dos and dont's of marital strife,
the musts and must nots of sexual convolutions. Add
excitement to marriage, the *Digest* instructed, do it under the
dining-table, on the dining-table, under the bed, in the
bathtub. My friend and I sighed with excitement. Oh to be
married! Light candles, the *Digest* urged, use perfume, open
the door for your husband one evening, naked! My friend
and I shivered. Could the excitement in marriage ever cease?
Never! Could one ever be done with all these experiments?
Impossible! But with all this going on how did married people
look so calm, so matter of fact, so unlike the exuberance of
the Daily Act? One historic day, my friend discovered a much-

thumbed paperback in her parents' room, which when they were out she read swiftly, terror-stricken at the prospect of their arrival, enthralled at the discoveries she was making. It was rather complicated, she told me later in hushed tones. Sex apparently, was divided into three stages – foreplay, meaning kissing; intercourse, meaning intercourse; climax, meaning some height; and orgasm, meaning some release. The art of kissing, one we had always thought so simple, seemed almost as fraught with complications as the act that followed. The book said it was not confined to the lips and required great expertise. The rest was hazy. We could not put action to any of the words. We pondered over the question of time. Ten minutes? Half an hour? One hour? Furtively we tried to imagine our parents doing it. But no, that was not possible. Parents were beyond such experiments, beyond such desires, beyond any heights, any releases. Mystified, frustrated, delighted, we stared at each other. It was a far more complex and lengthy process than we had anticipated and, therefore, certainly far more to be desired. Sex was something that one day would happen to the likes of us and then lightning would crack and the heavens would change colour. We would have our Rochesters and our Rhett Butlers, it was only a question of time. A question of time when our noses would become finer, our lips more sensual, our eyes large and liquid, our hair thick and luxurious, the kind men loved to run their fingers through. A question of time before the pimples would vanish gracefully, the breasts appear mysteriously, the hair on our arms and legs fall off quietly, our eyebrows arch and distance themselves silently. Only a question of time, of time. Not the time our mothers were subject to, who slept with bedroom doors wide open on beds three feet away from our fathers, who had slept that way ever since we could remember. No, not the time our mothers were subject to, who as brides, were even more ignorant than we were as children. I think now of these multitudes of mothers, once silent brides entering yellow and white flower-bedecked bedrooms after the wedding, against which their bridal sarees burnt red and gold. How did our fathers undress these women, so many of whom did not even know the reason for such a ritual? Did our mothers then protest, silently, silently? Or quietly, unprotestingly acquiesce to what some instinct told them had to be endured, hearing during the act, like incantations, the distant refrain of their mothers' voices, chanting, do what your husband tells you to, accept, endure. Or perhaps, stricken with shyness and the strangeness of it all, did our fathers speak falteringly to their brides, initiate them slowly, gently, assuming an experience they never had? Was there the possibility for love? And their stories lay untold, swollen like rivers after the monsoon rains. Years later, untold stories still, and our mothers like the parched, cracked countryside, waiting for rain that will never come.

'After raping me,' Sangeeta said, 'he dropped me home.' I recalled that evening, recalled that my mother was busy getting everything arranged for the women's sangeet. The house was decorated with rangoli and the kitchen, redolent with the smell of cooking. Two hours before the sangeet, Sangeeta entered the house and I remembered how strange she looked, her eyes swollen, face pale, her saree more crumpled than the heat warranted. She told our mother that the heat was bothering her and Ma shepherded her to the bedroom and urged her to hurry and get ready. And I remembered that she took two hours over her bath. Then our relatives and friends arrived in a glitter of gold and Kanchivaram sarees. Sangeeta, exquisite in a yellow and silver Benarasi saree with pearls, her hair covered with jasmine, sat mutely as someone played the dholak and everyone sang. As the songs turned sentimental, lamenting the daughter leaving her mother's house, my mother, predictably, began to cry, but Sangeeta, playing with the gold bangles on her wrist, did not. I remember there were gulab jamuns, pedas and rasmalai after dinner, and I with my passion for sweets and without my mother's eagle eye on me, rapidly consumed a meal composed entirely of sweets. Then, overcome by the weight of my pimples, my oily skin, lanky hair and my intense shyness, I went to our bedroom and slept.

Now, twenty years later, I try and imagine what would have happened had my sister told my parents about the rape. They would, of course, have called it off. And Sangeeta, with her lost virginity would have continued to live with our parents, a fallen woman, as people would say. Despoiled, she would have faded quietly away into the greyness of eternal spinsterhood, while my parents prayed that some nice man would come along and love her in spite of it all, not questing the unbroken hymen. Had I been older, I would have told my parents and watched them shrivel away with barely a rustle, accepting this as their karma for sins committed in their last births, cradling their first-born, bearing forever the burden of an unmarried and deflowered daughter. And the people, oh the people would have talked and talked and the fault would have been entirely hers.

And what of Nikhil, the groom-to-be? Twenty-five to Sangeeta's twenty, he was a man so tall, so attractive, so charming, that he put to shame Darcy, Rochester and almost, but not quite, Rhett Butler. Theirs was an arranged marriage and as is inevitably the case, they fell violently in love. What romance! What courtship! What a profusion of roses for Sangeeta, what an exchange of love letters! Though they lived in the same city, they wrote to each other every day, went out with parental approval every other day. A romantic though I was, I could not imagine what they could write about after meeting so often. Didn't they talk? If I received vicarious pleasure from my books, it was nothing to that which I received from their romance. But, consumed by shyness, I could barely talk to Nikhil or his brother Abhinay who was Sangeeta's age and almost as handsome as Nikhil. Their parents were kind to me. They would pat my head and declare that I was a polite and good girl. Which was true, for being shy, I could be nothing if not good and polite. Besides, what else could they

say about me? I had neither looks nor charm nor poise.
Sangeeta had all three. She made me giggle with her chatter,
let me use her old lipsticks, feel her silk sarees. She cooked
me my favourite dishes, told me stories about the excitement
and adventure in her world – the grown-up world. She bought
me books, usually ones I had long outgrown, but it didn't
matter. She was wildly extravagant and almost always happy.
She believed that money was meant to be spent and life was
meant to be enjoyed, and she did both with abandon. When
she was at home I didn't mind not reading; instead I watched
her and listened to her. I thought her the most beautiful
woman I had ever seen and her eyes were always brimming
with laughter. Unlike mine which were always sad and lost,
God knows why, for then I had nothing to be sad about.

That night Sangeeta and I put each other to sleep. I don't
think she slept, but I did, deeply, the sleep of the young. When
I awoke she was locking her six suitcases.

And so they were married late that night, on the auspicious
time the pandit had augured. The pandit chanted the shlokas
that nobody understood and my sister and Nikhil, under a
mandap decorated with marigolds and surrounded by matkas
painted green and red and white, went seven times around
the holy fire. Abhinay was sitting behind Nikhil, I behind
Sangeeta, and, as I cried, Abhinay patted my hand. I found
myself holding his finger and bending it back and I think I
would have broken it if he hadn't, in shock and pain, snatched
it away. No one noticed and I continued sobbing with all the
other weeping women.

The day after the wedding, Sangeeta and Nikhil came
home, she in a green Kanchivaram saree with a magenta
border, ruby drops in her ears, he in a spotless white silk
pyjama-kurta. 'Made for each other', as the cigarette ad said,
and I thought, 'It's all right, it's all right now,' relief washing
over me in waves. Then I saw her eyes, blank, listless. We all
sat in the puja room and my mother performed a short puja.
After it was over we ate and as my parents talked to Nikhil, my

sister took me to the bedroom, sat on the bed, sat me at her feet, and, looking away from me at the wall, began to talk, her voice flat, expressionless, compulsive. Nikhil hadn't done anything last night. She had recoiled and he had attributed it to natural shyness and apprehension. He had soothed her forehead and said, take your time. And she, shivering with distaste, lay awake all night. Nikhil sickened her, nauseated her. 'Didi,' I said, 'Didi, please don't. Still looking away from me, Sangeeta said, 'Do you know what Abhinay did?' 'No,' I said, rising, but she pushed me back to the floor, then described at length the rape and I listened, nausea rising, till the very end when I saw her lying bleeding on the cool floor. Then my mother came into the room, Sangeeta's expression changed to the sister I knew and she hugged me.

The following month Abhinay moved in with them. He needed coaching for his chartered accountancy exams and Nikhil, being a chartered accountant, would coach him. Their mother was pleased and fondly said that now Abhinay had a bhabi who would cook and look after him. When my sister told us this at her next visit, my mother's face grew grim with disapproval. It was unhealthy, she told my father after Sangeeta left. When Nikhil went to work Sangeeta and Abhinay would be together all day – it was unhealthy. My father, disturbed, cleared his throat.

Fear for my sister, coupled with guilt at my own behaviour, engulfed me. I had avoided being alone with her on the occasions she came home and refused to visit her in her house with my parents. When she came home I would sit in the living-room with everyone else, ignoring Sangeeta's plea that I should show her my books. Now, terrified at the new development, I went to the nearby temple and prayed. I told the Gods that if they made things all right for my sister I would never marry, sacrifice forever my Rochester-like husband. Not enough, not enough. I prayed that if things had to change, and in order to effect the change if I had to sacrifice what I most loved, I would sacrifice books, not all books (I was still in school), but fiction. I would stop reading fiction now, today. I prostrated myself before Ganesh, Lakshmi, Saraswati and Hanuman, and having appeased them all with coconuts, I came home.

Time stopped. Not being able to read, there was nothing to do. School was closed for the summer holiday and my only friend had gone to visit her grandparents. By the next evening I was in a ferment of boredom. I could not live without my books but I could not break my vow to the Gods. What to do? I finished a box of sweets in the fridge, stared hungrily at *Jane Eyre* which I had been reading for the third time (why hadn't I finished it before making my vow?) and fantasised about spending a day in the library. I stood for a long time before the bookshelf in my bedroom, closed my eyes, took out a book at random and opening it, smelled it deeply, the smell that still makes my stomach tighten with excitement and anticipation. Smelling wasn't breaking a vow. Then I thrust the book back. I took a walk to the nearby library, assured myself that I had read most of the books and that none were worth re-reading. Craving, tearful, I walked back home. There my father presented me with a heavy cardboard box. I opened it. Books, books, books. 'All second-hand,' my father said happily. 'I couldn't resist the bargain for my little girl.' 'But,' said my mother the disciplinarian, 'One at a time, *not* more than *one* a day, or else you'll get mental indigestion. Choose one,' she told me, 'and you lock the rest away,' she told my father. She knew too well my ability to drug myself with books and prescribed as low a dose as she possibly could, irritated by my state of stupor during my reading spells.

Watery-eyed, I looked away and said, 'No, I don't want to read, I've outgrown books.'

'You're learning to be sarcastic, aren't you?' my mother retorted. 'Talking this way won't get you more than one.'

'Don't want any,' I said and went to my bedroom, bereft, broken. My father followed me and sat beside me apprehensively. 'Are you unwell? Do you miss your sister?'

My sister. My sister. I had forgotten my sister. My sister. I began to wail and miraculously, Sangeeta entered the room. I caught hold of her saree palla. 'Come back home,' I cried, 'don't go back. Come back home.' I pulled her palla till the saree tore at her shoulders, screaming, 'I won't let you go back, I won't let you go back.' My mother, books forgotten, rocked me in her arms. Then Sangeeta cradled me in hers, whispering in my ear, 'If you tell anyone I'll deny it, I'll never talk to you, I'm finished.'

When I finally emerged from the room, a confused Nikhil patted me awkwardly and gave me a chocolate. Dinner was a quiet affair; my parents still shocked by my unprecedented behaviour. I went to bed immediately after dinner. Sangeeta followed me and sat on the bed. 'No,' I said, 'Didi, no.' Her head turned away from me, she told me that every morning when Nikhil was away on work, Abhinay raped her and at night Nikhil did.

'No, didi, don't.'

'Abhinay does it every single day. And, at night, after coaching him for his exams, Nikhil does the same thing. Only, Nikhil takes ten times as long because he thinks he's being patient, but it always hurts me, always, it doesn't matter how you do it ... it's the same thing. Nikhil's patience only prolongs the pain, I detest them ... .'

I put my fingers in my ears. Sangeeta turned to me and removed them. She held both her hands over mine and hissed, 'Listen, *listen*.' Then, still holding my hands, she continued, 'Nikhil thinks I've changed. He says I've lost my spontaneity, my warmth, lost it all, all of it. He doesn't understand me, he says.' And she became quiet, and almost wistful. I got out of bed and went to the living-room.

After they left I asked my mother how long one had to sacrifice something to the Gods in order for one's wish to be fulfilled. 'At least a year,' she said, then sighed, 'and sometimes, never.' My mother kept innumerable fasts and was forever giving up sweets or meat or something she loved as part of the many bargains she struck with God. If never, I asked, why didn't she stop? 'How can I?' she answered. 'After all these years.'

And so I took *Jane Eyre* and ravenously finished it for the third time. I asked my father for the books he had got for me, and frenzied, finished fourteen in a week. 'It's the summer holiday, so do what you want,' my mother snapped in exasperation.

Sangeeta came home on three occasions after that, each times in a saree brighter than the last, and each time I sat glued in my chair in the living-room with the rest of the family, ignoring her pleas to talk in the bedroom. 'Bad girl,' she said once, pouting. 'You don't love your sister.' My mother said, 'Go and talk to your sister, you don't have to sit with us.' I burst into tears. 'Everyone bosses me around,' I said inadequately. And Nikhil, dear Nikhil produced a chocolate, and, giving it to me, said, 'For heaven's sake, let her be'. I could see unhappiness writ large on his face and when I caught him looking at my sister, he looked bewildered. She talked non-stop when she came home, her hands moving, bangles tinkling and she wouldn't listen to anyone else. My parents obviously found nothing wrong and my mother once commented that she had become even more talkative after her marriage.

Then for some time, I think two weeks, Sangeeta didn't come home. One night I woke up screaming in my sleep, emerging from a nightmare where the sound of the shehenai mingled with the sound of Sangeeta moaning and I saw her covered with marigolds and Nikhil and Abhinay on either side of my dead sister. I woke to find my parents bending over me and in anguish I called out my sister's name. 'Didi's dead,' I told my parents. 'Didi's dead.' My mother held me as my body was racked with sobs and my father in his striped pyjamas looked bewildered.

The next morning my parents called my mother's younger sister home for lunch. Mala Mousi was a gynaecologist and my parents no doubt attributed my hysteria to some vague, ill-defined, ill-articulated problem, thought perhaps that my hormones were going awry, my periods on their way, imagined that in some obscure fashion I was jealous of my sister's fairy-tale marriage, wished her dead, that beneath my quiet exterior lay suppressed violence and anger. They had seen the change occurring after Sangeeta's marriage and, typically, refused to question me on matters so explosive, and handed me over to Mala Mousi. At thirty, Mala Mousi was twelve years younger than my mother. She was slim, attractive with pert, sharp features and short, dark hair, direct brown eyes and a nose so small and straight that I almost died of envy every time I saw it. She was brisk, sharp and cutting and everyone including my mother was a little scared of her. Sangeeta found her most intimidating – too direct, too crisp, too outspoken, too independent. Mala Mousi, she felt, had too many sharp edges and not enough of the softness and oozing affection she associated with our aunts. She found Mala Mousi's remarks too penetrating, her views shocking and her attitude to the world too serious to justify a life that was meant to be enjoyed. 'She thinks too much,' Sangeeta would tell our mother. 'There's no point philosophising on life and all that rubbish. She doesn't know how to have fun. And what's the point of all her philosophy and reading if she still isn't married?' For Mala Mousi at thirty was single and, to my horror and admiration, seemed none the worse for it. Mala Mousi did love life, but her love for life was of a different nature from Sangeeta's. It was serious, contemplative, silent. I found her optimism impossible to understand in the light of her two broken engagements, her constant fighting for her privacy and independence, the fact that she lived alone and that her family pitied her unmarried state and constantly reminded her of it. None of this seemed to affect Mala Mousi, who was quite ruthless with her six sisters and reminded them at regular intervals that she was the only one who wasn't using her education to cook. I could share my love of books with her since she too was a voracious reader. She listened to me quite seriously, never babied me, and on my questioning, was perfectly willing to talk to me about issues like God and the universe and what we were doing in it. She told me that she didn't believe in God and certainly not in Heaven and Hell, a revelation I tried hard to swallow with equanimity. According to her Heaven and Hell only existed on earth and as hard as I tried, I could never figure this out. In the convent where I studied, Heaven and Hell were realities you could not ignore, and I was sure Purgatory was the place for me, since I sinned by reading books that were forbidden. In school we had our Christian God, at home our Hindu ones, and I had no trouble in believing in both. When the nuns told us about the miracles Christ performed, I would chime in with the miracles Krishna performed, for I truly loved them both, and the nuns would listen, patient, amused, disbelieving. I loved the Bible almost as much as I loved the *Ramayana* and the *Mahabharata,* for they were all stories that stirred me deeply, moved me to inevitable tears. I wept when Lord Rama abandoned his pregnant wife in the forest. Unfair, unjust. All because he had overheard a conversation where one of his subjects questioned Sita's purity. All because Lord Rama wanted to show his subjects that he did care what they thought. And so, without telling Sita, and she pregnant, he sent his brother, Lakshmana to escort her to the forest and leave her there, alone, unprotected. '*How* could he, Ma, how *could* he?' I cried every time she told me this story. Once, my father, overhearing this said, 'Such are the Gods we worship.' I wept too for Draupadi, gambled away by her five husbands, the Pandavas, along with their kingdom, to their enemies, the Kauravas. I wept as Duryodhana ordered Dussasana to strip Draupadi naked, as Dussasana began pulling at her saree before the entire court, and Draupadi's five husbands, helpless, watched. '*How* could they, Ma?' I cried. '*How* could her husbands do it?' And my mother told me how Draupadi vowed that one day she would wash her hair in Dussasana's blood and till then her hair would lie loose and uncombed. Then I sighed with anger and anticipation. And my father, listening again, reaffirmed his disgust with the men in our mythology. The *Ramayana* and *Mahabharata* abounded in passion, intrigue, vengeance and retribution – stories within stories within stories, and ultimately, of course, Good always triumphed over Evil. They had to be true, I reasoned, they absolutely had to, for how could anyone possibly have the imagination to make it all up?

Mala Mousi, in addition to her apocalyptic views, also smoked, to my parents' disapproval and embarrassment. 'Decent women don't smoke,' my father would tell my mother, and my mother, torn between her assent and her love for her baby sister, would not reply. She even drank occasionally, and she did both with such grace and style that, in my bedroom, I would often go over each gesture, the elegant lift of her slim hand, the leisurely movement of her long fingers holding the cigarette, her magenta lips coolly exhaling smoke. I longed both to impress her and impress upon her that I too had views to express that were radical. But I did not. I didn't even argue with my parents, for, besides wanting to read more, there was nothing to argue about.

Yes, Mala Mousi fascinated me. But I didn't aspire to be like her because to do so would mean no marriage and no babies and I wanted both. However, not to be like her would mean to be like my mother who had marriage and babies and was fat, comforting, unexciting, exacting, loving, practical, oozing security and discontentment. And every woman I saw around me who was married was like my mother – totally, completely unromantic. Was there no in-between?

Before lunch Ma and Mala Mousi were closeted in my parents' bedroom and many years later I was told that the conversation went something like this:

Ma: Geeti's seriously disturbed. I don't know what to
        do.

Mousi: Talk to her. Find out.

Ma: Perhaps she's had her periods and doesn't know what do to?

Mousi: Ask her.

Ma: You're a gynaecologist. Check her up.

Mousi: What do you mean, check her up! She's your daughter for heaven's sake, and having her period isn't a disease. The poor child.

Ma: Mala, beti, please talk to her.

Mousi: Didi, you're being totally irresponsible. The poor child needs you, not me.

Ma: Mala, beti, I think she's seriously disturbed about Sangeeta's marriage.

Mousi: Why?

Ma: She's behaving in such a strange manner – she cries for no reason and yesterday she dreamt that Sangeeta was dead – do you think she wants her dead?

At this point my mother burst into tears. Then Mala Mousi lectured her on her repression, her stupidity, her utter blindness to my loneliness.

'But I wasn't lonely,' I tell her now, twenty years later. 'I can't recall ever having been lonely.'

'Rubbish,' Mala Mousi says. 'You were a solitary child with practically no friends. You were so lost in your world of books that the real world eluded you completely. And you were totally, horribly oblivious to the terrible burden placed on you by your selfish sister.'

'She had no one else,' I say. 'No one.'

'She had your parents,' Mala Mousi says. 'She had a choice. She chose to stay in that masochistic set-up and use you.' Suddenly her eyes fill and she murmurs, 'The poor child, poor, poor Geeti.'

I persist, 'She was terrified that no one would believe or understand. She wasn't even aware that a choice existed.' Things are so cut and dried for Mala Mousi. Mala Mousi says, 'Your beloved sister was weak. She accepted every bit of her suffering and that made her a masochist.'

But of that day, twenty years ago, Mala Mousi's lecture to my mother, the strained lunch ... After lunch Mala Mousi asked me to tell her about the books I was reading. We went to my bedroom, and in the middle of my talk on Jane Eyre's sad childhood, I faltered.

'Something is bothering you, Geeti,' Mala Mousi said.

'No,' I replied, for if I spoke my sister would die.

'Have you had your periods?'

I blushed, 'No.'

'Do you know why women have them?'

'Oh yes,' I said airily. 'If women have periods, then they can have babies.'

'Yes,' she answered and then told me about a woman's anatomy and reproductive organs, and then about a man's. After this, to my acute embarrassment, she told me about the sexual act, mixing it nicely with biology.

When she finished I said, 'I bet you don't know how *much* it hurts.'

'Rubbish,' said my aunt.

'*I* know,' I said. '*You* don't know.'

'Actually,' Mala Mousi said, 'I don't know. Why don't you tell me?'

'You'll know when you get married,' I said sadly.

'But you're not married, Geeti. How do you know?'

'I know people who are married, Mousi, friends,' I clarified hastily.

'And what do your married friends tell you?'

'I have one married friend,' I said, 'Whose brother-in-law raped her two days before the wedding.'

'And then?'

'Then her brother-in-law came to stay with them and now he rapes her in the morning and her husband rapes her at night.'

I noticed that Mala Mousi's hands were shaking. She said, 'Geeti, my child, is that woman your sister?'

I did not answer. I felt my throat was paralysed. My frightened face was answer enough. 'Don't tell Ma,' I said.

Mala Mousi took my hands in hers. 'Geeti, baby, trust me. Do you believe I'll never harm your sister?'

'Yes,' I whispered, the tears flowing.

She wiped my tears and said, 'We'll have to tell your mother and your father.'

'No.'

'Yes. They'll get your sister back home. She'll be safe. No one will harm her. They'll never let her go back. And *whatever* happens, I'll be with you.'

'Promise? Cross your heart and promise.'

'I cross my heart,' she echoed, doing it, 'and I promise.'

'Ma can't take it,' I said. 'She'll become hysterical.' Mala Mousi pressed my hand. 'But Daddy,' I said, 'will be brave and strong. He is,' I struggled for the word, 'an invulnerable man.'

For some time we sat together quietly, Mala Mousi, her arm around me, stroking my forehead. I was filled with a sense of peace and comfort I had never known before and have never known since. Then I looked up and saw that Mala Mousi, my strong, no-nonsense Mala Mousi, was crying quietly. The fear rushed back, making me dizzy and I looked at her with such terror that she covered my eyes with her wet fingers. She said, 'Nothing will happen to Sangeeta. I'm crying for you.'

I sighed deeply, then smiled. '*I'm* all right.' I looked up at her 'See, I'm all right.'

I really believed I was.

And so Mala Mousi called my parents to my bedroom and told them. I waited for Ma's loud tears and lamentations, but there were none. She sat limply against her chair, the faint lines around her mouth suddenly darker, her large eyes unfocused. It was my father who wept, not silently and soundlessly as I believed men cried, but in spasms of uncontrolled sounds, a sight so impossible, so unbearable, that I then felt the complete and irrevocable collapse of my world.

Mala Mousi helped me pack my suitcase and then we went to her apartment to stay for a week. She told me that my parents would get my sister back home and it would be better for me to stay with her for a short time.

That evening she told me with infinite gentleness, that my sister had died in her sleep.

After the first storm of grief, I lay in her arms and said, 'She must have died of a broken heart.' They didn't let me attend the cremation and Mala Mousi didn't either, but stayed with me, holding me during my periodic bursts of weeping.

Sangeeta did not die in her sleep and of course, she did not die of a broken heart. I discovered this four years after the event, and then only because my kid cousin, an irritating girl of great precocity, wanted me to tell her a story. I, absorbed in my book, had no intention of, or interest in indulging her. So she said, 'I bet no one told you that Sangeeta didi died because she hung herself from the fan.'

I put down my book.

'I knew I could stop you reading your stupid book,' she crowed.

I stared at her.

She grinned. 'And before she killed herself she cut of Abhinay's ... *thing* and he died bleeding.' And overcome with embarrassment at mentioning Abhinay's 'thing', she covered her mouth and giggled.

They all knew, all, all of them, our relatives, neighbours and the entire city where we had lived, and which we moved out of a month after her death. They all knew, since of course,

it made headlines in the local newspapers and there were the
police, the journalists and curious people like tidal waves
against our door. During that entire period I was at Mala
Mousi's, kept away from newspapers and people, and soon
after I left with my parents for another city, a place too distant
for our relatives to descend as regularly. They all knew that
when my parents entered Sangeeta's house (the front door
was unbolted), she was hanging from the fan, and Abhinay
lay below, next to the door.

How did she do it? When he was sleeping, probably, the
sleep of the satiated, the safe, knowing Nikhil was away on
work for a week. After that she must have locked the bedroom
door, watching and hearing him as he tried to crawl towards
it, watching and hearing him collapse. In the note she left for
me she wrote, 'Today Abhinay raped me for the fifty-second
time. I am pregnant. I can hear him dying and I like the
sound.' Did she then carefully place the note on the table,
and hands folded, patiently watch Abhinay die? Or did she,
as he screamed, trying to crawl towards the locked door,
whisper to him about the fifty-two times?

There was a bottle of Ganga water on the side table, which
she had drunk before stepping on to the chair.

It was Mala Mousi who finally told me all this. My parents,
when I confronted them, were of no use. In the kitchen I
held my mother and shook her, begging for the truth. My
mother, leaning against the kitchen wall, shook her head,
her face wet. I held her face in both my hands then, and forced
her to look at me; but her eyes, streaming, looked at the
ceiling. Then I went to my father who was sitting in the
veranda. He had heard me. Face averted, he said hoarsely,
'Don't ask me anything.' 'Tell me,' I shrieked, 'tell me!' The
next-door neighbour peeped out from her door and my
cousin cowered in the corner of the veranda. Then I went to
my parents' bedroom, opened my mother's saree trunk,
rummaged in the folds of her sarees till I found the money
carefully tucked away, my mother's only savings put away each

month from the household money. I counted four hundred
rupees in ten and five rupee notes. The next day I took the
train to the city where Mala Mousi lived, the city we had left
four years ago. My parents, unprotesting, let me go.

Mala Mousi also told me that my parents, ravaged with
grief and shock, had broken down completely, and that Nikhil
had looked after them for a week as a son would. Nikhil's
parents, though mad with grief and remorse, accepted their
son's fate as retribution. They too eventually left the city. Mala
Mousi showed me some of the women's magazines that had
written about Sangeeta, making the case an issue. One
compared her to Draupadi on the battlefield after the war
had been won by the Pandavas, washing her hair in the blood
of the man who had humiliated her, fulfilling her vow like a
woman possessed.

'But she was no Draupadi,' Mala Mousi tells me today,
twenty years after the event. 'She had no courage, no
endurance, no ability to sustain herself or others.' My aunt,
so kind and compassionate with me, does not spare my sister
or my mother. She tells me that my mother has been
irresponsible at each stage. 'First she hands you over to me to
find out what you're disturbed about, then she turns to
religion after Sangeeta's death, then she refuses to tell you
anything, leaving you to find out from that precocious cousin
of yours.'

I defend my mother, 'You can't expect her to discuss it
with any equilibrium.'

Mala Mousi grunts. 'No, I can't. So I do it for your parents
both times.' She pauses. 'She lets her children find out
through a series of inopportune accidents, as she herself did
when she got married. One would think her own experience
would sensitise her to her children, but no. Did you know
that the first time your mother was in labour, she took
medicine for stomach-ache?' She notes my aghast expression
with satisfaction. She rubs it in. 'Sangeeta's conception was
one big accidental discovery, her birth another.' Mala Mousi

has virtually stopped seeing my parents. 'My sister depresses me,' she says.

'You're not one for euphemisms, Mousi,' I murmur, and she smiles reluctantly. My mother doesn't merely depress Mala Mousi, she infuriates her, enrages her. My mother is now fanatically religious, praying and meditating for six hours a day. On my visits home (and they are increasingly briefer now), I hear her bed creak at 4 every morning, listen to the sounds of her entering her bathroom, bathing, emerging and getting dressed. Then the smell of incense drifts into my room. If I arrive unexpectedly at my parents' home and she is in the middle of her prayers, she does not come out to greet me, and I sit in my bedroom and await the end of her puja, while my father, still unable to make tea, hovers around me and says I've become thin. My mother is practising detachment, believing completely that attachments only bring sorrow. When she isn't praying, she asks about my work as a surgeon and about my separation in a desultory manner, not always listening to my response. My father, always a believer of sorts, is still, strangely, one. Once in a while he shakes his head and says, 'Nothing is understandable', then follows this with, 'God has His ways'. Mala Mousi says that in the process of my mother's prayers and my father's sighs they have lost whatever little ability they had to be responsible and make decisions. She sees the whole affair as the inevitable result of their attitudes and choices, rather than the act of a God who has His ways, as my father says, or as retribution for sins committed in the last birth, as my mother believes. But for all her raving, all her intolerance, Mala Mousi is a woman of great optimism, and, therefore, I feel, of great courage. She has no complaints about a cruel fate or a malevolent god, believing, of course, in neither, accepts it when things go wrong in her life, and for the rest, goes about delivering babies, tending to her garden and reading with great zest.

Was there no in-between, I asked at twelve. Yes, there is. I am the in-between; it was only a question of time. A question of time when my nose became finer, my eyes with kajal, larger, my hair actually thicker and longer. A question of time when the pimples vanished gracefully, the breasts appeared mysteriously, the hair on my arms and legs disappeared – waxed determinedly, my eye brows arched and distanced themselves, having been plucked painstakingly. It was only a question of time ... a time not still and stagnant like my mother's, but one entirely my own. Time passed as I waited for the man who would be my Rochester, my Rhett Butler, my Darcy, my David, my Sanjeevani, my life-giver, my healer. I foisted all these attributes on the man I eventually married, waited for his eye to turn dark with compassion and understanding as I told him the story of my life. Mad, obsessed, he said of me. Crazy, he said of my sister. The less he listened, the shriller I became. As I eventually turned away from him in bed, he said, it must be running in the family.

And so I went back to Mala Mousi. She listened. No questions here, no judgments. I spoke of Sangeeta, my parents, my husband, sobbed out my dreams and fantasies, my illusions and the reality. And when I stopped my outpouring, she began hers.

Yes, I am the in-between; not married, fat, discontented and accepting like my mother, or unmarried, uncompromising and independent like Mala Mousi, but separated for the time being from my uncomprehending, angry husband, having shed my old fantasies for another – that of empathy, tenderness and companionship. In my dreams I foist this on my resisting husband, unwilling to believe that he is as unlikely my Sanjeevani as I am his Gopi.

And like women possessed, Mala Mousi and I come back to Sangeeta every time we meet. Mala Mousi still hasn't got over the stricken twelve-year-old or the traumatised sixteen-year-old she looked after and counselled. When talking of it she speaks as though the child were not me but another girl in another time. She says she couldn't bear it then and can hardly bear it now. Sometimes, unconsciously, she talks of me in the third person. 'The poor child,' she tells me. 'The poor, poor child.' It is as though Mala Mousi has become twelve-year-old Geeti, recapitulating her experience for me, her thirty-two-year old friend, articulating all that the twelve-year-old never did. Then it is my turn, and I become Sangeeta, living every day and every night of my sister's marriage, recreating it to the last bloody day. Then, groaning, I tell Mala Mousi that perhaps I should be thankful for my husband. A statement that she promptly tears to shreds, berating me for acting out the wifely resignation epitaph of 'others have it worse'.

Mala Mousi's aphorisms, while sensible, were too practical for me, her philosophy of life – for her, solid and flourishing and protecting like a Banyan tree, was for me too frail a branch to hold. I wanted to believe my mother when she told me, 'It is all a delusion, everything. To think this is the real world, that is what leads us all astray.' Her eyes were bleak as she looked out of the kitchen windows.

'Rubbish,' Mala Mousi said when I repeated this to her. 'It is your mother who is deluded.' Her expression softened as she saw my face, 'I know. It allows her to continue living.'

Caught between my longing to believe my mother and my longing for Mala Mousi's approval, I alternated between hope and guilt. How did Mala Mousi cope? Where did she get her optimism from, how could she be so cheerful about her future, all alone, always alone? And I, how could I even begin freeing myself from the past, desperately loving all that I remembered of my sister, quietly loving Mala Mousi, and even against my will loving my husband, in spite of his Rhett Butlerish, Rochester-like qualities, seeing in his bewilderment, some hope?

And Nikhil. My chocolate-bearer, blind unwitting rapist, big, kind brother-in-law. Many years after Sangeeta's death he came to see me at Mala Mousi's house and for the first five minutes, so shocked was I at the change in him that I couldn't talk. He had greyed prematurely, had a slight stoop and had lost forever the charm that was so much part of him. He came to find out what Sangeeta had told me. All these years it had obsessed him, knowing that Sangeeta had talked to me, not knowing what she had said. Year after year he had visited Mala Mousi but she had refused to betray my confidence. My parents had refused to let him see me. Mala Mousi had told me of his visits but not the reason for them. 'I thought it would be too hard on you,' she said defensively. Dear Mala Mousi. All these years, Nikhil told me, he had waited to talk to me. What had Sangeeta told me? Why, how had she borne it? When had it begun? So I told him and his face shrivelled. Shuddering, he said, 'I thought she was inhibited. Oh God, I was no better than my brother.' Looking down, he whispered, 'Now I understand.' There was a long silence, then Nikhil looked at me, his eyes crazed with pain, and said, 'I thought you would tell me that she loved me. I came feeling that hearing this I could go away bearing it at last. But this, oh Geeti, this is beyond bearing, beyond going away from.' After that he could not speak. We sat mutely for fifteen minutes, he looking blindly out of the window. Finally, when he left he said, 'I will have to pray. I will go to Amarnath next month to pray that I can atone to her in my next birth.' As he turned to walk away he said, 'Before I met you I had hope.'

I went back to the living-room and sat on the divan, shaking with the old grief. Even today it takes me by surprise, this feeling, and I'm twelve again and uncomprehending once more. Ah the promise of our next births where we can atone for the sins committed in this one, accept our suffering in this birth, believing all our pain is our karma for the sins committed in the last one. There is much to say for Hindu philosophy, for belief brings with it acceptance and hope. It denies the eternal damnation of hell, makes explicable the inexplicable, is the only logical answer to the tormented why. By that logic, my parents, my sister, Nikhil and I must have sinned voluptuously, horribly, in our last births. I too, like Nikhil, pray; like my mother, I make promises to the Gods, but I do it surreptitiously. Mala Mousi would disown me if she knew, for she relegates the cycle of births to the same category as Heaven and Hell. I pray that Sangeeta's soul is resting, that if there is another birth, we will know each other again. What a ritual of secrecy and guilt my prayers are! There are times when I long for Mala Mousi's conviction of one life and one death and nothing before or after, long too, for her optimism and faith in herself. But if I had her conviction, I would not have her optimism, and could I then continue living, knowing that this is the end, that this is all? I pray, just in case.

The Wet-Nurse

Mahasweta Devi

My aunt who lived in the thicket
My aunt who lived far away,
My aunt never called me fondly
To give me peppermints or candy.

Jashoda cannot remember whether her own
aunt treated her as badly as the one in the children's rhyme,
or looked after her well. More likely, right from her birth she
has been just Kangalicharan's wife and the mother of twenty
children, if you count the living and the dead. She cannot
remember a time when she was not carrying a child in her
womb or when she was free from spells of morning sickness.
Nor can she recall the darkness of a single night, intensified
by the light of the small oil lamp, when Kangalicharan's body
did not bore into her like a geologist's drill.

Jashoda never had the time to decide whether she could
or couldn't tolerate motherhood. Interminable motherhood
was the only way she could keep her large family alive. She
was a professional mother; it was her career. She was not an
amateur in the game like the women in the bhadralog, babu

households. After all, this world is the monopoly of professionals. The city has no time for amateur beggars, pick-pockets, whores; even the street dogs and crows hanging around trash-cans, tempted by the garbage, will not yield an inch of their territory to an amateur newcomer. And so, perforce, Jashoda took up motherhood as a profession.

The responsibility for this, of course, lay with the Studebaker that belonged to the new son-in-law of the Halder household, and with Halderbabu's youngest son's sudden desire to drive a car in the middle of the day. The suddenness of the desire was nothing new: the boy was driven by all kinds of unexpected whims and physical impulses which would not let him rest until satisfied. Funnily enough, these strange desires surfaced in the noontime solitude to drive him relentlessly on, like the slave of a Caliph of Baghdad. Still, upto now Jashoda's taking to motherhood as a career was not in any way connected with what the young fellow did as a result of his afternoon vagaries.

For example, one day, driven by lust he assaulted the family cook. She was lethargic after a heavy meal of rice, fish-head (slyly hidden from her mistress's hawk eyes), and some delicious greens specially cooked, so she relaxed, lay back, and said, 'Do what you like.' At last the Baghdadi spirit released him from its grip and the boy shed tears of remorse, pleading with the cook, 'Don't tell anyone, mashi.' The cook shrugged off the whole incident, said, 'What is there to say about it?' and promptly went to sleep.

She would never have disclosed the story to anyone because she was quite pleased that her body had attracted the young man. But the guilty tend to become excessively sensitive; seeing extra large helpings of fish and other goodies on his plate, the boy became alarmed. He felt that he would be in the dock if the cook decided to expose him. So one afternoon, driven by his Baghdadi djinn, he stole his mother's ring and hid it inside the cook's pillow-case. He then raised a hue and cry, leading to her dismissal.

Another afternoon he stole his father's radio and sold it. It was difficult for his parents to see the link between the boy's capricious behaviour and the afternoon siesta, because in keeping with the tradition of the Harishal Halders, the father created his children only in the depth of the night, after duly consulting the almanac. (In fact, once you cross the gate you find that the household is still in the grip of the sixteenth century, and almanacs guide the days of cohabitation with one's wife.) But these are peripheral matters, mere bye-lanes to the real destination, which is Jashoda's story.

Kangalicharan worked in a sweet shop. He made sweets for those Brahmin pilgrims to the temple of Simhavahini (the Lion Goddess) who are proud of their caste and still observe the taboos regarding food. He would fry puris in keeping with the shop advertisement: 'Puris and curry prepared by a good Brahmin.' In the process, he would filch a bit of flour or this and that to help in the smooth running of his own household. One afternoon Kangalicharan was returning home after handing over charge of the shop to the owner. Tucked away in the folds of his dhoti were a few samosas and jalebis which he had pinched from the shop. (Returning home at mid-day is part of his daily routine; he and his wife Jashoda eat their daily lunch of rice at that time. His hunger appeased, he would be overcome by filial emotion towards Jashoda and fondle her full breasts a little before falling off to sleep.) On that particular afternoon, Kangalicharan was returning home, as was his wont, thinking of the pleasures that awaited him at home, and particularly of Jashoda's breasts. The thought filled him with ecstasy. At this moment of anticipated heavenly joy, the youngest Halder son in the Studebaker screeched to a halt, saving Kangalicharan by the skin of his teeth, but not quite able to save his feet. Both these were mangled beyond repair.

Crowds gathered in a trice. Nabin Panda shouted threateningly: 'We would have shed blood if the accident had happened anywhere other than in front of the Halder home!'

Nabin is a priest and a guide in the temple of the Goddess, who is a direct manifestation of Shakti, and so it is but natural that in the hot afternoon sun his temper took an upward swing. His bellowing succeeded in bringing everyone out of the Halder home.

Old man Halder started thrashing his son and screaming at him, 'You ass, you blockhead, do you want to kill a Brahmin?' The son-in-law, seeing his Studebaker just a little damaged, heaved a sigh of relief and proceeded to prove what a vastly superior human being he was compared to his in-laws, who may have amassed money but were totally devoid of any cultural refinement whatsoever. In a voice as fine as the finest cambric, he asked delicately: 'Will you let the man die? Won't you take him to the hospital?'

Kangali's employer was also in the crowd. Seeing the scattered samosas and jalebis, he was about to say: 'Shame on you Kangali that you should do this!' but he changed his mind and said guardedly, 'You do that, dada.' The son-in-law and Halder senior promptly took Kangalicharan to the hospital.

Old Halder felt genuinely sorry. During the Second World War he had assisted the anti-fascist war of the Allies by buying and selling scrap iron. Kangalicharan was then only in his teens. Respect for Brahmins was ingrained in him and he would start the day by touching a Brahmin's feet. If Chatterjee Babu was not available then he would take a grain of dust from Kangalicharan's cracked soles, Kangalicharan who was young enough to be his son. On festivals and special religious occasions, Kangalicharan and Jashoda came to the house and when the daughters-in-law became pregnant, a sari and sindur would be sent to Jashoda.

He brought himself back to the present, consoling Kangali, 'Do not worry, my son. As long as I am there I will not let you suffer.' Even as he said this, the thought that Kangali's feet had turned into mincemeat flitted through his mind and he realized that when he needed to, Kangali's feet would not be there for him to touch. Regret welled up within him and he cried, 'What did the sonofabitch of?' His eyes filled with tears. He appealed to the doctors at the hospital: 'Do everything possible for him. Don't worry about money.'

But the doctors could not return the soles of his feet to Kangali. He returned home a defective Brahmin. Old Halder ordered a pair of crutches for him. The day Kangali returned home armed with his crutches, he learnt that Jashoda had received a food parcel every day from the Halder household in his absence.

Nabin Panda was third in the line of temple priests. He was entitled to less than one-sixth from the sale of temple prasad and the constant, nagging unhappiness of this made him feel like a worm. After seeing a film on Ramakrishna, he was inspired by the saint's manner and started addressing the deity with great familiarity. He also started getting sozzled on ritual spirit in the good old tradition of Shakti worship.

He now informed Kangali, 'I offered flowers to my beti for your welfare. And the pagli said to me that in Kangali's house there is an incarnation of mine. It will be only because of her that Kangali will return home safe and sound.'

Wanting to recount this conversation to Jashoda, Kangali scolded her suspiciously, 'So this is what you were doing when I was absent? Carrying on with that rascal Nabin?' Jashoda clasped the mistrusting head between the two hemispheres of her body and assured him, 'Every night two maidservants from Halderbabu's place came and slept here in order to guard me. Why should I encourage that crook Nabin? Am I not your chaste wife?'

In fact, even when Kangali went to visit the Halder household, he had proof of the fiery glow of his wife's shining chastity. Jashoda threw herself at the feet of gods and godmen, she performed all kinds of rituals and sat in front of Simhavahini's temple without food and water till the Great Mother appeared to her in a dream in the form of a midwife, complete with a midwife's bag under her arm, and told her, 'Do not worry. Your husband will come back.'

Hearing all this Kangali was overwhelmed. Old Halder explained to him, 'Would you believe it Kangali, these cynics say that if Simhavahini had to appear, why would she do so in the guise of a midwife? I reasoned with them: as a mother she conceives and creates and as a midwife she brings children into the world and looks after them.'

After all this, Kangali ventured to speak to Halderbabu, 'Babu, how can I work any longer in the sweet shop? How will I stir with a ladle when I can only stand supported by a crutch under my arm? To me you are like a god. You are providing for so many people in so many ways. Please also provide me with some work. I do not want to presume on your goodness and beg.'

Halderbabu answered, 'Of course, Kangali, I have thought of a place for you. I will make a little shop for you in my front verandah. You can sell puffed rice, popped rice, candy sugar and dry food-stuff. Mother Simhavahini is right in front of us, the pilgrims come and go, so you won't lack customers. Just now there is a wedding in the house, so there will be a little delay in starting the shop. It is my seventh brat's marriage. So till that time a hamper of food will be sent to your house everyday.'

Hearing this, Kangali's feelings soared like the joyous mating flight of ants signalling the coming of the rains. Going back home, he told Jashoda, 'Do you remember that saying of Kalidas', 'You can have it because it is not there, if it was there, then could you have it?' This is true of our luck. Halderbabu has said that after his son's wedding is over, he will start a shop for me, covering a portion of his front verandah. Till that time he will send us food parcels. If my shanks were there would all these good things have happened? It is all the Great Mother's will.'

Clattering about on his crutches, Kangali spread the good tidings of his changing fortune to all and sundry. As a result, his former employer, Nabin Panda, Kesho Mahanti who ran a flower shop, Ulhas, the regular drummer in the temple, all acknowledged: 'What a miracle! You can't dismiss everything as Kaliyug. This after all is the Great Mother's realm. Here good deeds and virtue shall reign. Evil will be destroyed. Otherwise, why should Kangali lose his legs? Or, for that matter, why on earth should old Halder, fearing the curse of a Brahmin, take all this trouble? And the most important question is why should Mother appear as a midwife in Jashoda's dreams? It is all her will.'

Everyone was amazed that the Goddess Simhavahini, whose discovery and setting up in a temple was the result of a dream some hundred and fifty years ago, should manifest herself around Kangalicharan Patitunda in the fifth decade of this century. After all, old Halderbabu's change of heart was also the Mother's will.

It was well known that Halderbabu was quite selective about distributing his largesse. He was a citizen of free India, where all men were considered equal, where there is supposed to be no distinction between the states, language groups, castes, communities and classes of people. But he had made his pile during the British regime when divide and rule was the policy. That was when his mentality was moulded. As a result he did not trust Punjabis-Oriyas-Biharis-Gujaratis-Marathis-Muslims. His heart, well-ensconced in its layer of fat under a size 42 Gopal vest, did not itch with charity when he saw a Bihari child in distress or a starving Oriya beggar.

He was the patriotic son of Harishal, now in Bangladesh, so that even when he saw the common housefly of West bengal, he would exclaim: 'Ah! The flies at home were so fat and healthy. Here in this godforsaken place everything is so scrawny!' No wonder the hangers-on in and around the temple were astonished to see that same Halder drip with mercy over Kangalicharan who very much belonged to the Gangetic delta.

People could not stop talking about it. Halderbabu was such a chauvinist that when his nephews and grandchildren were studying the lives of the great sons of our motherland, he used to remark to his employees, 'Huh! Why do they teach them the lives of the Jessore-born, Dacca-born, Mymensingh-born great men? They should be taught the strength of the men of Harishal. The men of Harishal are made of the bones of Dadhichi. In time to come it will be revealed that the Vedas and the Upanishads were written by the Harishals. You will see.'

His underlings now told him, in a ridiculous mixture of Bengali and English, 'Sir you have had a change of heart. Otherwise how can you harbour so much kindness for a West Bengali? You will see, Sir, God must have some purpose behind this.' The boss was overjoyed to hear this and said, smiling broadly, 'A Brahmin is a Brahmin. There are no distinctions of West Bengal and East Bengal as far as a Brahmin is concerned. Even when he is shitting, if you were to see the sacred thread, you have to pay your respects.' He laughed loudly at his own joke.

So all around the air was perfumed with goodness-kindness-charity, all under the influence of the Great Mother's will. And in this heady atmosphere, whenever Nabin Panda thought about Simhavahini, the picture of the full-breasted heavy-hipped Jashoda floated in his mind's eye. He wondered whether the Mother was not appearing before him in the form of Jashoda, just as she appeared in Jashoda's dreams as a midwife. The priest who was entitled to fifty per cent of the temple's takings dismissed his fancies with the advice, 'You are pixillated. It's a disease that attacks both men and women. You better tie the root of a white aparajita on your ear while you are peeing.'

Nabin was not prepared to acknowledge this. One day, he told Kangali, 'I am a devotee of the Mother, I will not fool around with Shakti. But I have a great idea. There is no harm in Vaishnavite hanky-panky. I tell you. Spread the word that you have found a Gopal in a dream. My aunt brought me a stone image of a Gopal from Shrikshetra Puri. Let me give that to you. The moment it gets around that God has appeared to you as Gopal in a dream, there will be a great big splash and what's more, cash will come clinking in. Begin, because you need the dough and then you will see that holy thoughts will follow.'

Kangali admonished him, 'Shame on you, dada, how can you flim-flam with the gods?' So Nabin shooed him off with a 'Go to hell.' But subsequent events showed that Kangali would have done well to heed Nabin's advice. For Halderbabu suddenly died of a heart failure. It was the end of the world for Kangali and Jashoda. A Shakespearean welkin broke over their heads.

Halderbabu left Kangali a pauper. All the wishes of the Goddess uttered around Kangali, with Halderbabu as a via media, now disappeared into thin air like the blazing pre-election promises made by political parties, and the couple lost sight of the rosy prospect, just as the flight of a film heroine to some unknown destination, in a movie, is shrouded by some mysterious magic. The many-coloured balloon of Jashoda and Kangali's fantasy burst with a prick from a European witch's bodkin, and the two were utterly stranded.

The children, Gopal, Nepal and Radharani, continuously wailed for food and got a tongue-lashing from their mother. It was quite natural for the little ones to cry with hunger. Ever since Kangalicharan had lost his feet, they were accustomed to nice meals, thanks to the Halder food parcels.

Kangali also yearned for a scoop of rice. But when, in order to divert himself, he induced a feeling of filial love and rubbed his face against Jashoda's breasts like a little Gopal, he got a terrible scolding.

Jashoda was a true example of Indian womanhood. She was typical of a chaste and loving wife and devoted mother, ideals which defy intelligence and rational explanation, which involve sacrifice and dedication stretching the limits of imagination, and which have been kept alive in the popular Indian psyche through the ages, beginning with Sati-Savitri-Sita right down to Nirupa Roy and Chand Usmani in our times. Seeing such a woman, every Tom, Dick and Harry knows that the ancient Indian traditions are alive and kicking. Old sayings, celebrating the fortitude of women, were made to describe such females.

Actually, Jashoda did not wish to blame her husband one bit for their calamity. The same protective love that welled up within her for her children reached out to envelop her husband. She wanted to be transformed into an Earth Mother, rich in a harvest of fruits and grains, in order to feed her disabled husband and helpless children.

The ancient sages have depicted man and woman as the male and female principles in nature. They never described this maternal emotion that Jashoda felt towards her husband; but then, they existed in those long-forgotten times when they came into this peninsula from other countries. However, such is the chemistry of the soil of this land that all women turn into mothers here and all men choose to be eternal sons. All those who ignore the fact that in this country all men are Balgopals and all women Nandaranis, (Krishna's foster mother), and instead look on women in a different light such as 'eternal she', 'Mona Lisa', L'Apassionata', 'Simone de Beauvoir' etc., are mere amateurs in the act of pasting current posters over existing, tattered ones.

That is why, one observes, educated Babus harbour such liberated stereotypes about women outside their family fold. The moment these revolutionary women cross the Babu's domestic threshold, the men desire the old Nandarani in words and deeds. It is a complex process. Because Saratchandra understood it very well, he always made his heroines feed the heroes a good meal. In point of fact, the apparent simplicity of Saratchandra and writers of his ilk is, in reality, quite complicated and worthy of calm consideration of an evening while sipping a cold glass of bael panna. (In West Bengal, all those who engage in cerebral and intellectual work strongly experience the grip of amoebic dysentry, and on that account they should give due importance to bael. It is because we do not recognize the importance of traditional herbal medicines in our lives that we do not know what we are losing in the process.)

But let that pass. In recounting Jashoda's life story, we should not make all these detours. The reader's patience is surely not like the pot-holes of Calcutta's streets, given to increasing by leaps and bounds with every passing decade. The truth of the matter is that Jashoda was caught in a tight spot. After old Halderbabu's last rites were over (during which period the deprived family ate their fill), Jashoda went to meet Halderginni, clutching Radharani at her breast. She wanted to plead her case with the mistress of the house and secure employment with the family as a cook in their vegetarian kitchen.

Halderginni had been heartbroken by her husband's death. But just recently the family lawyer had informed her that the master had left the title deeds of the house and the ownership of the wholesale rice business in her name. And so, heartened by this secret strength, she once again took up the helms of her household. In the beginning she had been very depressed at having to give up the choicest pieces of fish and delicacies such as fish-heads. But gradually, she found that one can continue to exist with the help of the purest ghee made from cow's milk, rich kheer, the best kinds of bananas, and sweetened curds and sandesh from such well-known shops as Gunguram.

And so, sitting on a stool, Halderginni reigned supreme over her household and glowed with the well-being of her good living and power. Ensconced on her lap was her six-month old grandson. Upto now, six of her sons had been married off, and because the almanac prescribes intercourse with one's wife almost every month, the row of rooms located on the ground floor of her house, which had been specially set aside for confinements, were hardly ever empty. The lady doctor and the midwife, Sarala, were permanent visitors to the household. The old lady had six daughters. They also bred regularly at eighteen-month intervals, and so the Halder home was infested with an epidemic of Kanthas and diapers, feeding bottles and pacifiers, rubber sheets and Baby Johnson powder.

Mrs Halder was exasperated by the struggle to feed her infant grandson lying on her lap. Seeing Jashoda, she was overcome with relief and exclaimed, 'Ma, you are a godsend! Please nurse him a bit, I beg of you. His mother is unwell, and he is such a stubborn creature that he will not touch the bottle.'

Jashoda stayed back in that house till nine at night. She nursed the infant at her breast from time to time in answer to the old lady's pleas. The cook was asked to reach a generously-filled pot of rice and curry to Jashoda's family.

During the day, while nursing the child, Jashoda posed the question to the mistress of the house: 'Ma, the master promised so many things but he is no longer there and so I don't want to rake up the past. But you know that your poor Brahmin son has been crippled. I don't care about myself. But I worry about my husband and children and it is on their behalf that I am requesting you for a job – any job. May be you could employ me in your kitchen.'

Halderginni did not feel the same devotion towards Brahmins as her husband, so the replied, 'Wait a while. Let me think about it.' Halderginni did not quite accept the fact that Kangali's loss of feet was in any way connected with her youngest son's noontime quirks. It was as much a question of Kangali's fate. Otherwise why should he have been walking down that road, smiling euphorically in that blazing noonday sun?

Halderginni cast a sideward glance, filled with both admiration and envy, at Jashoda's mammary projections. She admitted ruefully; 'Really! God has created you to be a Kamadhenu, a divine milch-cow. Your tits yield milk with the slightest touch. The creatures whom I have brought into my own house are almost dry. They do not have even a fraction of the milk that you do.'

Jashoda acknowledged the compliment with great self-assurance: 'That goes without saying, Ma. I remember, Gopal was weaned away when he was three years old and this little one had not come into my womb then. Even so, my breasts would be flooded with milk. I wonder where it comes from? I am hardly able to take any special care of myself or get any proper nourishment.'

At night Jashoda's flowing milk-bar was the subject of much heated discussion among the women of the household. And finally, even the men got to hear about it. The second son, whose wife was unwell and whose infant son was nursed by Jashoda, was particularly wife-oriented. He differed from his brothers in that, while they made children with their wives – after duly consulting the almanac for an auspicious time, and at that moment filled with love for their spouses, or indifference, or even disgust, or for that matter preoccupied with the nuts and bolts of business – the second son made his wife pregnant with the same frequency, but a deep love for her drove him to it all the time.

That his wife got high with child repeatedly was all God's will, but he was eager that she remain good to look at. He had always worried about how to combine beauty with repeated childbearing but was at his wit's end regarding a solution. Now when he heard from his wife about Jashoda's surplus milk supply, he suddenly exclaimed:

'Ah! I've found a way.'

'Way for what?' the wife asked.

'A way to relieve you of your troubles.'

'Relieve me of my troubles? How is that possible? My troubles will be over only when I am on the funeral pyre. How can my health survive an annual turn of childbed.'

'You health will recover. It will recover for sure. I have just discovered a divine machinery. Even though you will have a child every year your figure will remain perfect.'

And so the husband and wife confabulated. In the morning the husband went to his mother's room and held some serious discussions with her. She was at first reluctant to heed the son's whispered suggestion, but when she thought it over for a while, she felt it was a million-rupee proposal. Daughters-in-law have come into the house and because of the ineluctable laws of nature, they will become mothers. And as mothers, they will nurse their babies. Inevitably, they would continue to be mothers as long as it was possible, and it therefore automatically followed that if they continued to breastfeed, they would lose their figures. As a result if her sons did a bit of skirtchasing outside the house or if they ran after the maid-servants at home, she would have no one to blame: it was only natural that they should search for greener pastures outside the house.

So if Jashoda became a wet-nurse to all the new-borns of the family, the problem would be solved by sending her a daily hamper, giving her clothes for special festive occasions and paying her a few rupees at the end of every month. Besides, all kinds of rituals were a regular occurrence at her home and a Brahmin woman had a special role to play on such occasions. Jashoda could easily double-up. Moreover, her son was responsible for Jashoda's plight; this would be a good way of absolving themselves.

When Halderginni made the proposal to Jashoda, the poor woman felt that she had been offered a cabinet ministry. She began to think of her breasts as precious objects. At night when Kangalicharan started making approaches, she warned him, 'Look, I will keep the household running on the strength of these. So you had better use them carefully.' That night Kangalicharan gave up his usual practice reluctantly. But when he saw the quantity of rice, dal, oil and vegetables in the hamper, he lost all traces of the tender, filial emotions of a Gopal for his mother, and instead became charged as Brahma the Creator.

He explained to Jashoda, 'Your breasts will be filled with milk only if there is a child in your womb. Keeping that in mind, you will have to suffer a lot of problems. You are a good woman, a virtuous woman. It is because the goddess had foreknowledge that you will become pregnant, have children whom you will nurse yourself, that the Great Mother appeared before you as a midwife.'

Jashoda appreciated Kangali's arguments and her eyes filled with tears of penitence. She said, 'You are my lord and master as well as my teacher, my guru. If I ever forget my place and say no to you, you must correct me. Don't talk of suffering. Where is the suffering in child-bearing? Didn't Halderginnima have thirteen deliveries? Does a tree suffer when bearing fruit?'

And so that rule was established. Kangalicharan became a professional father while Jashoda became a mother professionally. In fact, looking at Jashoda, the greatest sceptic was converted into ardently believing in the message of that famous Bengali devotional song which goes something like this: 'It isn't easy to be a mother/Just having kids isn't enough.'

On the ground floor of the Halder house, around the huge, square courtyard, some dozen or so healthy cows of fine breed were always kept tied to their stakes. Two Bhojpuris, considering them to be Sacred Mothers, tended them very carefully. Mounds of grass, fodder, cattlefeed, oilcakes and molasses were brought to the house for them. Halderginni was of the opinion that the milk yield of the cows would increase in proportion to their feed.

But now, Jashoda's position in the household was even more exalted than those sacred creatures, the more so because Halderginni's sons created offspring like Brahma, the creator of the world. And Jashoda nurtured them. The old lady kept a strict check on things so that nothing stemmed her milk supply. One day she called Kangalicharan and told him, 'Look son, in the sweet shop you were accustomed to preparing food. Why don't you take charge of the cooking at home now and give my girl a little rest? She has two of her own and there are three kids here. After nursing five, is it possible for her to go home and cook?'

Wisdom dawned on Kangalicharan, and when he came down, the two Bhojpuris gave him a pinch of tobacco to chew and exclaimed, 'The mistress is quite right! Just watch how we look after our sacred cows whom we treat as our mothers, and your wife, she is mother to the whole world!'

Kangalicharan started cooking for the family, and made his children his assistants. In time, he perfected the most difficult delicacies of Bengali cuisine, such as the special dals, the sweet and sour fish, the dried vegetable preparation from the plantain tree trunk. He even prepared a fabulous curry from the sacrificial goat-head from the temple of Simhavahini, and made his way into the heart of the drunk and dope-addicted Nabin through his stomach. As a result Nabin fixed him up in the Nakuleshwar Shiva temple.

Jashoda started bloating up like a PWD officer's bank account as a result of being served hot, ready-cooked meals at home. Besides, Halderginni allotted her a daily drink of milk, and whenever she started expecting a child, the old lady sent her pickles, chutneys, relishes and preserves. Even the unbelievers started toying with the idea that only for this had the goddess Simhavahini appeared in Jashoda's dreams as a midwife with a bag under her arm. Otherwise who on earth had ever heard of or seen such repeated pregnancies and deliveries, this unlimited nursing of other people's children, yielding milk like a great big cow. All the dirty fantasizing that Nabin had been indulging in about Jashoda, vanished. Imbibing such stimulating stuff as ritual spirit, hash and spicy curried goat's-head did not help to excite Nabin's cooling ardour. Instead, he was filled with an emotion close to piety, so that whenever he met Jashoda, he addressed her as mother. Consequently, there was a revival of faith in the whole area in the greatness of Simhavahini, and the electrifying currents of that faith filled the air in the locality.

Everyone's respect and devotion towards Jashoda became so intense that she started playing a prominent part in all the womanly rituals connected with marriage, childbirth, thread ceremony, and so on. The special feelings towards Jashoda were now extended to her offspring: her sons, Nepal, Gopal, Neno, Boncha, Patel, began to don the sacred thread as they grew up and started touting for pilgrims visiting the temple. Kangali did not have to search for grooms for his daughters, Radharani, Altarani, Padmarani. Nabin found husbands for them with great alacrity and the chaste daughters of a chaste mother, like the true satis that they were, went to make homes for their Shivas.

Jashoda's worth increased in the Halder household. Nowadays, the daughters-in-law did not get weak with alarm when they saw their husbands consult the almanac, and this in itself pleased the sons of the house. They could act the eternal child, Gopal, in bed because their own children were being nursed at Jashoda's breasts; the wives had no grounds to reject their advances.

The wives in turn were happy because they could keep their figure in shape. They could wear cholis of fashionable cut and bras in the latest style. On Shivaratri, they could watch films the whole night because they didn't have to bother about feeding their babies, and all this was possible because of Jashoda.

Inevitably Jashoda was filled with a sense of her own importance and began taking the liberty of voicing her opinions. She would be sitting in the old lady's room, feeding the infants endlessly while making sarcastic comments like, 'Women are made to have babies. Whoever has heard of calling in doctors, checking blood pressures, having tonics prescribed for something so natural! Great big fusspots if you ask me. Look at me. Here I am, a baby every year. Is it affecting my health or drying up the milk? Disgraceful! Here they are having the milk dried up with injections! Never heard of such a shameful thing in my life.'

It had been the custom in the Halder household that the boys, as soon as they were in their teens, started making passes at the maid-servants in the house. This pattern changed with the present generation of adolescents. They had been nursed by Jashoda and thought of her as a mother-substitute. Now they adopted the same attitude towards the other women servants in the household and, instead, started hanging around the girls' school. Relieved of their unwanted attention the maids acclaimed Jashoda saying, 'Joshi, you are great. It is because of you that the whole household had changed.'

One day, the youngest Halder son was squatting in front of Jashoda and watching her nurse an infant, when she addressed him, 'Son, you have brought me an enormous amount of luck. It was because you crippled my man that all these comforts came to me. Can you tell me whose will all this is?'

The boy replied, 'It is Mother Simhavahini's.' He wanted to know very badly how the legless Kangali played the role of Brahma, but since the conversation turned to matters spiritual, he forgot to raise the question. It was all the will of Simhavahini.

Kangali's legs were amputated in the fifties. From then we have reached present times. In the intervening twenty-five years or, to be more precise, say, thirty years, Jashoda had taken to childbed some twenty times. The last few pregnancies did not serve their purpose because, somehow, fresh winds of change started blowing away the old cobwebs in the Halder household. But let me first deal with the major events of the intervening years.

When this story started Jashoda was the mother of three. After that she had seventeen confinements. Meanwhile, old Halderginni also died. The old lady played one favourite wishing game: she wanted at least one of her daughters-in-law to have the same sort of experience that her mother-in-law had had. It was customary in the family that, if one had twenty children, then the couple had to go through the entire wedding ceremony once again, with all the related pomp and circumstance.

But Halderginni's daughters-in-law were not prepared to fulfill this desire. They cried Halt after a dozen or so. Thanks to some unfortunate wicked thinking on their part, they were able to convince their husbands and went into hospitals to take the necessary steps. All this was the fault of new trends sweeping through society.

Through the ages, thinkers and sages have never allowed the winds of change to enter the citadel of the family. My grandmother used to tell me the story of a respectable gentleman who came to her house to read through the rather startling literary magazine, *Sanibarer Chithi.* He would not dream of allowing the journal into his own home! 'The moment wives, mothers, sisters start reading that magazine, they will claim that they are women first and last, not mothers, sisters, wives.' And if he was asked what would happen as a result, he would reply, 'They will start cooking meals wearing slippers in the kitchen.' It is an age-old custom: new fashions, new fads always destroy domestic peace.

The sixteenth century continued to reign in the Halder household, but suddenly, because of a proliferation of family members, some of the men broke away from the joint family and set up households of their own in other localities. They flew the nest. Even this could be tolerated, but what was most objectionable was that the old lady's granddaughters-in-law came into the family with completely different notions of Motherhood from Halderginni's.

In vain the old lady argued, there is no lack of food or cash. The old master had had a secret dream of filling up half of Calcutta with Halders. But the younger women were unwilling to oblige. Defying the old lady, they discarded the family homestead and accompanied their husbands to their places of work. Meanwhile, following a fracas among the temple priests, an unidentified person or group turned the Simhavahini image around.

The news of the goddess turning her face away broke the old lady's heart, and one midsummer day, after eating an

enormous quantity of overripe jackfruit, she died of gastro-
enteritis. In dying, the old lady found her release. The burden
of living was far more irksome than passing over to the other
side. Jashoda grieved over Halderginni's death, really and
truly. Basini, the long-time maid-servant of the household,
was well-known in the locality for her professional mourning
but with Mrs. Halder's expiry, Jashoda surprised everyone with
the vehemence of her performance. The reason, of course,
was that with the departure of Halderginni, Jashoda would
lose her meal-ticket.

Basini howled, 'Oh ma! Where are you now? Ma, you had
such a fill of good fortune! You were the jewel in the crown
after the master's death! It was you who kept a tight control
and held everything together! Ma! What sins have we
committed that you should leave us? I pleaded with you not
to eat so much jackfruit, but you paid no heed!'

Jashoda bided her time and when Basini paused to catch
her breath, she wailed with redoubled strength, 'Ma! Why
should you remain here? You, who were so blessed, why
should you put up with this sinful world? There was a throne
established here for you to reign but then your daughters-
in-law discarded it. Isn't it a terrible sin for the tree to refuse
to bear fruit? Is it possible that a virtuous woman like you
can tolerate such evil? And to top it all Simhavahini turned
her face away, ma. You realised that a virtuous home has
turned into an ungodly den. Is it conceivable that you could
go on living here? After the master had left this world, I
could see that you also wanted to join him. But I realised
that in the interests of your family, you kept your body and
soul together.'

Jashoda addressed the daughters-in-law, weeping as she
did so, 'Get some alta and take her footprints. Those footprints
will act as a talisman for your family. The goddess Lakshmi
will never desert the household as long as the footprints are
there. Every morning if you do your obeisance there before
starting the day, it will ward off all sickness and disaster.'

Jashoda followed the funeral procession to the burning ghat, weeping and wailing at the loss of her employer. When she returned, she claimed emphatically, 'Saw it with my own eyes, cross my heart. A chariot came down from heaven and snatched the mistress' body right out of the funeral pyre and whisked it upwards in a matter of seconds.'

After the last rites and prescribed period of mourning were over, the eldest daughter-in-law spoke to Jashoda, 'Bamin didi, I must talk to you. The family is breaking up. The second and third brother's families are moving into the Beliaghata house. The fourth and the fifth are shifting to Maniktala-Bagmari. The youngest will be setting up his home in our house in Dakshineswar.'

'Who will stay here?'

'We are going to stay put here. But we will be renting out the ground floor rooms. We will reduce our establishment and cut expenditure. We must. You have been wet-nurse to the family, you have nursed the children, and in return, a daily hamper of food had been sent to your house. Even after the last child had been weaned, my mother-in-law continued to send you the food parcel for eight years. She did as she pleased and her sons also never objected. But I will not be able to continue in the same style!'

'What will happen to me, Boudi?'

'If you cook and look after the kitchen for my family, you will make enough to support yourself. But what about the rest at home? What will you do about them?'

'What shall I do?'

'It is for you to say. You are the mother of twelve living children. The girls have been married off. The boys, I am told, help to bring pilgrims to the temple. They also eat the temple prasad and sleep in the courtyard. The Brahmin, your man, I hear is doing quite well at the Nakuleswar temple. What is your problem? You do not have to worry about anything.' Jashoda wiped her eyes and murmured, 'Let me see. I will speak to my husband.'

Kangalicharan's temple was a scene of hectic activity. He brusquely asked Jashoda, 'What will you do in my temple?'

'What does Nabin's niece do?'

'She looks after the temple household, cooks the prasad. You have not done any cooking for so long even at home. How can you look after the heavy kitchen work of the temple?'

'The food parcels are going to be stopped. Has that entered your thick head, you bum? What will you do for a meal?'

Kangali answered, 'You don't have to worry about that.'

'Why did you let me do the worrying for so long? A lot of money seems to be rolling in at the temple, isn't that so? You have saved every bit of it and lived like a parasite on my hard work.'

'Who did the cooking at home?'

Jashoda answered with a contemptuous gesture, 'The men bring in the food, the women cook. That is the age-old pattern. But in my case everything is reversed. You have lived off me all these years, so now you feed me. That is only right.'

Kangali retorted sharply, 'How did you manage to get the food in the first place? Would you have had entry into the Halder home? You were lucky to have the doors opened to you only because I lost my legs. You seem to have forgotten everything, you hussy.'

'Hussy yourself! Living off his wife and calls himself a man.'

Following this, the two got into a terrible fight. Invectives and curses flowed fast and furious between them, and at last Kangali exploded 'Beat it! I don't want to see your face again.'

'So you don't want to see me again, do you? That's fine by me.' Jashoda left the room in a rage. Meanwhile, the various shareholding priests in the temple had discussed the urgent need to restore the goddess to her old position, and so a puja of atonement was being celebrated with great pomp in the temple.

Jashoda threw herself at the feet of the goddess. Her grief seemed to burst through her flabby, middle-aged, milk-dried breasts. She wanted Mother Simhavahini to understand her hopeless state and show her the way out of her misery.

For three days and nights Jashoda lay prone in the temple courtyard. But Simhavahini herself must have been affected by all the new ways, the changes in the air, for she did not bother to appear in Jashoda's dreams. In fact, when Jashoda went home, shivering with weakness after three days of fasting, her youngest son informed her, 'Father says he will stay in the temple. He has asked me and Naba to ring the bells there. He says we will get some money and can eat the prasad.'

'I see. Where is your father?'

'He is lying down. Golapi Masi is scratching the prickly heat rash on his back. He gave us some money to buy lollipops and leave him alone. So I ran home to come and tell you.'

Jashoda realised that it was not just the Halder household but Kangali also who had outgrown the need for her. After quieting her gnawing hunger with a drink of water and a bit of candy sugar, she went out to complain to Nabin. It was he who had turned the Simhavahini image around and after negotiating satisfactorily with the other priests on the division of the takings on special festival days, he reinstated the image to her original position. As a result, he had massaged his aching body with alcohol and was high on hash. He was busy hectoring the local candidate for the elections with dire threats, 'You did not bother to make your special offerings. The Mother's powers have returned. Let's see how you win this time.'

That the days of miracles were not yet over and extended to the temple precincts can be evidenced from Nabin himself. It was he who had turned the image because he felt that the priests were not aligning themselves into a united front like the political parties before elections, and afterwards had begun to believe that the goddess had turned her face away. And now that the image had been re-established, he made himself believe that she had returned of her own accord. Jashoda accosted him, 'What rubbish are you talking?'

'I am talking of the greatness and powers of the Devi,' replied Nabin.

Jashoda was still aggressive. 'You think I don't know that it was you who turned the goddess around?'

Nabin shushed her. 'Shut up, Joshi. Wasn't it the goddess who gave me the strength and the imagination? Otherwise how could I have carried it out?'

'It was in your hands that the goddess lost her powers,' Jashoda stated flatly.

'Lost her powers! Pah! There is a fan circulating over your head, and you are enjoying that cool breeze. Has it happened before? Have you ever had an electric fan in the temple courtyard?'

'Hmm. A likely story. But tell me, what have I done to you? Why have you ruined my life, destroyed my future?'

'What's the matter, Kangali is not dead.'

'Why should he kick the bucket? Oh no! It's much worse than that.'

'What has happened?'

Jashoda wiped her eyes and spoke in a voice choking with unshed tears, 'I have given birth to so many and that is why I was the permanent wet-nurse in the Halder household, the overflowing milk-bar. It is not that you do not know everything. I have never strayed, always on the straight and narrow.'

'God bless me. How can you utter such things. You are the great Mother's incarnation.'

'Well, the Mother has done pretty well by herself, what with offerings and worship but the incarnation is about to die of starvation. The Halder meals are drying up.'

'But why did you have to go and pick a quarrel with Kangali? After all he is a man. How do you expect him to react when you flaunt the fact that you have been the breadwinner?'

'True, but why did you have to plant your niece there?'

'That, after all, is the will of the goddess. Golapi used to go to the temple for darshan and pray for hours. Gradually

Kangali realised that he was Bhairav and she his Bahiravi in the true tantrik tradition.'

'Bhairavi be hanged! Even now I can horsewhip her and drag my husband away.'

Nabin exclaimed, 'That is not possible any longer. Kangali is a virile man. You won't be able to satisfy him any longer. Besides Golapi's brother is a notorious goonda. He is keeping guard there. He even threw me out. If I smoke ten drags of hush, he smokes twenty. Gave me one kick in my ass. I had gone to plead your case. Kangali would not listen. Said not to mention your name. She does not appreciate her husband but runs after her employer's family. The employers are her gods. Let her go there.'

'Fine, that is what I will do.'

With this parting shot, Jashoda, half-crazed by the injustices meted out to her by life, returned home. But it was difficult for her to settle down in the empty house. She felt desolate; it was difficult to fall asleep without a child curled up against her. Motherhood is a terrible addiction; once you are hooked it is difficult to withdraw even after the milk has run dry.

Swallowing her self-respect, Jashoda appealed to Mrs. Halder, the new mistress of the household. She said, 'I'll cook and serve. If you wish to pay me, well and good, if not then don't. But you will have to let me stay here. That good for nothing husband of mine is living in the temple. And the kids, they are such ungrateful wretches, Ma, they have joined him. For whom then should I keep maintaining the room?'

'You may stay here,' said the new mistress generously. 'You have nursed the young ones and, on top of that, you are a Brahmin. Stay, but I must warn you, it will be difficult for you. You will have to share the same room with Basini and the rest. You will have to learn to adjust and not quarrel with anyone. As you know, Babu, the new master is hot-tempered. To make matters worse the third son has gone to Bombay and married a local chit. So already he is nettled. If there are squabbles to add to all this, he will be beside himself.'

Jashoda's fertility had been her fortune. With that over, she had her first brush with hard times. The chaste, respected Jashoda, rich in her milk yield, cherished by all the local mothers, now found her luck was down. But human nature is contrary. During bad times, one is not prepared to swallow ones overweening pride and accept with humility the raw deal meted out by life. And so, buoyed by an old arrogance, one is ready to pick a fight over small issues only to have one's nose rubbed in the dirt by the lowliest.

Jashoda suffered the same fate. In the old days, Basini and the rest had been real bootlickers, ready to fawn on her for her favours. Now Basini declared without batting an eyelid, 'You wash you own plate and glass. Are you my employer that I should do your menial work for you? You are a servant the same as me. No difference.'

'Don't forget who I am,' shouted Jashoda in a rage. But she was put in her place by the new mistress. 'This is what I was afraid of,' she said, 'my mother-in-law has pampered her no end. Listen Didi, I did not beg you to join my service, you came on your own. So now keep to yourself and don't make trouble.'

Jashoda realised that she no longer had a voice in the household. No one was prepared to listen to anything she had to say. Keeping her counsel she cooked and served and when evening came she went to the temple yard and silently shed tears of bitterness. She could not even lighten her burden by crying openly. After the evening worship at the Nakuleshwar temple was over and Jashoda had heard the drums and bells and cymbals, she wiped her eyes and returned home. She whispered, 'Have mercy on me, Great Mother. In the end do I have to sit on the roadside with a tin bowl begging for alms? Is that what you want?'

Jashoda could have spent the rest of her days cooking for the Halders and unburdening her sorrows at the temple. But fate had decreed otherwise. She began to feel that her body could not cope any longer. She could not quite put her finger

on why she felt so depressed. Her mind became confused.
While she was cooking she was constantly assailed by the
thought that she had been the wet-nurse in this household.

Images float through her mind. She remembers going
home with the food hamper wearing a wide-bordered saree.
Her breasts feel empty, wasted. She had never dreamt that
there would come a time when no babies would suck at her
nipples.

She became absent-minded. She cooked and served the
meals but forgot to eat herself. Sometimes she would appeal
to Nakuleshwar Shiva. 'If Mother does not take me back to
herself, you put an end to all my troubles. You take me back.
I can't bear to live any longer.'

In the end it was the new mistress's sons who informed
their mother, 'Ma, is our nurse ill? She does not seem to be
herself.'

'I'll take a look,' she assured them.

Her husband interjected, 'Yes, you should. After all she is
a Brahmin and if something happens to her the sin would be
laid at our door.'

The mistress went to find out. She saw that Jashoda had
put the rice on the stove to cook, spread out a part of her
saree on the kitchen floor and was lying down.

Seeing her exposed body, the lady of the house exclaimed,
'Oh dear, didi. What is that red patch on your breast, Good
God! It's such an angry red.'

'God only knows what it is. It's big and hard like a pebble
and feels as hard as stone.'

'What is wrong?'

'I wouldn't know. Maybe this is the result of all those infants
that I suckled.'

'Rubbish! You get such inflammations only when there is
milk in your breast. But even your youngest is at least ten
years old.'

'Oh, the youngest is no longer there. He passed away soon
after birth, and a good thing too. It's a wicked world.'

'Wait, tomorrow the doctor is coming to examine my grandson. I'll ask him. It doesn't look right to me.'

Jashoda closed her eyes in pain and said, 'It feels like a breast made of stone or filled with stones. Earlier the hard lump used to move about, now the whole breast feels heavy and inert.'

'Shall I ask the doctor to take a look?'

'Oh no! No Boudi, I won't be able to expose myself before a male doctor.'

That night the doctor came. Speaking through her son, the lady recounted Jashoda's problems. 'There is no pain or burning but for some reason she seems to be getting more and more listless.'

The doctor enquired, 'Find out if the nipple is crinkled and if there are glands under the arm like a swollen ball.'

Hearing such words as nipple and ball, the lady thought to herself, 'How crude', but she went to investigate on the spot. She returned to report, 'The woman says that she has had these symptoms that you mention for a long time.'

'How old is she?'

'If you count from the age of the eldest son, she should be fifty-five.'

'I'll prescribe some medicine', the doctor said. On his way out he told the master of the house, 'I hear there is something wrong with your cook's breast. I think it would be a good idea to take her to the cancer hospital for a check-up. I have not seen her personally, but from all that I hear it could be a cancer of the mammary gland.'

Until very recently, the eldest Halder had been living in the sixteenth century. He had entered the twentieth century only a very little while ago. Of his thirteen children, he had married off his daughters; his sons had grown up, or were growing up, and making their own way in life according to their lights. But even now Mr. Halder's brain cells were steeped in the dark ignorance of pre-Bengal renaissance days.

He still would not get vaccinated against smallpox saying, 'Smallpox attacks the lower classes. I don't need to be vaccinated. In upper class families, among those who respect the gods and Brahmins, such filthy diseases never occur.'

He pooh-poohed the suggestion of cancer contemptuously, 'Huh! Of all things, cancer! Highly unlikely. God alone knows what was said and what you heard. Go and prescribe some ointment and I am sure it will heal. I am not prepared to send a Brahmin woman to the hospital on your say-so.' On hearing the word hospital, Jashoda also refused saying, 'I will not be able to go there for sure. It would be far easier for me to give up my life. I did not go to the hospital for all these child-births, and now you want me to go there? It was only because that rotter went to the hospital that he returned minus his two legs.'

Mrs. Halder replied, 'Let me bring you some magic ointment prepared by a sadhu. It is sure to bring relief. The suppressed boil will come to a head and burst.'

But the panacea, and magic balm, failed to work. In course of time Jashoda lost her appetite and could not eat. She grew progressively weaker. She could not cover her left breast any longer with the end of her saree. Sometimes she thought it was burning, at other times she felt it was paining. There were lesions on the skin and the whole area became an open sore. Jashoda took to her bed.

Seeing these developments Mr. Halder became nervous. He was afraid that a Brahmin woman would die under his roof and the sin be visited on him. He called Jashoda's sons and scolded them, 'It is your own mother and she has brought you up and looked after you for so long and now she is dying. You has better take her with you. Is it right that when she has all of you, she should die in a Kayastha house?'

Kangali cried copiously when he heard this. He came to visit Jashoda, lying in her room in semi-darkness. He pleaded with her, 'Wife, you were chaste as Sita and good as Lakshmi. I have suffered for ill-treating you. Within two years the temple plates were stolen, I had boils on my back and that bitch Golapi got around Nepal and broke open the cash box. She made off with the money and set up shop in Tarakeshwar. Come home and I will look after you. I'll do all I can to keep you in comfort.'

Jashoda listened and then said quietly, 'Light the lamp.' Kangali lit the oil lamp.

Jashoda showed him her bare, ulcerated left breast. 'Have you seen the sore?' she asked, 'do you know the stench it gives out? What will you do with me if you take me home now? And in any case why did you come now to take me back?'

'The master told us to.'

'Ah! Then the master does not want to keep me here any longer.' Jashoda sighed and said, 'I will not be of any earthly use to anyone, how will you manage if you take me back?'

'It doesn't matter. I'll take you home tomorrow. Today I will clean out the room. Tomorrow I'll take you back, as sure as I am standing here.'

'Are the boys all right? Earlier, Nawal and Gour used to drop in occasionally. But now even they have stopped coming.'

'Selfish bastards, each one of them. After all they are born of my seed. No wonder they are heartless like me.'

'Will you come tomorrow?'

'I will, I will, I will, I promise.'

Suddenly Jashoda smiled. It was a wistful smile of the kind which touches the core of one's being and revives memories. She asked shyly, 'Do you remember?'

'Remember what, my dear?'

'Remember how you used to caress these breasts? You could not close your eyes otherwise. My lap was never empty and there would be a never-ending line of infants to suckle. On top of that there would be the babies of the master's family whom I had to nurse. How did I manage, I wonder.'

'I remember everything, my dear.'

At that moment Kangali meant what he said. Seeing Jashoda's diseased, worn-out body, pity welled up in the greedy, self-centred, self-indulgent Kangali to whom his own physical gratification had always been of prime importance. Stirred by a deep sadness, he held Jashoda's hand and remarked, 'You have fever?'

'Yes, I always have fever. I think it is because of the inflammation.'

'Where is this awful stink coming from?'

'From my wound', Jashoda answered closing her eyes. Then she added, 'Perhaps you had better call in Sannyasi doctor. He had cured Gopal's typhoid with homeopathic medicine.'

'I'll call him. I'll take you home tomorrow itself.'

Kangali left that day. But Jashoda could not hear the tap-tapping of his crutch when he went out. With her eyes closed, thinking Kangali was still in the room, she whispered softly, 'It is all lies what they say, that you are a mother if you suckle a baby. Look at me. The boys, Nepal, Gopal and the rest hardly bother to come in and neither do the boys in the Halder family make any enquiries about my health. No one cares.'

The multiple lesions on Jashoda's cancerous breast, open and oozing, seemed to ridicule her sorrow. 'Listen', she called, and opened her eyes, but realised that Kangali had gone away.

That night itself, she got Basini to buy her a cake of Lifebuoy soap and went to have a bath the next morning. What a foul smell, a godawful stink. It's the kind of fetid smell that one gets when carcasses of cats and dogs rot in the neighbourhood garbage cans. All her life, because she had had to nurse the children of the Halders, Jashoda had looked after her breasts, massaging them with oil and cleaning the nipples with soap and water. Those breasts that she had cared for so well had in the end betrayed her. She wondered why.

Her skin burned when it came in contact with the harsh soap. Even so, Jashoda soaped herself thoroughly, but when she finished her head was swimming, her eyes were blurred and everything became dim all around her. Her head and body seemed to be on fire. The black floor looked so inviting and cool. Jashoda spread one end of her saree on the floor and lay down. Her breasts seemed to weigh a ton and she could not continue standing under their weight.

The moment she lay down, she lost all consciousness. Kangali came the next day just as he had promised. But seeing Jashoda's condition he lost his head and did not know what to do. At last Nabin came and shouted, 'Are these people fit to call themselves human beings! Here was this woman who nursed all their babies and they could not even call a doctor. I'll go and call Hari doctor just now.'

The moment Hari doctor saw the patient he declared, 'Hospital!'

Normally patients in such extreme conditions are not admitted, but Jashoda got in through Halderbabu's efforts and influence.

'What has happened? Oh daktarbabu, please tell me what has happened?' cried Kangali like a little boy.

'Cancer!'

'Is it possible to have cancer in the breast?'

'How else did it happen?'

'... twenty of her own and at least thirty from the Halder household. She had a lot of milk, daktarbabu.'

'What did you say? How many has she nursed?'

'Oh! Fifty easily.'

'F-i-f-t-y?'

'Yes sir.'

'She has had twenty children?'

'Yes sir.'

'God!'

'Sir?'

'What do you want?'

'Did this happen because she suckled so many ...?'

'That cannot be said for certain. No one can say what is the cause of cancer. However, those who do a lot of breastfeeding ... why did you not realise her state earlier? This could not have happened in one day.'

'She was not living with me, sir. There was a quarrel ...'

'O.K. I have understood.'

'How do you see her? Will she get well?'

'Get well? Start counting the days before she goes. You have brought her here at the last stage. No one comes out of this alive.'

Kangali returned home crying. In the evening, distressed by his tears and laments, Halderbabu's second son went and talked to the doctor. The boy was not in the least anxious about Jashoda but he went because his father gave him a dressing down and he was still economically dependent on him.

The doctor explained everything. Something like this did not come up suddenly, it developed over a long period of time. How did it happen? No one can say for sure. How can one find out if there is breast cancer? First there is a small lump which can move about. Then the lump gets harder, bigger and spreads over a large area inside the breast. The skin on the surface is likely to get reddish just as the crinkling of the nipple is a possible symptom. The gland in the armpit may possibly get inflamed. Ulceration occurs in the last stage. Fever? That takes second or third place in the order of importance of symptoms. If there is an open sore on the body, temperature is only natural, it's a secondary symptom.

The boy was quite confused by all this expert explaining and could only ask, 'Will she live?'

'No.'

'Then how long will she suffer?'

'Oh! I don't think it will be very long now.'

'But if there is no hope, how will you treat her?'

'I'll prescribe some painkillers, sedatives, some antibiotics for the fever. Physically, she is very run down.'

'She had stopped eating.'

'Didn't you call in a doctor?'

'Yes, we did.'

'Did he not say anything?'

'He did.'

'What was his diagnosis?'

'He said that possibly it was cancer. He suggested that we take her to a hospital. She refused.'

'Why should she want to go to a hospital? In that case how can she die?'

The second son came home and reported, 'That time when Arun daktar said she had cancer, if we had taken her to the hospital then, she may have lived.'

Angry at the implicit accusation, the mother shouted, 'If you knew so much then why didn't you take her there? Did I forbid you to?'

Somehow in the minds of the mother and son, an indefinable sense of guilt and remorse came to a head and broke instantly like the gaseous eruptions bubbling on the surface of dank, scummy, stagnant waters. The sense of guilt kept drilling the words into the mind, 'She was living under our roof. We did not even bother to look in and see how she was. God alone knows when the illness started, never gave it any importance. She did not know what was happening. After all, she looked after so many of us and we did not look after her in return. And now, when she has so many people to call her own, she has gone to die in a hospital. So many sons, a husband, but she clung to us, and so it was our responsibility...! What a strong body she had, what enviable health! The milk would simply spill out of her breasts. Never for a moment did one think that she would be struck with a disease like this.'

But the next moment, a more reassuring justification took over: 'Who can overrule fate? She was destined to die of cancer, no one can set aside one's fate. If she were to die here, the blame would fall on us. Her husband and children would ask questions about her death. Now we have been saved from that blame. No one can say anything.'

Halderbabu senior also reassured them, saying, 'Arun daktar has told me that no one can survive an attack of cancer. Since Didi had cancer, the doctors would do surgery and remove her breasts and uterus but even after all this people die of cancer. See here, father used to give them due respect because they were Brahmins and we are managing to exist because of father's blessings. If Didi died here, we would have to do special pujas of atonement because a Brahmin would have died within our own household.'

Patients admitted into hospital in a far less advanced stage of cancer have died much sooner. Jashoda, to the great surprise of her doctors, lived on for a month longer. In the beginning, Kangali, her sons, Nabin, used to visit her regularly, but Jashoda's condition continued unchanged – comatose, burning with fever, senseless. The sores were getting bigger and bigger and the whole breast took on the appearance of one big naked wound. Although dressed with surgical gauze soaked in antiseptic, the decaying odour from the rotting flesh spiralled through the room and filled it like the perfumed smoke from a burning agarbatti.

Kangali's first flush of concern ebbed somewhat after seeing all this. He said to the doctor, 'She doesn't respond to our call.'

'Isn't that better? One can hardly bear this excruciating pain when one is unconscious, it would be impossible to live with it when conscious.'

'Does she know that we are coming to visit her?'
'That's difficult to say.'
'Is she eating anything?'
'Through tubes and drips.'
'Can people live like that?'
'Why this interest now?'
The doctor realised that his irrational anger was caused by Jashoda's condition. His rage covered Jashoda, Kangali,

and those women who do not take the early symptoms of breast cancer seriously and suffer such terrible agonies in the end.

Kangali left the room since he did not get a satisfactory answer to his questions. He came to the temple and told Nabin and his sons, 'There is no point in going to hospital and visiting her. She does not recognize anyone, does not open her eyes, does not even know who is coming and going. The doctor is doing everything he can.'

'If she dies...' ventured Nabin.

'Halderbabu's telephone number is with them. They will inform us.'

'Just suppose she wants to see you one last time, Kangali. She has been a good wife to you, completely devoted. Who would say that she was the mother of so many? Her body – but she never strayed, never glanced at another man, not for a moment.'

After this outburst, Nabin shut up and sank into himself, ruminating. In fact, since seeing Jashoda lying unconscious with the sores on her breasts exposed, many philosophic thoughts crossed Nabin's mind, aided by a whole host of stimulants, like the rhythmic swaying of mating snakes. Thoughts like – there was such yearning, such longing for her – god, what an end to those beautiful, fascinating breasts – Dammit! The human body is nothing – anyone who loses his balance over it is mad to begin with.

Kangali had no time for Nabin's advice. There was already a sense of rejection in his mind as far as Jashoda was concerned. He was genuinely concerned for her when he first saw her that evening in the Halder house and during the first few days in hospital, but gradually there was a cooling off of the first welling of compassion. The moment the doctor said that Jashoda would not live, Kangali dismissed her from his mind without a twinge of pain. Her sons were his sons also. Moreover, a distance had already grown between the mother and the sons. The mother they had known, a woman of strong personality, her hair tied high into a neat topknot, her dazzling white saree, was not the same woman lying prostrate on the hospital bed.

The comatose brain as a result of the breast cancer was a welcome relief for Jashoda. She realized that she was in hospital, and she also realized that this torpor, this state of oblivion, was induced by drugs. She was greatly relieved. And in her weakened condition, her dazed mind wondered whether one of the Halder boys had become a doctor. He must have been suckled by her and was repaying the debt by making her last days comfortable. But the boys of that family go into business as soon as they finish school. Whatever it is, why don't they release her from this foul smell rising up from her breast? What an unbelievable stink, what a betrayal. Knowing that these breasts were her tools of trade, how diligently she strove to keep them filled with milk. After all, that was what a breast was for – to contain milk. How she washed and kept them clean with good toilet soap. She never wore a blouse even when she was young because they were so heavy.

When the effect of the sedation wore off, Jashoda screamed with pain, 'A-a-a-a-i-ee,' and, with clouded eyes, she looked desperately for the doctor and the nurse. When the doctor came, she muttered in a hurt tone, 'You have grown so big on my milk and now you are making me suffer like this.'

'She sees the whole world as her nurseling,' the doctor observed. Then once more an injection, and once again the cherished oblivion. Pain, tormenting pain, the spreading cancer at the expense of the human host. In the course of time the open sore on Jashoda's breast took on the appearance of a volcanic crater. The emanating stench made it difficult to go near her.

Finally, one night, Jashoda felt that her hands and feet were getting cold. She realized that death was approaching. She could not open her eyes but she understood that someone was feeling her hands. That prick of an injection needle on her arm. Difficulty in breathing. Inevitable. Who were the people looking after her? Were they her own people?

Jashoda thought that she had nursed her own children because she had brought them into the world; she had nursed the Halder children for a living; she had nursed the whole world; in that case would they let her die alone, unaccompanied? The doctor who was treating her, the one who would pull the sheet over her face, the attendant who would take her out on a trolley and the man who would place her on the funeral pyre, the dom who would burn her earthly remains, were all her foster children. One had to be a Jashoda to nurse the world. One also had to die alone, friendless, without a single person whom one could call one's own to hold one's hand at the end and to make the last journey easier. But wasn't there a promise or something of someone being there with her at the last moment. Who could it have been? Who? Who ...?

Jashoda died that night at 11 p.m.

A phone call was made to Halderbabu's house, but they disconnected their phone at night: it did not ring.

After lying in the morgue as per the rules, Jashoda Devi, Hindu female, was carted in due course to the cremation grounds and cremated in good time. The dom burned her. Whatever Jashoda had thought had come true. She was like god in this respect: whatever was in her mind was executed by others. This time also was no exception, Jashoda's death was god's death. In this world, it was always happened that when a person takes on godhood upon himself, he is rejected by everyone and is left to die alone.

Translated from the original Bengali by Ella Dutta

A Kitchen in the Corner of the House

Ambai

ৎৡ ৵৶

It seems that Kishan's father had bought the land at the rate of eight annas per square yard and built the house upon it. A row of rooms like railway carriages. Right at the end, the kitchen, stuck on in a careless manner. Two windows. Underneath one, the tap and basin. The latter was too small to place even a single plate in it. Underneath that, the drainage area, without any ledge. As soon as the taps above were opened, the feet standing beneath would begin to tingle. Within ten minutes there would be a small flood underfoot. Soles and heels would start cracking from that constant wetness. Kishan's mother – called Jiji by everyone – would present a soothing ointment for chapped heels on the very first day one entered the kitchen, cooked a meal and was given the traditional gold bangle.

There were green mountains outside the windows that looked eastward from the kitchen. Somewhere on top of them there was a white dot of a temple. A temple to Ganesha. The cooking area was beneath this very window. The green mountains might have made one forget one's chapped heels. But since the clothesline was directly beyond this window, trousers, shirts, pajamas, saris and petticoats spread out to obscure the view.

As one looked up from turning the pieces of meat which had been sprinkled with coriander, chilli powder and garam masala, spread with ground turmeric and ginger, and marinated in curd, what one encountered might well be a pair of pajamas with their drawstring hanging down. But nobody seemed to object to this.

Their style of life did indeed encompass the kitchen; was woven around the concept of the kitchen. The lineage had a reputation for its love of food and drink. They were people who enjoyed the pleasures and experiences of life. In fact, at their wedding – Kishan's and hers – the one thing the Ajmer relations objected to was that no sort of alcoholic drink was served to anyone.

Even the prasad for their clan goddess, Amba, was spirits. Whatever was opened, whether it was Scotch whisky or country liquor, it was drunk only after first being sprinkled on the walls with the words, 'Jai Ambe.' The first thing to enter a new-born baby's mouth was a finger dipped in spirits. When such was the case, what sort of marriage celebration was this? Very well. Perhaps there was no need for rum, gin or whisky. But what about the orange coloured Kesar Kasturi made in their own Ajmer? After all it had a kick that went straight to one's head! Tch. Tch. How could you get married like this, they asked him; without the horse and the drink that is appropriate to a warrior, how can it be a wedding? Older women, whose heavily pleated and hugely flowered skirts in deep earth-brown, green, orange and bright red, flared and swayed from their wide swollen hips, lifted silver-edged veils to ask him: Isn't there anything to drink?

In the days when Jiji could get about, she would start cooking pappads at the stroke of seven. Papaji would be ready and waiting in the outside verandah, having finished all his other business. Jiji would bring him pungent spiced pappads stacked on a plate. As soon as the pappads were finished, there

would be Bikaner sev, sharp upon the tongue. If they tired of
that, then pakoras of sweetcorn. Or groundnuts dipped in
chillies and besan and deep fried. They would sit opposite
each other, and begin with 'Jai Ambe'. If the sons and
daughters were there, the entire family would join in. Jiji would
sing country songs. 'If you go to the fair, bring me tassels for
my hair ... and a bright coloured dupatta for me to wear.'
Papaji would laugh. 'Do you still care for these things?'

On a small stove, in the corner of the kitchen, there was
always water boiling for tea. If anybody they knew appeared
at the threshold of the house at meal times, first they received
ice-cold water. Then, Papaji would begin.

'You must eat with us. Give Uncle a plate.'

'O no, thank you. I just dropped in.'

'Yes, quite so. But what about a cup of tea?'

'No, thanks.'

'Coffee, then?'

'This water is plenty.'

'How can we allow you to drink plain water? At least have
some sherbet.'

'Very well.'

Jiji would get up.

'Just put a couple of kebabs for him on a plate to go with
his cold drink.'

Even before Jiji reached the kitchen, Papaji would
remember the methi parathas which were made that morning.
'Suniye ji,' he would call to his wife. 'Warm up a couple of
those methi parathas and butter them,' he would say. 'Let
Uncle just have a taste.'

The visitor would be forced to accept defeat. 'All right
then. Let me eat my meal with you.'

Jiji would go into the kitchen in any case, to fry up a couple
of eggs, sprinkled with salt and pepper. Suppose there was
not enough to go round?

All the same, the actual details, the concrete facts of the
kitchen and its space didn't seem to matter to them. It was

almost as if such things didn't actually exist. In their family houses, one crossed the wide stone-paved front courtyard and the main room before reaching the kitchen in a dark corner. A zero watt light bulb hung there. The women appeared there like shadows, their heads covered, their deep coloured skirts melting into the darkness of the room, slapping and kneading the chappati dough or stirring the fragrant, spicy dal. The kitchen was not a place; it was essentially a set of beliefs. It was really as if all that delicious food which enslaved the tongue appeared as from a magic carpet.

On one occasion, when they were eating, Minakshi raised the subject. Papaji was building a room above the garage at that time.

'Papaji, why don't you extend the verandah outside the kitchen? If you widen it, we could have some chairs out there. If you then build a wash place to the left, you could have a really wide basin for cleaning the vessels. And then beyond that, you could put up some aluminium wire for drying the clothes.'

Papaji looked for a moment as if he had been assaulted by the words expressing this opinion. Jiji in her turn looked at him, shocked. Daughters-in-law had not thus far offered their own opinions in that house. Radha bhabhiji stared fixedly at her plate. Kusuma straightened her veil to hide her agitation. Papaji turned to Kishan. Kishan continued to eat calmly. At last Papaji cleared his throat and asked, 'Why?'

'The basin in the kitchen is extremely small. And the drainage is poor. If the servant woman washes the vessels there, the whole kitchen gets flooded. And, Papaji, if you hang the clothes outside the window, the mountain is hidden.'

Again he looked at Kishan. And that skilled architect agreed with his wife.

'What she says is right, Papaji. Why don't we do it?'

'And when did you go near the kitchen?'

'When she cooked up that Mysore-style meal, it was he who sliced the onions and chillies for her,' said Jiji.

'It seems we might as well present you with a gold bangle and be done with it.'

'Never mind the bangle, Papaji. You could give me a ring, though.' Papaji laughed.

The new room was completed. The state of the kitchen remained unchanged. Two more nylon lines were added, for drying clothes. Outside the window. Papaji's silent retort: Woman, woman of Mysore, you who have not lived here for many generations, why do you need mountains? Why do you need its greenness? What possible connection is there between Rajasthani food customs, and the window, and the washing up basin? Dark skinned woman, you who refuse to cover your head, you who talk too much, you who have enticed my son ... .

* * *

At the first fading of the night as early as three o'clock, the peacocks began to call. One after the other, with their harsh discordant voices; broken music. When she and Kishan came to the open terrace at five-thirty in the morning, a peacock in the tree opposite spread its tail, wide as Siva's spread locks. As it turned, there were sudden flashes of soft green, then dark blue, and then again, the deepest of deep green. Most unexpectedly it flew over to the terrace and sat upon the parapet wall, trailing its tail feathers. Then two more came, without extended tails. Before you could turn around there were another two, this time with tail feathers as long as whips. A gentleness and coolness spread within one, as of a weight being eased. Those dark-blue and green icicle-like feathers, seemed instantly to calm all unruly passions. She ran her tongue along Kishan's mouth and kissed him very gently. A kiss like a snowflake, the passion contained within.

The door to the terrace creaked. Bari-Jiji had woken. She had come to collect charcoal from the big drum near the door, and to light the portable stove. Bari-Jiji was Papaji's stepmother. When Papaji was seventeen, his father had married a second time, a young girl who was also seventeen years old. In the following years five daughters were born to her. Papaji had been her mainstay and comfort. She was only Bari-Jiji in name. Between her and Jiji there was only a difference of two years. She was now completely toothless. She refused to have false teeth, claiming that she didn't need teeth anymore, now that she had given up eating meat.

Bari-Jiji left, her heavy silver anklets clinking on the stone steps.

'Shall I bring up some tea, Mina?'

'Hm.'

As soon as he had gone, she turned on the tap of the water tank in the terrace, washed her face and cleaned her teeth.

Kishan brought the tea in a kettle, covered with cosy. When he set it down and poured the tea into two cups, the delicate smell of ginger and basil rose from it. A single morning star shone in the sky. The peacock sprayed its green and blue. The tea descended, warm to the throat.

When they went downstairs, Bari-Jiji sat in the corner of the kitchen, blowing upon the hot tea which Kishan had poured for her, and holding the hot tumbler with the end of her dupatta. Radha Bhabhiji was pouring hot water into another large kettle with tea leaves in it.

'Shall I mix the dough for breakfast?' asked Bari-Jiji.

'Papaji has gone for a walk. He'll bring samosas and jilebis. We'll only need some toast. I'll do that in the toaster. What sort of cuisine shall it be today? Our style or Mysore style?'

'She and Kishan bought vegetables and coconut yesterday.'

'What sort of bland food is that, with coconut. Just do one thing, Bari-Jiji. Grind up some turmeric and ginger. We'll do a mutton pulao. Grate some of the gourd for me. We'll make a few koftas. Then I want you to peel the colocasia. You must also pound some cardamom, pepper, cinnamon bark, coriander seeds and cloves. Really fine, please. I also want some coriander pounded separately for the alu-gobi tonight.'

Radha Bhabhiji came out of the kitchen carrying a tray with the teapot and cups.

'Well, Miña, what are the going to cook today?'

'Nothing whatsoever. We are going to the Ganesh Mandir mountain.'

'Very well.'

Minakshi went into the kitchen to prepare another round of tea. Bari-Jiji opened her toothless mouth to smile. She held out her brass tumbler.

'I want some tea too.'

'Shall I add some ginger, Bari-Jiji?'

'Yes please. I love the tea you make.'

A command was spoken from outside the kitchen, to everyone in general. 'I've brought the samosas and jilebis. Put a few jilebis into hot milk.' Minakshi took the packet of jilebis into the kitchen and began to open it.

'Sh... here... here.'

Minakshi turned around.

'Give me four,' said Bari-Jiji.

It was a food war. The chief protagonists were: Jiji, Bari-Jiji. When grandfather was alive, Bari-Jiji ruled absolutely and tyrannically. Jiji kneaded mountains of chappati dough. She sliced baskets of onions and kilos of meat. She roasted pappads in the evening while Bari-Jiji drank her Kesar Kasturi. She made the pakoras. Then grandfather died. Within ten days Jiji was sworn into power. Bari-Jiji lost her rights to kumkumam, betel leaves, meat and spirits; she also lost in the matter of everyday meals. Everyday there was meat cooked in the kitchen. In a democratic spirit, the vegetarians in the family (actually only Bari-Jiji) were served potatoes. Bari-Jiji celebrated her loss in the battlefield with loud belching all night long, by breaking wind as if her whole body was tearing apart, and then whimpering in the toilet. Before she could be attacked again, she then started a second offensive of her own. Once in six months, Bari-Jiji began to be possessed by Amba.

Amba always chose the moments when Jiji and Papaji were seated at evening times with their pappads and their drinks. At first there would be a deep 'Hé' sound which came from the pit of the stomach. When they came running to her, panting with fear, she would yell in anger, 'Have you forgotten me?' The instant Jiji bent low and asked reverently, 'Command us, Ambé,' the orders would come. 'Give me the drink that is due to me. I want Kesar Kasturi. I want a kilo of barfi. I want fried meat ... ah ... ah.' When she was given all these things, she would say, 'Go away, all of you.' And for a while there would be loud celebratory noises emerging from Bari-Jiji's room.

The next morning Bari-Jiji would appear in the kitchen lifting her alcohol-heavy eyelids with difficult and smiling her toothless smile. 'Amba tormented me very much,' she would say.

It might have been possible to bandy words with Bari-Jiji, but Jiji did not have the courage to question Amba.

'Give me jilebis,' said Bari-Jiji.

Minakshi gave her four jilebis. When the jilebis were served to all the family, Bari-Jiji would get her fair share. This was for pure greed. At first, Minakshi used to wonder where Bari-Jiji hid away these things. It was only later that she realized that there were a couple of secret pockets in the heavily pleated four-yard skirts that Bari-Jiji wore. She had shown them to Minakshi. She put the cover on the teapot.

'Give me the masala ingredients before you go,' said Bari-Jiji. 'And I need ghee as well. For the mutton pulao.'

This was a recent thrust of the battle. Jiji's asthma and blood pressure had restricted her activities somewhat. Next to her bed was the wooden cabinet in which were kept cloves, saffron, cinnamon, peppercorns, raisins, cardamom, sugar, ghee, cashew nuts. You could not get to any of these things without going past her. Before that you were subjected to a severe catechism: Why do you need the ghee? What happened to the ghee I gave you yesterday? If there is half a katora left after spreading on the chappatis, a quarter katora should be sufficient now. Show me all the masala ingredients you have taken out before you go. That saffron was specially ordered from Kashmir. Don't dump it into the pulao. What are you cooking for the vegetarians today? Wasn't there anything left over for them from yesterday? What is the use of just eating and then going to the toilet?

From that dimly-lit, narrow-windowed kitchen, there were hands reaching out to control, like the eight tentacles of the octopus which lives in the sea. They reached out to bind them, tightly, tightly; and the women accepted their bonds with joy. If their waists were bound, they called them jewelled belts; if their feet were held back, they called them anklets, if they touched their foreheads, they called them crowns. The women entered a world that was enclosed by wire on all four sides and reigned there proudly; it was their kingdom. They made earth-shaking decisions; today we'll have mutton pulao; tomorrow let it be puri-masala. Impotent authority.

When the window was opened to gather in the mountain, the open air, the blue and the green, it was as if their strength was sucked out of them. Like Vina Mausi, Kishan's aunt. She was now fifty and had been a widow from the age of fifteen. She was a teacher in a village. She had a room and a kitchen at one end of the garden belonging to the owners of the school. An asoka tree stood in front of the house, and behind the kitchen, a champakam tree, with its creamy flowers and yellow stems. Flower-laden creepers entered through her windows freely. In the evenings, all the neighbouring children would come to visit their teacher. Otherwise there was the koel song from the asoka tree. But Vina Mausi would still say, 'I don't have any authority.' The little ones surrounded her,

calling out, 'Teacher, teacher'. She had the entire
responsibility for primary education at the school. She could
walk down to the bazaar at will. If she put a charpoy under
the asoka tree, she could share the companionship of the
koel and its calling voice until her longing ceased. In the early
mornings the white flowers were at touching distance the
minute she opened her door. But Vina Mausi's breath caught
in her chest. As soon as she reached open spaces, something
in her moved towards the earth. Her nipples and her womb
became as stone. Heavy. Pulling her down. Descending,
descending, descending to the earth in surrender. Forcing
her to stand stock still, her feet buried deep.

* * *

From the edge of the lake white wings were raised, lowered
and tilted as the birds began to move. Minakshi was shaken
with astonishment on the very first instant that they came into
view. As the birds circled over the entire spread of the lake,
coming to rest upon its waters, their red beaks shone through
the distance. Then they rose again, smoothly separating their
wide wings, tilting to the left and then to the right, now
gliding ... the swish of their wings was very near, almost in
one's face. Their coral beaks were flat and thrust forward.
Russian birds. They came to Anasagar Lake for a few months;
sudden visitors.

The picnic to the lake had been decided upon only the
previous evening. The plan was for all the relations to make a
trip to the lake together. For twenty people: a hundred puris,
with enough potato and tomato chutney; a hundred
sandwiches, things to munch, bottles of milk for the babies,
hot water in flasks. A portable stove to cook hot pakoras in
the evening. Oil, besan, onions, chilli powder, salt and green
chillies for bhajis.

A light burnt in the kitchen from four o'clock when dawn
broke. On a large tray, Jiji began to mix the wheat flour into

dough. Kusuma was heating oil in a pan, ready to cook the rolled out puris. Radha Bhabhiji was spreading bread with butter and chutney, the packets of bread opened, surrounding her. Bari-Jiji was filling small plastic bags with things to nibble and rubber banding them.

Mina had not thought about this whole aspect of the trip to the lake.

'O, Mina, are you up?' said Radha Bhabiji. Her hair was glued together with sweat. 'Will you make some tea?'

Mina started to make tea for all of them. She put basil leaves into the hot water. Kishan, joining them after brushing his teeth, put out the cups on a tray.

Radha Bhabhiji was muttering to herself, 'The children have to be bathed. It might be a good idea to take two or three extra pants in a plastic bag. Priya sometimes forgets to ask. I must roll up five or six rugs for spreading on the grass. How many tiny babies will there be? Four. Milk powder. Glaxo for Minoo. Archana's baby takes Lactogen. Mustn't forget the packet of biscuits. Mine only likes salty ones. If there aren't any, we'll stop on the way. Otherwise the child won't stop crying. And he hates that. Sugar. Mustn't forget the spoon. Serving spoons. Plates. Kusuma, take that bottle of soap to wash the plates. There's a tap there. Bari-Jiji, please slice ten or fifteen onions. If we take them in a plastic bag, the pakoras will be done in minutes. Mina, please, will you bathe the children?'

'Bhabhiji, it's only six o'clock now. They'll cry if they are woken up. Why doesn't Gopal Bhaisaheb give them their baths later?'

'O yes, he'll bathe them. Keep thinking that.'

Mina handed her her tea. She poured some tea into Bari-Jiji's brass tumbler. She understood Radha Bhabhiji's sarcasm. Radha was brilliant at Maths. Because her family would not consent to her taking up further studies in this subject, she was working in a bank, in quite a high position. A few months before this, she and Gopal Bhaisaheb had invited Kishan and Minakshi to spend a few days with them in Jodhpur. Gopal Bhaisaheb was a doctor at the hospital there. It had been really hot at the time. The midday meal had not been ready.

'The heat in these parts absolutely burns you up. It's impossible to do anything. Radha was out of town recently, for a couple of days, on her bank work. I was completely helpless. I couldn't so much as stand in the kitchen. And you can't even get servants over here. Can you imagine what it was like, Kishan. I couldn't even stand in the kitchen long enough to make a cup of tea.'

Kishan said quietly, 'Isn't Radha Bhabiji who also has a job at the bank, cooking in the same kitchen at this very moment?'

'Certainly. So what? After all, women are used to it.'

True. You could not expect Gopal Bhaisaheb to wake up early during his vacation in order to bathe his children.

'Radha Bhabhiji, what sari are you going to wear?' asked Kusuma.

'My red silk. I pressed it last night, and then did his clothes and the children's.'

'I was thinking of wearing my white sari with the black spots, but my choli needs ironing. Mina, will you lend me your black choli?'

'Why not? Do have it. But it is sleeveless.'

'O dear. In that case please iron my choli for me, Mina. I cannot wear a sleeveless choli. I haven't shaved under my arms.'

'Make sure you have left a long enough pallav, and just cover yourself with it. After all, who is going to come and peer under your arms?'

'Look here, Mina, don't try to be funny. Are you going to set up the iron?'

'All right, all right.'

Jiji came in very slowly, holding on to the walls, and opened the large pickle jar.

'Whatever are you trying to do, Jiji? Go and lie down quietly,' Radha Bhabhiji scolded.

'But they'll all enjoy some pickle. Let me put some out.'

'What's all that racket in the kitchen. You are not allowing us to get any sleep,' came a voice.

Immediate silence.

Then, in hushed tones, 'Mina, will you put the potatoes to boil on the little stove?'

'Radha Bhabiji, why don't you spice them and put them in the pressure cooker? Then you won't have to boil them first and then peel them.'

'You do that then. Leave Bari-Jiji to fry the rest of the puris.'

By the time eight o'clock struck, all necks and underarms were raining sweat. Cholis were stuck to bodies. Oil smoke irritated their eyes. Their eyelids were heavy from lack of sleep. Papaji peeped into the kitchen.

'As soon as the trip to the lake was mentioned, the lot of you began to leap with enthusiasm.' He laughed aloud.

Chirping and clucking, the small birds floated on the water, yellow and black. All of a sudden, white wings swirled above, coral shadowed.

Upon the rugs, card games. A few of the women were playing too, until children tugged at them, clutching their backside and pleading, 'Mummyji, dirty.' Then off they went with old newspaper in their hands. There would be a swift knock on the child's head, enough to hurt. When the mothers got up, the younger girls took their places. Every now and then they rose, offering the men water to drink.

Radha Bhabiji and Kusuma washed the plates. Then the stove was lit to make pakoras.

'Arre, what a marvellous smell! Two for me please, with only green chillies.'

Intermittently there was conversation with the children:

'Raju, what are you going to be, when you grow up?'

'A pilot, z-o-i-n-g.'

'You, Priya?'

'I... I... I'll make the thapatis in my house.'

'How cleverly she talks,' Jiji laughed.

'I've climbed all the mountains which surround Ajmer,' said Papaji.

'Jiji, what about you?' asked Minakshi.

'Every time he climbed a mountain, I was carrying a child,' Jiji laughed whole-heartedly. Everyone laughed with her. Jiji had borne fourteen children.

At last, they gathered up everything, firmly changed the minds of the children who were wondering whether they should go 'dirty' one last time, and started homewards.

Kusuma lingered, 'Mina, walk a bit slowly. I haven't even seen the birds properly yet.'

'Shall I call Satish?'

'No, no. Let him go. Otherwise there will be trouble.'

They walked on slowly.

'I was ten days late. Just as I was thinking of going to the doctor, it's come on.'

'Did you come prepared? If you had said, we could have stopped by the shops.'

'O yes, I came prepared. Even so, it's a white sari. Can you just have a look?'

'It's all right. Nothing's happened.'

'Should we walk a bit faster? There's no time to sit by the lake shore. I have to peel the garlic for the evening meal.'

'Just come. Don't talk.'

She silenced Kusuma and made her sit by the lake. She had asked Jiji once, 'What sort of daughter-in-law would you like, when your third son marries?' Jiji had answered at once: educated, fair skinned, quiet. 'Well said,' Papaji had agreed. Minakshi had refused to believe that such a girl existed. She had assumed that Jiji's answer had been a continuation of that afternoon's incident. A friend of Papaji had visited them, an expert in skin diseases. At that time, Minakshi had found a few itchy, whitish spots on her hand. Papaji introduced her to the skin specialist. This is Kishan's wife. She never stops roaming the town. She always has a book in her hand. A chatterbox. Examine her hands.

The expert's advice: Just stay at home. Be like the other women. Everything will come out all right. If people live as they ought why should anyone fall a prey to disease?

'Aha,' said Papaji, in admiration.

She had thought that what Jiji said was a kind of joke, following upon this. But when Kusuma was found, she was like a fine illustration and commentary to Jiji's exposition.

An M.A. in Politics. A diploma in French. It wasn't quite clear why she had studied French. It seemed that collecting a diploma in some language or the other was a necessary part of waiting for marriage. If the bridegroom had a job in foreign parts, then it seems the knowledge of a foreign language would come in useful. During this time of waiting, Kusuma had also embroidered cushions and pillow cases, handcrafted small objects, decorated saris with lace and embroidery. She had not missed out on classes in flower arrangement, bakery, sewing and in making jam, juice and pickles. She had learnt all these skills. She was the perfect daughter-in-law.

As if they had remembered them suddenly, the white crowd that had gone a long distance, rose high, wheeled about, and flew in towards their left. They came floating, at a moderate speed now, circling by them.

Kusuma wept.

'That beak ... what a red,' she sobbed.

Winged coral floated against a reddening sky.

The unpeeled garlic ...

Wings opened to the beat of another circle.

The unformed foetus ...

One, two, three, four, five – in series they slid gracefully into the water and began to float.

Kusuma sobbed quietly.

* * *

Jiji's worst attack happened when they came to Ajmer for the Holi holidays. One afternoon she sorted out the ingredients needed for the cooking, tucked in her keys at her waist, and came walking slowly towards the fridge to check what was left there. Before she could reach it, her breath caught, and then came in loud dragging sighs. Before the family could come rushing to her aid, her heavy body had fallen to the ground. She was streaming with sweat and was drenched in her own urine.

'I am going ... I am going ... My daughters-in-law are all elsewhere ... That wretched Bari-Jiji will rule in the kitchen ... Hé Bhagwan.' She kept turning her head from one side to the other. The doctor who lived downstairs came in haste to give her an injection. At last she began to breathe evenly once more; her eyelids dropped and she fell asleep.

When she opened her eyes again, she first made sure her keys were as usual at her waist. 'What are you cooking for the evening meal?' she asked. When they answered, Beans, she grumbled, 'Why? Didn't I say cauliflower? Did she change it? Did she think I was going to die?'

'No, no, Jiji. It was just that there was no cauliflower available in the bazaar.'

'My sari ... give me ... another sari,' she said.

Kusuma opened Jiji's wardrobe and took out a green sari, a green underskirt and a pale yellow choli. She placed them by Jiji's bed. Jiji turned her head to see. She asked in a feeble voice, 'Where are my bangles?' Minakshi opened the bangle box to take out some green glass bangles.

They closed the door and removed Jiji's clothes. Her body was like a fruit that has passed its full ruddy ripeness and is now wilting. Upon the backs of her wizened hands, the veins stood out. Heavy lines ran along the palms. There were scars of childbirth on her lower abdomen, as if she had been deeply ploughed there. Her public hair, whitened, hung in wisps. Buttocks and thighs, once rounded, now shrunken, hung loose with deep creases. The upper part of her inner thigh was like withered and blackened banana skin. Dry nipples hung low, like raisins. On her neck were dark lines, caused by heavy gold chains. A wide, polished scar as if she were going bald, shone at the lower edge of her centre parting, where the gold band with its heavy pendant had constantly pressed.

A body that had lived. A body that had expelled urine, faeces, blood, children. A body with so many imprints.

As soon as the sari was on, Radha Bhabhiji combed Jiji's hair and plaited it with a dark string finished with coloured tassels. Kusuma tucked the cabinet keys at her waist. Jiji leaned back on her bed.

After the others had left, Minakshi sat by Jiji's side. Jiji's hands burrowed at her waist. The room was darkened, the curtains drawn.

Jiji began to speak. Because of the medicines, her tiredness, and the onset of sleep, her voice was deep, yet it seemed curiously weightless, as if it had roamed about in the wind and then returned.

'A red skirt.'

'What is it, Jiji?'

'My wedding skirt. It was bright red, with gold and silver decorations all over. Twelve gold bangles. Two necklaces. Earstuds in pearls and red and green gemstones. Another set of earstuds in coral. Five sovereigns worth of centrepiece to the gold headband. A silver key-hook. I was just fifteen years old. At the time of my bidai, when my parents sent me to my new home, my mother spoke to me in my ear. The memory of that bidai is still heavy in my heart. With her head covered, she leaned over me and held me to her. Her big nose ring was sharp against my face. "Take control over the kitchen. Never forget to make yourself attractive. Those two rules will give you all the strength and authority you will need." '

'Let it be, Jiji. You sleep now.'

'I ... remember ... everything. There were thirty people in the household. I used to mix five kilos of atta to make three hundred chappatis. On that first day, the palms of both my hands were blue with bruises. There were shooting pains in my shoulder blades. Papaji said ... shabash. You are an excellent worker.'

She let out a huge breath.

'We had a baby, a son, even before Gopal. Did you know that? He died at the age of one. There was a puja that day. Everyone was in the kitchen. The baby had climbed the stairs and fallen off the parapet wall. He had crawled up thirty steps ... I heard that huge scream just as I was putting the puris into the hot oil ... It seemed to knock me in the pit of my stomach ... The base of his skull was split ... His brains were splattered all over the stone pavement, like white droppings ... After all the men returned ... I fried ... Mina, are you listening ... I fried the rest of the puris.'

Minakshi stroked Jiji's forehead.

'After Father-in-law died, I slipped the keys onto my silver waist hook. Mina ... see how much I gained. I am like a queen ... Don't you think?' Jiji muttered. She was almost asleep.

Minakshi bent low to those withered earlobes wearing flower shaped earstuds covered in pearls and brightly coloured gemstones. They were alone, Jiji and she; alone as Maha Vishnu on his serpent bed floating upon the widespread sea. In that darkened room, there was a feeling like that of the cutting of an umbilical cord. We cannot be certain whether this conversation was actually started by her, or whether it happened on its own, or whether it only seemed to her to have occurred because she had imagined it so often. It is not even certain whether that conversation was between the two of them – Jiji and herself alone.

Jiji, no strength comes to you from that kitchen; nor from that necklace nor bangle nor headband nor forehead jewel.

Authority cannot come to you from these things.

That authority is Papaji's.

From all that

be free

be free
be free.
But if I free myself ... then ... what is left?
You alone, having renounced your jewellery, your children and Papaji. Yourself, cut free. Just Dularibai, alone. And from that, strength. Authority.
And when I have renounced all that, then who am I?
Find out. Dip in and see.
Dip into what?
Into your own inner well.
But there is nothing to hold on to ... I'm frigh ... .
Dip in deeper, deeper. Find out the relationship between Dularibai and the world.
Had there not been those three hundred chappatis to cook every day, nor those fourteen children who once kicked in your womb.
If your thoughts had not been confined to mutton pulao, masala, puri-alu, dhania powder, salt, sugar, milk, oil, ghee.
If you had not had these constant cares: once every four days the wick to the stove has to be pulled up; whenever kerosene is available it has to be bought and stored; in the rainy season the rice has to be watched and the dal might be full of insects; pickles must be made in the mango-season; when the fruit is ripe it will be time for sherbet, juice and jam; old clothes can be bartered for new pots and pans; once a fortnight the drainage area in the kitchen must be spread with lime; if one's periods come it will be a worry; if they don't come it will be a worry.
If all this clutter had not filled up the drawers of your mind.
Perhaps you too might have seen the apple fall; the steam gathering at the kettle's spout; might have discovered new continents; written a poem while sitting upon Mount Kailasam. Might have painted upon the walls of caves. Might have flown. Might have made a world without wars, prisons, gallows, chemical warfare.
Where did you go away, Jiji?

How could you think that
your strength came
from food that was given in the appropriate measure
and jewellery that weighs down ears and neck and
forehead?

Sink deeper still
When you touch bottom you will reach the universal waters.
You will connect yourself with the world that surrounds you.
Your womb and your breasts will fall away from you. The
smell of cooking will vanish away. The sparkle of jewellery
will disappear. And there will be you. Not trapped nor
diminished by gender, but freed.
So touch the waters, Jiji
and rise
rise
rise.

Jiji turned, searched for and held fast to Minakshi's hand.

Translated by Lakshmi Holmstrom.

Thirst

Vandana Singh

In the dream there were snakes coiling about her, dark and glossy as the hairs on her head, and an altar, and the smell of sandalwood incense, her mother's favourite kind. When her eyes opened she could not remember for a moment who she was. Even the familiar room, with the whitewash peeling off the walls and summer dust on the sill of the open window, the sag of the bed, the curve of the man's shoulders as he lay in sleep with his back to her – all that seemed imbued with remoteness, as though it had nothing whatever to do with her. Slowly her name came to her: Susheela, and with it the full weight of her misery returned. Her husband stirred in sleep, but he did not turn towards her. She might as well be dead, she thought bitterly, for all the notice he took of her.

And on the heels of that thought came another (as she sat up very carefully so as not to wake her husband), that tomorrow was the day of Naag Panchami, the Snake Festival, and that was why the dream had come. The monsoons were late, and this was the hottest summer ever. Perhaps it would rain tomorrow. A Festival day rain would be a good thing. She slipped out of bed, bathed quickly using an inadequate half a bucket of water and dressed in a pink cotton sari. An early morning hush lay deep over the house; the ceiling fans had wound down during the night (another power failure) and even the birds in the bougainvillea outside the window seemed reluctant to break the silence. As Susheela entered the kitchen she heard the creak of her mother-in-law's bed from the other end of the house, and the old woman's plastic slippers slapping the bare floor as she shuffled to the bathroom. Susheela's son was very likely still asleep in his grandmother's bed; she could see him in her mind's eye, forehead beaded with sweat, plump hands closed into fists, cheeks flushed with heat, lips tremulous with the passage of some childish dream. For a moment she wanted desperately to see him and hold him, but she could not face the old lady just yet. Instead she put the tea water on to boil and turned on the tap so that when the water came (one precious hour in the morning and one in the evening) the buckets would begin to fill for the day's use. Now the tap only belched warm air; heat came in from the small window like the breath of a hungry animal.

She stood at the window, looking out into the courtyard and the untended garden behind it. The drought had reduced the back garden to a mass of dead, spiny shrubs dotting withered grass. Only the little harsingar tree stood proud, its young, leafy branches dotted with tiny orange and white flowers. It had survived on a daily cupful of water and her love.

Afterwards, as she rolled paratha dough for her husband's breakfast, hoping she would not (again) make him late for office, she heard the household stir; and the water came gurgling out of the tap. She felt the old hunger in her as though she was waiting for something. As the earth waits for rain, she thought, licking her dry lips.

She thought of the lake in the park, and – despite herself – the thin face of the gardener who worked there, and the way he said 'namaste' so respectfully while his eyes looked at her in a way that dissolved all distance between them, all barriers of class and caste and propriety ... She really shouldn't go there so often. But Kishore loves it, her mind said rebelliously, and she thought of how her little boy loved to walk under the trees and watch the parakeets eat the neem berries. She would make up stories for him about imaginary people who lived in the ruins around the lake and ate nothing but milk-sweets all day.

The park was on the way to the vegetable market that came up in the late afternoon like a miniature city on the sidewalks, complete with towers of jewel-toned purple eggplants and cascades of coriander leaves and citadels of fat, shiny little onions. The market was her excuse for surreptitious visits to the lake in the park, with her boy (poor, innocent boy!) as chaperone and protector. Sweat rolled off her temples; she dabbed at it with the free end of her sari and thought of the translucent coolness of the lake, the lips of the water against her bare toes. I am a cursed woman, she thought to herself with a shudder. My mother-in-law is right, the water draws me and draws me, to what other thing but death. Curses do run in families. She thought of her own mother, and her maternal grandmother, and she resolved that today she would not go to the lake, even though that would make Kishore cry.

In the end she broke her promise to herself, as she had done many times before. In the dry, breathless heat of the day, Susheela felt as though the air in her lungs had turned solid. She went blindly about her tasks, cooking and serving lunch, piling the steel dishes noisily in the sink for the servant boy to wash when he came in the evening. The grandmother took Kishore off for his afternoon nap. Susheela collected the kitchen leavings – potato peels, turnip ends and scraps from lunch – into a battered tin and went up the short driveway to the front gate. Dead leaves crunched under her feet. Piling the refuse by the side of the gate, she waited for Muniya, the milkman's ancient cow, to come meandering down the lane.

The lane shimmered in the heat. The three shisham trees in the garden stood very still, their small, round leaves drooping. Behind her the house crouched like a yellow cat. Plaster flaked off its front, revealing an underflesh of burnt red brick. Susheela leaned on the gate. A breeze, no more than a breath, stirred the dead leaves on the trees, smelling of dust. But Susheela smelled – or imagined she smelled – water.

Suddenly she made up her mind. She crept into the still, dark house and saw with relief that the grandmother had fallen asleep with Kishore. The two lay together like exhausted children, damp with sweat, the old lady's arm protectively around the boy. I have not been a good mother, Susheela thought. Her eyes burned with tears. She went out into the bright and dusty afternoon.

In less than ten minutes she was at the iron fence, with the rusty, indecipherable Archeological Survey of India sign leaning over the entrance. She paused for a moment, looking around her a little apprehensively. A bicycle-repairman sat nodding under a tree with his paraphernalia around him, but there was no one else about. She let herself into the gap in the fence where there had once been a gate; inside, tall neem trees made deep shadows. A clerk or two lay sleeping in the shade. Then she saw the gardener, sleeping, his turban spread out over his face. The bullock that had been pulling the lawn mower lay beside him like a white, humped mountain, chewing cud. Susheela crept soundlessly to the lake's edge.

The lake itself was small, more like a large pond. The edge was paved with stone, brown and weathered with age; at one end there was the old ruin with crumbling steps leading down into the quiet, green water. What ancients had built and frequented the place Susheela did not know, but it was tranquil here, under the neem trees. The water had receded with the heat of summer, but there was enough to allow a few fragile blue lotuses to bloom in the shade.

She leaned against a tree trunk, savouring the peace. Then she slipped a slender brown foot out of her embroidered shoe, over the sun-warmed stone paving into the water. She felt the cool silk of the water on her foot, and a tremendous longing arose within her, a desire to feel the water lick the dry heat from her body, to envelop her in its fluid embrace ...

Some small sound jolted her back into herself. She withdrew her foot hurriedly from the water, wiped it on the stone. What had she been about to do? A bead of sweat ran down her cheek to the corner of her mouth. Then she saw that there was something in the water, making ripples as it swam towards her. A turtle, perhaps – or a snake? She leaned forward, peering. In the emerald depths, apparitions of pale fish scattered as the thing came closer. It was a snake – a cobra.

Just as she identified it she saw a stone skimming over the water, falling a few feet short. The snake dived and disappeared.

Her skin prickled. The gardener was standing beside her. 'They say it is good to see a cobra the day before the Snake Festival,' he said. He wiped the sweat off his face with his turban. 'It means rain. But better not to let the Naag Lords get too close, behen. Would you like some flowers? Amaltas blooms, yellow as sunlight, lovely tied in your bun, against your neck ... or would you prefer ... a delicate twig of harsingar?'

She edged away nervously. For a moment she imagined his fingers on the nape of her neck.

'No, I don't want anything,' she said shortly. He was looking at her without any shame, as though she were a woman of his own class, not a respectably married housewife. But respectably married housewives didn't wander about parks alone.

'If ever there is anything you need... I will be happy to serve you. But tell me, where is your little boy?'

Oh why hadn't she brought Kishore? She looked around her, terrified, and was reassured to see a young couple enter the park, holding hands surreptitiously. Some of her fear abated.

'I have to go,' she said, drawing herself up. The gardener put his palms together, accepting her dismissal, his gaze licking at her face. 'Achha, behen-ji,' he said. Yes, sister. He watched her leave. She was conscious of the movement of her hips, the slight swing of her arms, the dust she raised with every step. She did not draw breath until she was out in the lane.

She had grown up off-balance. All her life she had carried inside her an empty space that disturbed her centre of gravity, that drew her to the sheltering closeness of trees, walls, wilderness. Nothing she had done in her life – not her studentship, not marriage, not even the birth of her son – had assuaged that emptiness, that feeling of the earth waiting for rain. She was still waiting.

In her childhood the Snake Festival had been special. It was the one day she had always understood to be her own. Here in this small town where her husband had grown up, Naag Panchami would be marked only by a visit to the temple and prayers to the gods to prevent death by snakebite. But in her hometown of Ujjain, tomorrow, there would be special ceremonies and processions in the streets ... .

In her parents' house, every Festival day, the child Susheela had helped her mother arrange flowers and sweet offerings on the kitchen altar. Dressed in silks, Susheela had sat with her brother on the flower-strewn floor, watching as their mother lit the oil diyas. In the flickering light, her mother would become remote and solemn, chanting the ancient Sanskrit phrases: homage to the snakes of the earth. Homage to the snakes in the rays of sun, the tree-snakes. Homage to the snakes of the waters, homage to them all. The names of the Snake lords were then recited: Anantha, who supports the earth in his coils, Vasuki the king, who rules their fabulous, gem-studded underworld city. Takshaka, Muchilinda, all the greater and the lesser lords. They bring us life, her mother would say; they foster fertility and renewal. They bring also death. They are in the fire of Agni and in the primeval ocean.

Her mother would turn from the altar to her children and take the child Susheela onto her lap. Then the stories would come, wondrous tales, fierce or sad; about the Snake divinities speaking to gods and mingling secretly with humans; about their exquisite underwater palaces, where they kept the knowledge and wisdom they had accumulated, waiting until humankind was ready for the gift. As her mother spoke her hands would rise and fall in smooth and sudden gestures, and the stories, built thus of words and hands, would come to life in the fragrant air. Her mother's urbanized Hindi would give way to the sing-song village dialect she had spoken as a girl. Even as a five-year-old, Susheela was aware that what was being passed on to them on these occasions was meant particularly for her; that her brother, sitting wistful-eyed across from them was in some inexplicable way, excluded.

But the most wonderful thing about it all was that the three of them were sheltered for a while, in a cocoon of mystery and ceremony, from the mundane, silent bitterness between her parents. Her father kept away from them during Naag Panchami, leaving them to an unfamiliar peace. As she grew older, it became increasingly clear to Susheela that the undercurrents of ill-feeling in the house, the raised voices (mainly her father's) behind locked doors in the night, the misery, guilt and yearning in her mother's eyes – were all her fault. Her father treated her with a distant regard; his love he kept for his son, expressing it with his eyes whenever he looked at the boy, unaware that the boy feared him and longed to escape.

Coming home from school – she remembered how it felt to enter the dark, polished hallway, the high-arched ceilings – how the house diminished her. The respite of the garden and the parakeets in the guava trees, the three harsingar trees (her favourite kind) bright with tiny flowers ... And then quite

suddenly she was grown up and her marriage arranged with a
stranger she had met only three times. He had come once for
tea in the garden, and later they had walked together,
chaperoned by her mother and aunts. She had lost her reserve,
pointing out to him the trees and flowers and her favourite
shady spot under the jamun tree, and he had impressed her
with the way his hands touched the blossoms, the ripe fruit,
so gently for such a big, quiet man. She had wanted him to
touch her like that ...

For the five years of her marriage the Festival had brought
her nothing but shadows from the past, and a small
remembrance from her brother. Only this year – this year
was different. The intensity of the old dream, the tightness in
her chest, the feeling of breathless anticipation ... Entering
the dim stillness of the house, Susheela found herself longing
for her son. But he was still asleep in his grandmother's bed.
She wanted to hold him forever because she feared that she
would not hesitate to leave him for the nameless hunger that
was in her.

In the late afternoon, when the heat had abated a little,
Susheela's husband came home from work. His name was
Prakash, but she couldn't think of him by his name, only by
the way he made her feel, a mixture of bewilderment and
yearning.

Kishore ran up to him at the doorway, calling 'Baba!' in
his high voice. The child had sulked all afternoon when she
told him they were not going to the park. Finally she had
made him a paper boat and told him he could play in the
washing-up water. Now he held out the damp boat to his
father. A brief smile broke the serious cast of her husband's
face, accentuating the lines that made him look older than
he was. He glanced at Susheela quickly, non-committally, and
went into the back to wash his hands, leaving in his wake a
faint odour of musty offices and old ledgers. Standing in the
silence and heat of the dining room, with the silver teapot

and the array of delicacies arranged on the table, Susheela felt suddenly bereft of hope.

How had she come to this?

Once she had almost loved him. Not at first – she remembered sitting terrified before the nuptial fire under a canopy of marigolds in the front lawn, with this man that she hardly knew. Her father had died the previous year. She had left the large suburban bungalow, the luxuriant garden that had been her refuge, and her mother, alone, serene now after years of unhappiness, but with a haunted, fragile air about her – all that, for the life of a senior accountant's wife in a strange town. Still, in the beginning, her husband's gentleness had won her over. He had been loving and attentive, filling her with a joyous, incredulous relief, allaying her fears that her married life would be as dreary and bereft of happiness as her mother's had been. She had started to fall in love with him, with his patience, his long, contemplative silences, and the inexplicable, endearing seriousness with which he took his work. But then, quite soon after the birth (nearly painless) of their son, everything had changed. Her husband suddenly began to avoid her as much as was possible, and sometimes she had caught him giving her peculiar, wary, sidelong glances that she could not fathom. It had disturbed the healthy, animal joyfulness of motherhood.

He had evaded her questions, meeting her pleas, tears and anger with a pained silence. Finally she had come to accept that things would stay this way between them. Four years later, he was still the kind, quiet man she'd known, but he had kept his distance; he no longer looked at her much, even when they (infrequently) made love.

The evening wore on – dark fell and mosquitoes came swarming in through cracks in the shutters. The power was still out so her husband lit candles in the rooms that cast large, tremulous shadows. The air was thick as a blanket.

There was a sudden loud crash in the house, and the sound of water splashing. Her mother-in-law screamed, 'Susheela?

Arrey Susheela! Look what your son just did! Don't cry, my darling ... '

In the kitchen, which was lit dimly by a candle, Kishore stood soaked to the skin in the washing-up water. The bucket lay overturned on the floor. He was crying noisily, holding the soggy remains of the paper boat. As Susheela picked him up, her mother-in-law shook her head. 'It's the curse on your family!' she said. 'Drawn to water – and to death! He had climbed into the bucket with his boat. He would have drowned if I had not come in just then. My poor boy, what will become of him!'

'Let her be, Ma-ji,' her husband said. He was standing in the doorway. He gave Susheela a quick, shy look. When she came towards the door with their son he laid his hand on the boy's dripping head.

'Susheela?'

He spoke her name tentatively, questioningly, but her eyes were already filling with tears. She stepped past him with her burden. In the bedroom she stood Kishore on the bed to dry him down and change his clothes.

'I'll make you another boat tomorrow,' she told him, glad that the semi-darkness hid her tears.

Curses did run in families ... She remembered her brother's escapades to the pond at the end of their street when they had been children, and how their father had scolded him as he stood dripping and half-naked on the polished floor of the hall. Nothing he said had made a difference to the boy; the next afternoon he would be gone again with the servant children, diving and splashing in the pond among gleaming green lilypads, coming reluctantly home in the evenings through the dining room window, all aglow with his adventure, swearing her to secrecy ... .

The power came back suddenly. Susheela blinked in the light. The ceiling fans began their laborious circumlocutions, and the still air began to move. Her son laughed, jumped off the bed and went to find his father, holding out his little arms like airplane wings.

Late that evening, after the servant-boy had finished doing the dinner dishes and been dismissed, Susheela stood alone in the kitchen, finishing the day's chores. She could hear the low sound of the TV from the drawing room. In the small bedroom that her son shared with his grandmother, her mother-in-law was singing some old, half-remembered lullaby. In the storeroom, above the bins and sacks of grain, the gods gazed at Susheela from the altar – a brass statuette of Vishnu the Creator, reclining under the sheltering hood of the great serpent Ananth; Krishna with his flute, a meditative Buddha and a print of Lord Shiva. She cleaned the altar of dead flowers, lit an incense stick and watched the smoke curl up to the rough, white-washed ceiling.

One more task remained. She filled a steel bowl with cold milk, put the rest of the milk into the small fridge, and took the flashlight. She had watched her mother do this every night for years in their home in Ujjain. Now, with her mother gone, the ritual gave her comfort. She went into the silent, moonlit courtyard behind the house, staying close to the wall. She walked up to the harsingar tree, which stood green and proud amidst the detritus of dead bushes and thorny shrubs. It always bloomed out of season, as though it obeyed the laws of some other universe. Under the tree lay a great stone, upon which she set down the steel bowl of milk. She turned off the flashlight. Would the snakes come, as her mother had always said? Usually she'd leave the milk on the stone and go back into the house, but today she wanted to wait.

The fragrance of the harsingar flowers filled her nostrils. The little tree was doing well. It had appeared last winter, the day before the festival of Diwali. She had just returned from the market with her mother-in-law. The servant boy did not know who had come into the compound in the afternoon and planted the tree. Susheela's mother-in-law said it must be the gardener who worked in the park – he had been trying to hire himself out in the neighborhood. Or maybe it was the lady from the Big House, the wife of Susheela's husband's supervisor, who had the huge ornamental garden that her mother-in-law had frequently admired. That is what Susheela wanted to believe.

The tree itself was innocent of its origins. She had loved it from the first moment she had seen it. Now it stood partly shading the great stone, beautiful in the moonlight. She shut her eyes and breathed in its scent. There was a sound – a soft, dry, sliding sound, scales against stone. When she opened her eyes the gleam of moonlight on the steel bowl vanished abruptly, and she thought she could see dark, coiled shapes against the stone. Let there be rain tomorrow, she said in her mind. She could not name the nebulous other thing she desired.

Very carefully she gathered half a handful of flowers from the tree and walked back to the house without turning on the flashlight. Inside she put the flowers on the altar in the kitchen. I will put some in my hair tomorrow, she told herself, switching off the light.

That night Susheela fell asleep thinking of her mother's mother, the grandmother she had never known except from old family pictures. This grandmother had brought up six children in a huge, old-fashioned house in the ancestral village. One day the river had broken its banks and filled the emptiness of the big house. The family took refuge on the rooftop terrace. The eldest son was missing – he had been visiting a neighbour. Grandfather had injured his leg so Grandmother went in the little boat, steering with a long pole, in the muddy water full of debris, pots and pans and bewildered river fish. She found her son, delivered him, then went to the aid of her neighbours. She rescued a woman stuck in a tree, several other people clinging to hutroofs, and a variety of animals, including dogs, goat-kids and muskrats. In the evening she cooked dinner on the rooftop over a coal fire, quite calmly, as though nothing unusual had happened.

As darkness fell, she told her eldest son, who was still awake, that she had to go do one more thing. She looked on the sleeping, exhausted family one more time, got into the boat, pushed off with the pole, and disappeared over the murky water. She was never seen again.

Stories gathered around the legendary grandmother like moths about a candle flame. She had given herself to the river, people said, so the floods would not come again. Susheela's mother, the youngest child, had been a teenager at the time of the disappearance; she remembered it well, years later, but she did not like to talk about it. Her face would fall slack with the memory. Then Susheela would gaze into her mother's eyes and think she saw what her mother saw: the flood, the dark water, the sole woman in the boat, steering herself away between the drowned houses, under a silent sky.

Her mother was a haunted woman, she knew. Soon after Susheela's marriage she had heard that her mother had gone to visit her ancestral home. At this, Susheela had felt a vague presentiment of disaster. But newly married, and pregnant, she had not been permitted to leave. A month later, Susheela had heard from her brother that their mother had walked to the river one morning, with flowers for worship, and that later that day, her clothes had been found floating some distance downriver from the house. Not long after that, Susheela had received a letter from her mother written a few days before the tragedy; the address on the envelope was nearly illegible and the ink was blurry and unreadable, as though the pages had been left out in the rain. Susheela had felt very clearly then that some intangible thing had passed from her mother's life into her own. For nearly five years it had been a heavy, mysterious presence within her.

She had seen that great river once, as a child. Now it came into her dreams, broad, serpentine, flowing between fragile cities, open fields and wilderness. She dreamed of floods, earthquakes, buildings tottering, the earth heaving, throwing off its old coverings, revealing roots, rocks, darkness. Twice she woke, and lay in the dark, trembling, her eyes wide open, listening to her husband breathe beside her. I must go, she thought, even if it is death that calls me.

Morning filled the house with a pale gray light; a cool breeze came in from the open windows, smelling of dust and anticipation. Susheela, breathless and light-headed, moved from room to room, distractedly applying the dust-cloth. In the kitchen she picked up a few of the harsingar flowers from the altar, hesitated, then put them down the front of her blouse for the fragrance. She did not have the patience to make a flower chain to weave in her hair. When her mother-in-law came into the kitchen Susheela was already rolling paratha dough for breakfast. She fed the family; she herself had no appetite. Her husband pushed away his empty plate with a sigh and unfolded the Sunday newspaper.

Susheela went to the front window in the drawing-room and perched on the cold sill. An army of storm-clouds was poised in the sky, and the breeze rattled the dry leaves on the trees. The raindrops fell, slowly at first, making pockmarks in the dust of the long summer; but in only a few minutes the dust became liquid mud, and the roadside ditches became torrents, and an aroma rose from the earth like a moist, cool breath of relief. All sounds were lost in the music of the rain. Neighbours gathered at their doorways, smiling, watching indulgently as children ran out of the houses and danced in the flooded, sparkling street. Then the clouds rumbled and lightning jagged across the sky. Parents called out to their children. Susheela, watching the rain, tried to decipher what message, if any, lay in its watery speech; what did it sing, as it drummed on the flat rooftops and gurgled in the ditches? She could not bear the thought that after all her waiting it would have nothing to say to her. Listening, she did not at first notice that Kishore was missing.

He'd been sulking; she had not let him go out with the neighbourhood children. He must have slipped away while she sat dreaming on the sill. She raised an alarm, feeling her knees beginning to shake. Her husband set down his cup, spilling tea, grabbed an umbrella and went into the storm.

But Susheela knew just where he would be, in the park that sloped down to the lake, their favourite walk. She gathered her sari about her ankles and went into the blinding rain. Her shoes were light and flimsy, they soon filled with muddy water, but she stumbled on. On this day of all days, to lose him like this!

The lake was a blur; the rain fell like thick needles. She looked fearfully around, shading her eyes from the rain. There he was – huddled by one of the neem trees that grew on the lake's edge. He was too heavy to pick up, he bent his head against the rain and sobbed wordlessly, but he let her set him on his feet. She thought she felt or heard something from the direction of the lake, but when she looked back, there was nothing.

She held Kishore to her in a tight grip, half-sobbing in her relief, babbling words of reassurance as she walked him back through the mud and rain to the house. She heard her husband call, saw him running up to them. Kishore looked up at her through a curtain of rain, and she thought she saw wonder in his face, then fear. He left her side and ran to his father, crying. Her mother-in-law was already at the front door with towels, scolding in her relief. Susheela stepped forward to follow her husband and son, anxious to reassure her little boy; what could make him look at her like that? But something made her hesitate on the top step. The rain streamed down her face, running in rivulets down her neck, between her breasts. Her bun had come undone and her hair lay wetly against her neck. Her sari was plastered to her skin. She itched all over. She saw now that there was a faint silvering all along her forearm, spreading rapidly over her skin. A tremor went through her.

She felt it now like a gravitational pull, as if whatever thread bound her to the lake was at last drawing her in. She turned, stumbled down the steps and began to run through the downpour. Behind her she heard her husband cry out her name, but her steps did not falter. Splashing through the water on the street and in the park, she stood at last, panting, on the lake's edge.

She had lost her shoes on the way and the stone paving felt slippery under her bare feet. There was only the sound of rain, sparkling on the lake's surface, drumming on the earth. Susheela put one foot into the water. A great shudder of desire went through her. She stepped into the lake, slipping a little on the stones. Mud squelched between her toes. The water rose to envelop her – it embraced her hips, her chest, her neck. As the water closed over her head she felt the change, like an electric current through her.

Her first feeling was that of sheer terror, as though something alien had invaded her mind and body. She thrashed about, rearing out of the water and falling back again with a splash, trying to see what or who was holding her arms to her sides, drowning her, but the rain fell in great curtains, obscuring everything. A spasm shook her from head to foot; as she lost consciousness she felt warm currents coursing painlessly through her, stretching and squeezing, shaping and moulding, as though she were a lump of clay in a potter's wheel.

When she came to, she found herself afloat in the water, conscious only of a great need to fill her lungs with air. She struggled to free herself of her clothes, turning and twisting until she swam out from the limp, wet folds of her sari, raised her head into the rain, and breathed. She turned slowly, and saw that her new body was long, limbless and lithe. Her senses registered a thousand unfamiliar impressions: the agitation of water against her scales; the completely alien sensation of being able to feel, through her skin, tiny reverberations that hinted of life swarming all about her; and the presence, inside her mouth, of a strange tongue, forked and unbearably sensitive. An exultation rose inside her; she became aware of other presences around her, long, sinuous shapes, ancient, powerful, familiar. Their bodies were dark, their heads narrow, their eyes black, beckoning, alive. She turned smoothly in the water and saw that her underbelly was pale, like theirs. Now they were leading her, diving underwater. She took a breath of air and followed them into the depths of the lake, brushing against stone; she sensed she was swimming through the passageways of some underwater structure. Memories that were not her own, yet belonged to her in some mysterious way, came crowding into her mind: warm, narrow spaces in the earth, fluid darkness, the coilings of other bodies beside her. The earth, the womb, shutting out the wide emptiness of the world.

The snakes swam around her, guiding her with gentle nudges. In the dark water they were like slender, graceful ghosts. One touched his head with hers, wheeling around her in an intricate spiral. They went up to the surface together to breathe, and taste the rain. The water was sensuous against her skin, and when the cobra leaned his head close to hers, with bright, ardent, questioning eyes, she felt a small explosion in her chest, as though a dam had burst, letting out all the needs and desires of her barren other life. That life, which she could scarcely remember now, seemed a distant dream; what was real was the movement of scale against scale, coil against coil, the flaring of her partner's majestic hood as they danced, braided about each other in the ancient, intimate rite of procreation. When at last they moved gracefully apart, to lie companionably in the water, spent but not exhausted, a picture came rudely into her mind, an alien intrusion: a small, hot, dusty room, a man asleep, his back to her, unreachable as a distant mountain. It was incomprehensible and disturbing, and she dismissed it sharply. The other snakes were coming up below her, swimming to the surface for air, and she joined them, moving playfully among them, dodging the raindrops. A feeling came to her then that she must have done this before, that this was all familiar, the snakes, the rain, the coupling in the water. That couldn't be – but the seed of a realization took root in her mind, and slowly flowered into certainty: that her mother had once done this. That this was how Susheela had been conceived... It was too enormous a discovery to comprehend all at once. When the snakes dived again, calling to her in their wordless tongue, she followed them into the submerged ruins. She understood it was a place of pilgrimage, sacred to her companions, and that they remembered its history in fragments that had been passed on from generation to generation. The pictures that arose in her mind hinted of calamitous events, heroic battles and long, golden periods of peace and prosperity. They were making her a gift of their story, she realized. She had no stories of her own but the memory of her mother and grandmother, which they accepted, she thought, with generosity.

But now the rain was slowing. She swam up to the surface and saw the sun emerge from behind the clouds. The other snakes swam sedately away from her, their farewells echoing in her mind. Until next time, she thought they said, whenever that was, and she had so many questions, so much to ask. But they were already gone, gliding over the ancient paving at the edge of the lake, disappearing into cracks and crevices in the old ruin, and into bushes, tree-holes, and other secret places. All that remained of their presence were wide ripples spreading and crisscrossing on the lake's sunlit surface. Why had they left her alone?

Rainwater dripped off the neem trees; in their shade a small emerald-green frog perched on a lotus leaf. She drifted in the middle of the lake, feeling bewildered, abandoned. Then she remembered as if from long ago, the small, heavy weight of her son on her lap, the way he tilted his chin up to her to ask for a story, his upper lip rimmed with milk. She turned and began to swim back to the lake's edge, feeling herself grow heavier and heavier, until she could feel her arms again, and her naked, muddy skin, from which the scales were already fading. Her body felt strange, awkward; at last she stood in knee-deep water, looking at her brown arms glowing in the sunshine, her mudstreaked breasts, the shiny stretchmarks on the slight, taut curve of her belly. The world swam into focus; she felt her head clear a little. She passed her tongue over her lips, and felt the slight notch on its tip that had not been there before. Behind her, under the shimmering green surface of the lake, lay the promise of that other world. She looked around and saw that her sari, blouse and undergarments were floating near her, amidst a sprinkling of harsingar flowers.

For a while she stood quietly in the water, feeling dazed and new, thinking, but not in words, or words she had known before. She knew her mother had stood thus once, filled with excitement and confusion, feeling the new life she had made stir inside her. At last she could stand inside her mother's skin and sense what she had gone through – the dilemma of choosing between two worlds, the prison she had made for herself, of love and guilt. Her brother's wistfulness; like her own son, he had been fathered by a man; he would always hear the call of his mother's kind, but could never transform, never know what it was like to turn underwater in an exquisite dance, to taste the world through his skin, to be life-giver, rain-bringer, death-lord. This new child she carried would be like her, an entity capable of existing in two worlds.

Two worlds ... Pictures rose in her mind: the warm yellow house, the harsingar tree. She remembered the rhythms of the day, the slow course of the white cow Muniya's morning journey from house to house, the taste of fresh milk. And Kishore ... No, she was not quite ready to leave it all behind. It was not yet time for that. She would come back to the lake again tomorrow, to begin to learn how to parcel her life between water and earth, fire and shadow, until it was time for the final leave-taking. Slowly, dazedly, she gathered her clothes and emerged from the lake. She went behind a bush and began to squeeze the water from her sari.

Her skin prickled; she sensed the gardener's presence a moment before he came around the bush. His eyes were filled with wonder and desire – he came slowly towards her as though she were a dream that would dissolve with the first stumble. She watched him curiously, without fear, still in the twilight state between her two worlds. He put trembling hands on her bare shoulders. She let him draw her close so that her breasts flattened against his wet shirt; she felt the angular roughness of his chin against her cheek. 'Lady,' he said, and she tasted his skin, his smell with her tongue, and remembered, with the suddenness of a thunderclap, the old fear and confusion. A bitter taste filled her mouth; as he pulled her down into the wet grass she reached up blindly and bit the side of his neck.

She watched him thrashing about on the ground. After he had stopped she spat and rubbed her face with her hands to try to clear her head. Then she gathered her clothes, squeezed and shook the water from them and dressed. Her hair was wet and tangled, but she managed to comb it back with her fingers and tie it into a bun. She looked once more at the gardener's still body, feeling the beginnings of a vague uneasiness.

She began to walk slowly home, looking about her like a child, letting the sights, sounds and smells wash over her: men on bicycles, ringing their bells, children splashing into rainwater puddles, shouting in their clear, shrill voices, cars all shiny and wet, honking, lurching as they negotiated potholes, the smell of wet earth and the vapours already rising from the moist ground, the drip of rainwater from the tree branches above her. Slowly it came back to her. The way home. It was familiar and strange all at once.

And there, meandering down the street was Muniya the cow. She caught up with the great white bovine matriarch and stretched her arm toward her, but the cow shied away from her as though stung, and began to edge away, fear in her dark eyes. Dismayed, Susheela stood there helplessly, tears welling up in her eyes. She made a small, experimental, cajoling sound, thinking of the way Kishore had looked at her last. The cow let out a breath redolent with the odour of grass and carrot ends, and let Susheela come up to her. She shuddered as Susheela stroked her back, but did not move away.

Susheela felt an urgent need now to see her son. Taking leave of Muniya she began to walk rapidly, knowing that passersby were staring at her, with her dishevelled hair and sodden clothes. She had to win back her little boy, to take that look from his eyes. She would do it, she thought in the wordless tongue, with patience, with stories, but – it came back to her now with horrifying clarity: the body of the gardener in the wet grass – how to protect her family from what she had become? What would she tell them? She couldn't even begin to articulate it, she realized in terror. People on the street were talking, laughing, and they might as well have been speaking some incomprehensible foreign language, because their speech had no meaning for her.

Then, slowly, she remembered the words, and understood them. It was Naag Panchami, the Festival of Snakes, and the monsoons had arrived at last. A car went by, fast, and two glittering arcs of water rose in its wake. There was the house; the shisham trees, their round leaves glistening, the trunks dark with moisture. Through the open front window she could see her husband's profile as he waited, reading his paper, one brown hand on the sunlit sill.

A picture came into her mind's eye: that brown hand scooping up earth, making a hollow like a womb for the roots of the harsingar tree, patting the soil in place. She trembled, as though a string had been plucked deep inside her. The door was open. She walked into the house as if for the first time.

The Offspring

Indira Goswami

Pitambar Mahajan was sitting in front of his house. His shoes were covered with a thick layer of mud, but he did not remove them. He looked at them with pride – only he and the Gossain of the Satra possessed shoes in this remote village.

Pitambar was in his early fifties. Once a robust man, his worries had slowly emaciated his healthy body. Folds of skin hung loose beneath his chin. He talked to others with eyes averted and head bowed. His gaze was always directed to the ground beneath his feet as if he were looking for something.

Heavy rain had soaked the ground and water had collected on both sides of the village. Half-naked children played in the water or stood here and there, fishing with bamboo-poles in their hands. With the rains, there was a rank growth everywhere of all sorts of plants and creepers like balechi and nalakochu. Flying fogs leapt from puddle to puddle and sometimes hit against the legs of passers-by.

Pitambar was staring intently at a chubby, naked boy trying to disentangle his fishing line from the leaves of a nalakochu plant. Suddenly his thoughts were interrupted by the grating voice of the village priest, Krishnakanta – 'You have no child to call your own! Why do you devour that child with envious eyes? Each time I have gone to and returned from the temple, I have seen you sitting there like this! What about your wife? Is she better now?'

Pitambar replied hesitantly, 'Several times I have taken her to the Civil Hospital at Gauhati but it is useless. Her whole body is swelling up now.'

'So there is not hope of an issue, is it? Very sad, indeed. There will be no one to continue your family line.'

Pitambar remained silent. The priest stood near him for some time. He was wearing an old dhoti well above his knees, and a punjabi made of endi cloth, the colour of dried sheepskin. His shoulders were covered with a cotton chaddar. As Krishnakanta had only two teeth left in his mouth, his cheeks had caved in and created two hollows in his face. When he spoke, his face presented a peculiarly comic expression. His small eyes always shone with a cunning glint. His sparse hair was parted in the middle. He bent down and whispered in Pitambar's ears, 'What about another marriage, eh?'

Pitambar removed his chaddar and wiped his face with one end. Before he could reply, the eyes of the two men were drawn towards a young woman passing by. She was Damayanti, the widow of a young priest from the Satra. Her rain-drenched clothes clung to her body. The colour of her skin was like the dazzling foam of boiling sugarcane juice. Though her figure was rather ample, she was immensely attractive. People said all sorts of things about her. Some even called her a prostitute. Perhaps the first Brahmin prostitute of the Satra!

Krishnakanta called out, 'Hey, Damayanti, where are you coming from?'

'Can't you see these cocoons?'

'So, now you have started mixing with that crowd of Marwari merchants, eh! When the need arises, one stoops to washing even goat's legs as the saying goes, is it not?'

Damayanti did not reply, but bent down to squeeze out the water from the wet folds of her mekhala. Her blouse had stretched tight and was pulled up, revealing the white flesh which, to the two men, looked as tempting as the meat dressed and hung up on iron hooks in a butcher's shop! Krishnakanta turned his eyes away almost immediately, a little self-consciously, but Pitambar kept looking, enthralled by the sight. Damayanti straightened up and, without glancing at them, walked away, her mekhala rustling.

'I hear that she eats meat, fish, everything.'

Krishnakanta nodded and said, 'This girl has brought disgrace to Bangara Brahmins. She has thrown to the winds all restrictions and rituals prescribed for widows.'

'Yes, yes! I have myself seen her once exchanging two baskets of paddy for a pair of khariya fish!'

The priest exclaimed, 'Hai! Hai! A widow and khariya fish! Chee, chee! Kalyuga! Kalyuga!'

'Shut up, you Brahmin! Why do you want the whole world to know about a Brahmin widow eating fish? It is the same everywhere, I hear. On both the north and south banks of the Brahmaputra. These old customs should be scrapped ...'

Pitambar stopped to swat some flies buzzing around him with the corner of his chaddar. In the meantime, Krishnakanta sat down with a sigh on the stump of a severed tree nearby. Pitambar asked,

'What about your jajamans for whom you perform religious ceremonies? How do they look upon you nowadays?'

'You know everything, still you ask me! My elder brother quarreled with me and made off with most of the business. I am now ruined!'

'Bapu! You don't know Sanskrit well. Your brother has spread this news everywhere and that's why your jajamanas do not want you any more.'

Krishnakanta hotly denied this, 'Ah! Ah! Now you tell me, how many Brahmins on the north bank can speak Sanskrit like Narahari Bhagwati? We studied together in the Sanskrit *tol*. He used to receive a cane-beating very often but not once did I. I know why I have lost so many jajamans. Even the

Brahmins well-versed in all the four Vedas are starving to death. It was once easy to get a sacred thread, two dhotis and five rupees every month from each jajaman's house. Nowadays, they don't want to observe the rituals. To avoid expenditure, our old jajaman, Manikanta Sarma, took his two sons to Kamakhya and performed their thread ceremony there! Mysanpur's jajamans have now started performing the shraaddh of their fathers and mothers at the same time.'

As Krishnakanta went on, Pitambar did not say one word either of assent or dissent. All the while, his mind hovered around the brief glimpse he had had of Damayanti's white flesh. He had never seen such soft burnished flesh before. It was not as if he had not seen or touched a woman's flesh. There was his first wife, then he had brought a second one with the hope of getting a child. Now she lay bedridden with rheumatism. Her whole body had become rickety – she was like a bundle of bones dumped in a corner of the bed. He had trodden the road to the hospital at Gauhati so many times that the soles of his shoes had worn out. He was numbed by the fear that he might have to die without an issue to continue the family line.

This gnawing fear had been further heightened by the constant nagging of the priest and others rubbing salt into his wounds. All this had affected his mental peace.

Pitambar's ailing wife, lying in bed in the mud-walled house, could see the priest standing outside. She signalled with a movement of her eyes to a servant standing nearby that he should carry one of the mooras outside for the priest to sit on. Pitambar, absorbed in himself, neither noticed the moora nor knew when and how it came to be there.

Krishnakanta stood up and said, 'People of the village are gossiping about you that you have gone off your head. What do you think? Don't you know that there are many people in this world who are childless like you? Just try to look at it in a different way. After all, it is all maya, illusion!'

Pitambar's head drooped. The priest could see the grey hair on it. His clothes looked worn and untended. Only his shoes, though muddy, were intact. He felt a kind of pity for this man. Once upon a time he was so handsome that people called him gora paltan. Now he had money, a granary full of paddy, everything. Still he was not happy! Suddenly Krishnakanta was struck by a thought. He looked around. He could see the open door of Pitambar's bedroom and the reclining body of his wife. He could even see her eyes, burning like those of an animal in a dark jungle, as if she were straining with all her might to catch what he was saying to her husband. The intensity of those glowing eyes, even after traversing that long distance, was heart-rending! The priest would not have believed it possible.

He made up his mind. Bending down, he whispered into Pitambar's ear, 'I can help you out of this agony.'

'Another solution again?'

'Yes, this time it is absolutely pakka!'

'I don't understand you...'

'This time there is no question of an unsuccessful pregnancy! She has gone through four abortions and every time she has buried those evil things in the bamboo grove behind her house.'

Startled, Pitambar cried out, 'Are you talking about Damayanti?'

'Yes! Yes! Nowadays Brahmin girls are even marrying fishermen. The daughter of the Gossain on the Dhaneshwari riverbank married a Muslim boy! Gandhi Maharaj has shown us the path. That's why I am telling you ...'

Pitambar exclaimed in a surge of excitement, 'What is it you are saying?'

'It you want, you can make Damayanti your own!'

Krishnakanta turned his head and looked again towards Pitambar's bedridden wife. He could still see the two glowing embers in her face. She was staring steadfastly at him. Pitambar stood up. Here was Krishnakanta putting what he could only

dream about into clear-cut words! He went up to him, trying
to seize his hand in an excess of gratitude but Krishnakanta
shrank back. He had just taken his bath and he had to go and
do the daily washing-ceremony of Murlidhar in Gossain's
house. If this man touched him, then he would have to bathe
again.

Pitambar's condition was like that of a drowning man
suddenly sighting a colourful sail. He did not know whether
to touch the priest's hands or his feet.

'So you had this in mind for quite a long time, did you?'

Krishnakanta again cast a glance at the invalid woman.
This time her eyes were shut tight probably in a spasm of
pain. Pitambar knelt down near the priest's feet and entreated
him earnestly, 'Only you can do it! Please help me with this
girl! She is a Brahmin. I will keep her in all comfort!'

A cunning smile played for a moment on Krishnakanta's
toothless mouth. 'Hum, well...er... I'll see about it. I'll have
to come again a couple of times. Then there are her two little
daughters to be taken care of.'

Pitambar got up with confused emotions and made his
way to the bedroom. When he entered, he saw his wife open
her eyes and look at him. She now saw him opening the
wooden box where they kept money and other valuables. A
little later, he closed the box and went back to the priest.

Krishnakanta took the money, twenty rupees in cash, and
went away humming under his breath.

A week had passed. Pitambar waited anxiously for the
priest, his whole being on tenterhooks. In these past seven
days, he had seen Damayanti passing by his house on her way
to Gossain's place, carrying cotton for making sacred threads.
The sight of her body heightened the turmoil in his mind.
His obsession for her created strange hallucinations. Before
his maddened eyes. Damayanti's clothes seemed to disappear
each time revealing more and more of her beautiful white-
fleshed body.

People said that she was born at Rauta on the banks of the Dhaneshwari river in Kamrup. There is a belief that nowhere else can you find girls as beautiful as the Brahmin girls born on the banks of the Dhaneshwari. Pitambar was now convinced that this was absolutely true.

Pitambar started sitting outside his house every day. At this time of the year, Damayanti came regularly to gather kollmu and vegetables which grew wild along the drains bordering the road. Her two little daughters, skinny and naked, usually trailed behind her. Their thin and undernourished bodies looked incongruous against their mother's healthy and voluptuous body. Damayanti's long and reddish-brown hair often caught Pitambar's eyes.

One day, Pitambar gathered enough courage to go near her when she was plucking green leaves and said, 'You will catch cold if you stand like this in muddy water every day.'

Damayanti looked back, her eyes opening wide with astonishment. But she did not reply.

Pitambar said again, 'I'll send the servant. You tell him to collect as many greens as you want and ...'

But his sentence remained unfinished. She looked back and Pitambar's eyes fell before her intense, disdainful gaze. He left the place hurriedly and went and sat down on the tree-stump in front of his house. He could see his wife lying again on the bed like a bird with broken wings. In the morning, she had seemed better, even moved around the room a little, but now the bed had claimed her again. Anger welled up inside him. He threw a look of undiluted fury in her direction. Sometimes he felt he could hear her dried-up joints creaking in her ailing frame. He looked at her with disgust. It was time for the next dose of her medicine but he did not get up. He looked at his shoes, took out his handkerchief and started cleaning them. He glanced often at the road, impatient for the sight of Krishnakanta. Suddenly he heard the krr krr sound of cart wheels. He knew what it was. His tenants were bringing his share of Boka Bhan, that variety of rice harvested in July, grown on his land. Normally, he would have been very happy at the sight of the carts laden with paddy. He would inhale with great pleasure and satisfaction the fresh fragrance of newly harvested paddy and rush to the carts to count the number of baskets as they were unloaded. But today he remained where he was. His servants, however, came out immediately and started carrying the baskets to the granary. When this was done, the tenants were offered tea, jaggery and parched rice which they gulped down with obvious enjoyment. They then went to the well, washed their hands and partook of the paan and betelnut kept separately for them. The tenants now approached Pitambar to take leave of him, but were perturbed to find him indifferent and unresponsive. 'Ah! You don't have children. All your granaries are now overflowing with paddy! Who will eat it? And you are growing old. Now is the time to worship God and offer charity and alms,' they seemed to be saying.

Pitambar went inside the house and brought out the money. He made their payment one by one and sent them off in complete silence. He then returned to his original place and sat down again. His eyes turned to the open door through which he could see his bedridden wife. Her eyes were open. A tumbler lay below the bed. Perhaps she had taken a drink of water. It was long past her usual medicine time.

Pitambar got up to go inside and give her the medicine. He removed his shoes and placed them in a corner. As he was about to cross the threshold, he heard a coughing behind him. Krishnakanta at last! He ran back and put on his shoes. His wife's eyes had followed him, expecting her medicine, but now she closed them wearily again. The fire in her eyes was extinguished, only the ashes remained.

Pitambar asked impatiently, 'Bapu! What news have you brought for me? Tell me quickly!'

In his excitement he even forgot to offer him a seat.

'Tell me! What is the news?'

The priest glanced round in all four directions. The invalid was lying on her bed like a corpse. She was not going to hear anything!

He whispered into Pitambar's ears, 'Just listen! I have dug up some information. Right now her womb is empty – it is not even one month since she buried the evil fruit of her last adventure. Her little daughter said that this time her mother had used a crowbar given by that student, who goes to Sariali college on bicycle, to dig the grave. He is a boy without character from a very rich household. During college hours, he used to go straight to Damayanti's place and hide his textbooks in the basket of rice. His college fees went for her cosmetics.'

The priest lowered his voice still further and barely whispered, 'On the bare floor! In front of the little girls! Hari, Hari! They copulated shamelessly. This time it was obviously that student's child.'

Pitambar heard everything in ice-cold silence.

The priest continued, 'I told her about you. She was infuriated! She spat out. "That pariah! How dare he send this proposal to me! Doesn't he know that I am from the jajamani Brahmin caste and he, the vermin, is a low-caste Mahajan?" I told her that when she was wallowing in the slime of sin, how could she talk of high caste or low caste? She was not getting any proposals for marriage from Brahmin boys. Who will marry a widow? That too with daughters. At least you are prepared to marry her, who is like a piece of sugarcane, chewed and thrown away. I told her straightaway that you would take the panchayat's consent, arrange a havan and marry her with due formalities. She questioned me about your wife. I told her you were the only man in the Satra who wears a pair of costly shoes! Suddenly she started crying. I don't know why she cried. They she wiped away her tears with her chaddar and said, "Nowadays, I don't keep well. I would like to lean on something solid and permanent." I told her, "How can you remain in good health? I have heard that you have got rid of those evil things from your womb four or five times. If the panchayat takes up this matter, it will be a terrible thing for the Satra. Even if somebody goes to your door for a glass of water, he will be fined twenty rupees. You have been spared only because you are a Brahmin. But for how long?" She replied, "What can I do? I had to live. They even stopped their orders for sacred threads and puffed rice. They considered me impure, contaminated! And those tenants! They have turned thieves and don't give me my share of paddy. They take advantage of my helplessness. In these circumstances, where should I have gone with my two tiny daughters? I have not paid the land revenue. The land, too, will be auctioned off! What can I do?" '

Pitambar grew impatient. 'What about my proposal?'

'Yes, yes! I am coming to that. She wants to meet you. On the full moon night. At her dhekal, the room in the backyard for pounding the paddy.'

Pitambar was overwhelmed. Krishnakanta took this opportunity to whisper in his ear, 'Come, take out forty rupees for me! The mosquitoes are playing havoc. I want to buy a mosquito net.'

Pitambar went inside the house. He saw that his wife was awake. He did not care, and went straight to the wooden box. He took out the money and turned round to go out of the room. The sick woman was staring at him. He burst out enraged, 'Why are you staring at me like that? I will scoop out your eyes!'

Krishnakanta heard everything, understood everything. Taking the money, he whispered to Pitambar, 'Look, if she stares too much, give her a dose of opium. Like your first wife, she is not quarrelsome. She probably feels deeply guilty for not bearing you a child.'

And he laughed toothlessly. The invalid lying on her bed closed her eyes again. The priest, becoming serious, continued, 'But that bitch, Damayanti, has great hunger for money! It's all right now. You can touch her in the dhekal ...'

Pitambar threw a glance at the sleeping woman inside. Even from that distance he could clearly see small beads of perspiration on her forehead.

It was a full moon night in the month of August. Pitambar took out his best clothes. He lovingly wiped his shoes clean with his hand. He took the looking glass out into the open yard and scanned his face. He had shaved in the morning. Peering into the glass, he saw the criss-cross of wrinkles on his face. He thought it look like a fish caught in a net.

He set out for Damayanti's house. He had to cross a thick sal forest. Her house lay beyond the forest on the outer edge of the village. It was an ideal place for Damayanti to carry out her nefarious activities.

In the moonlit sky, he could see mushroom-coloured clouds shaped like a canon. He felt that the moon looked like somebody had skinned and quartered a deer and placed in it the sky. It was so temptingly lustrous. Suddenly the moon became the naked voluptuous body of Damayanti in Pitambar's eyes. He tried to imagine the shape of her breasts. They would be like the soft rounded stomach of a pregnant goat. And the shaft of her body like a tender bamboo shoot. He lowered his eyes. No, no, he could not look at the sky any longer. He walked faster.

Near the sal forest, a pack of jackals flashed across the path. He reached the gate. Silently he slipped inside and entered the courtyard. He peered in and saw a child fast asleep near a cluster of jack-fruit and baskets of rice. The other girl was writing something on a small slate.

Damayanti was observing his movements from the adekal. She called out, 'Hey! Here! This way!'

Like a duty-bound soldier, he turned round on the quick and went towards her. A clay lamp of mustard-oil was burning near the pounding horse. She was leaning against a ramshackle wall. Pitambar did not dare look into her eyes: he was afraid. Suddenly it struck him that it was all an illusion!

Her figure before him in the dim light was also an illusion. But his thoughts were cut short. He heard her say, 'Have you brought some money?'

He was stunned. He did not expect her first question to be this. He said quickly, 'Here! Take this! Whatever I have is yours now.' He took out a small string purse from his waist and put it in her hand. Damayanti thrust the purse into the cleavage of her blouse. She took the lamp and guided him to the room where earlier the little girl had been doing her lessons. They found both girls fast asleep, clinging to each other. Damayanti then took Pitambar to an adjacent room, damp and dark. In it was a low cot, made of guava wood. It had been given to her deceased husband at the time of Gossain's funeral ceremony. She blew out the lamp ... .

Two months had passed. It was late evening. Pitambar left the dark in haste to get back to his house. Damayanti went to the well languidly and started taking a bath. Just then, the priest entered the courtyard. He remarked sarcastically, 'You never used to take a bath after sleeping with the Brahmin boy. What has happened now?'

Damayanti did not reply.

'Eh! He is from the lower caste, is that it ....?'

Suddenly Damayanti came running out as she was, in drenched clothes, and rushed to the far corner of the courtyard. She bent over and started vomiting. Krishnakanta stood still for a moment, stupefied. Then he shuffled up to her and said gently, 'This must surely be Pitambar's ...'

Damayanti still remained silent. 'Ah! This is good news indeed! That man was yearning for a child.'

Even now she did not say a word.

'So I will go now and give him the good news. He can now wed you openly.'

He came up to her and whispered, 'People are shocked and horrified by what is going on in this house. There was talk, off and on, of calling a meeting of the Panchayat. And listen! There was another thing. Something very serious! That three-month old foetus you buried behind the bijulee bamboos ... one day a fox dug it out, swallowed part of it and left a half-eaten limb in the Gossain's priest's courtyard. You know, the one who washes the Gossain's Murlidhar. He had a hard time getting himself purified – had to swallow two glasses of cowdung water.'

Damayanti started vomiting again making sounds of auk, auk, her mouth wide open.

The priest continued, 'Knowing all this, Pitambar is prepared to marry you. Listen, with my hands on the sacred thread, I tell you, this time if you do not save yourself from sin by taking this chance, you will surely burn in hell-fire!'

After giving the best news of his life to Pitambar, Krishnakanta said, 'So, at last, your dreams may come true. If she does not destroy this child, then you can rest assured that she will marry you.'

Pitambar was sitting on the tree-stump in front of his house, as usual, wearing his prized possession – his shoes. When he heard Krishnakanta's words, his whole body trembled. Was it really true? Could it be his own, his very own child in that woman's womb? It must be the truth! This Brahmin could not possibly utter lies. It is really my child!

He stood up, restless and agitated, and started pacing up and down in front of his house.

Krishnakanta said, 'At this age! To become a father! It's really a fortune, a miracle!'

Pitambar knelt at the priest's feet and entreated, 'Please, Bapu! Don't let my hopes be shattered. You know my background. My forefathers were brave warriors. They fought those Burmese invaders. You know that! If this lineage is snapped, if there is no son to carry it forward, only this doomed sufferer knows what tortures my soul will go through. And now this seductive sorceress holds my life in her fist. Oh Bapu, tell me! What should I do?'

Krishnakanta lifted one hand in consolation and said, 'Like the vulture keeping vigil over a corpse, I'll guard that woman. Not only that, I'll issue a strict warning to that old hag not to give her any of her evil herbs and roots for an abortion. But all this is not possible without money. I'll require lots of money!'

This time Pitambar did not have to go inside the house for it. Only that morning, he had sold all the jackfruit from his seven trees to a merchant from Orput, and he had the entire roll of currency notes in his pocket. He took it out and placed it in Krishnakanta's outstretched palm. The priest blessed him and left.

When Pitambar entered his house he again encountered the piercing, unblinking gaze of the sick woman. He was perturbed by those accusing eyes but only for a moment. Then he was his usual blunt and callous self again. He growled, 'You barren bitch! Why are you staring at me like that?'

Pitambar became almost insane with happiness. He would sit in his favourite place outside the house and dream about his child in Damayanti's womb. He imagined the different stages of his growth: he dreamed that his son, in the flush of youth, was taking him for a walk along the river bank. It appeared to him that the long golden thread of his family lineage was pulling them forward into a glorious future. He dreamed that both father and son were moving into a bright light where heaven and earth fused together on the distant horizon.

With the help of his servant he took out an old box perched on the rafter of his bedroom. He cleaned the dust and the cobwebs sticking to the box and, taking it to a corner of the room, opened it stealthily. Inside there was a package wrapped in cloth. It contained some half-burnt pieces of his father's bones and a string of gold beads his father used to wear around his neck. On his death-bed, his father had given the string to him telling him that the gold beads would be like golden steps which his son would mount, carrying the family flag.

Pitambar gazed at the relics for some time, then repacked them carefully in the same cloth and placed the box in its original place on the rafter.

Days passed. Pitambar became impatient. He has heard that a five-month-old foetus in a mother's womb cannot be destroyed. He waited, nervous and agitated, for this precarious period to be over. Each day was like a mountain which stood before him. Every day he imagined that he heard the footsteps of Damayanti coming towards him. He heard her telling him to make arrangements for the havan. She would say plaintively, 'I cannot stir out of the house now. Look how big my stomach has grown. I have been thinking! Hindu, Muslim, Brahmin or Kayastha – all these are like pieces of an earthen pot. There is no meaning in these words. I only want a man from whose body real blood flows when his flesh is cut open.'

In Pitambar's overwrought mind, the spectre of Damayanti became all too vivid and beautiful. He even imagined that he heard the musical notes of anklets from her smooth bamboo shoot-like ankles.

Three months passed. Now almost every day Pitambar strolled along the banks of the Dhaneshwari with the youthful son of his hallucinations. The dream pursued him persistently, day and night.

It was the month of August. The storm had broken in the afternoon and it was raining heavily. Pitambar went to the room near the dhekal to close the door. His wife was staring at him. He stood still. The wide open eyes were like shining snakes in the dark. Suddenly, the storm lashed out. All the oil lamps flickered and died out. It was pitch black. Over the roar of the storm, he heard crashing sounds. What was that? Surely lightning had struck a tree in his courtyard and split it in two. Which tree was it, he wondered? He rushed out helter-skelter. His servants were already there shifting the heap of coconuts from the verandah to the dhekal.

Gradually the thunder and lightning abated but the rain continued to come down in sheets. Suddenly Pitambar heard somebody calling out to him. Lantern in hand, he rushed out to see who it was. A figure loomed into view, completely drenched, dhoti held high above his knees. He had an old torn umbrella in his hand. The man was very thin, almost skeletal. He came towards Pitambar. What was it now? Holding the lantern higher, Pitambar looked closely at him. It was Krishnakanta! Pitambar exclaimed, 'Bapu, you? What is it? Why have you come in this foul weather?'

With great difficulty the priest reached the verandah and shut his umbrella. His hands were trembling. He looked extremely agitated. He squeezed out the water from his dhoti and said, 'Your first wife died under an inauspicious star, Pitambar. That must be the reason for what has happened now.'

'What? What did you say? What is wrong now?'

'It is said in the Shastras that when a person dies under this star even the shortest blade of grass in the courtyard burns to ashes. For you now everything has become ashes!'

Pitambar cried out in alarm, 'What has happened? For God's sake, tell me quickly!'

'Alas! She has destroyed it. She has got rid of the unborn child. She will not carry the seed of a low-caste. She is a Brahmin of Shandilya gotra. Oh, Pitambar! Pitambar! She has destroyed your child!'

The youth walking along the Dhaneswari had suddenly slipped and fallen into the river ....

One day, in the middle of the night, Damayanti woke up with a start, disturbed by some sounds coming from the backyard, as if someone was digging up the earth. Alarmed and frightened, she woke up her elder daughter. Both strained their ears. Yes, yes, there were distinct sounds of digging coming from the direction of the bamboo grove behind the house. That was the very spot where both mother and daughter had, some nights before, dug a pit for the aborted child! Yes, that was the night when both mother and daughter

were terrified by the frequent howling of the foxes as the
daughter held the earthen lamp and Damayanti dug the earth
with a crow-bar in jerking movements and scooped out the
loose earth with nervous hands.

Thuk! Thuk! Thuk!

They opened the window cautiously and looked out. They
saw a man digging in the dim light of a lantern hung from a
bamboo tree nearby.

Damayanti's heart started beating fast. Was it Pitambar out
there? Yes, it was! He was digging the earth with single-minded
determination. Gradually, the tempo of the digging increased.
The Mahajan's whole body and face assumed a terrible, violent
aspect. He dug and clawed the earth frantically with frenzied
energy.

Damayanti's body started trembling from head to foot.
Her heart beat violently. What should she do? Should she
shout? Should she keep quiet? A terrible thing was happening!

'Mahajan! Mahajan!'

There was no response!

Thuk! Thuk! Thuk! Thuk!

'Why are you digging, Mahajan?'

Pitambar looked up, but did not reply.

Thuk! Thuk! Thuk! Thuk!

Damayanti became frantic. She shouted furiously, 'What
will you get from there? Yes, I have buried it! It was a boy! But
he is just a lump of flesh, blood and mud! Stop it! Stop it!

Pitambar raised his head. His eyes were burning. 'I'll touch
that flesh with these hands of mine. He was the scion of my
lineage, a part of my flesh and blood! I will touch him!'

Translated by the author

The Last Song

Temsula Ao

It seemed that the little girl was born to sing. Her motner often recalled that when she was a baby, she would carry her piggyback to community singing events on festival days. As soon as the singers took up a tune and when gradually their collective voices began to swell in volume and harmony, her daughter would twist herself this way and that and start singing her own version of the song mostly consisting of loud shrieks and screams. Though amusing at first, her daughter's antics irritated the spectators and the singers as well, and often, she had to withdraw from the gathering in embarrassment. What the mother considered unreasonable behaviour in a child barely a year old, was actually the first indications of the singing genius that she had given birth to.

When Apenyo, as the little girl was called, could walk and talk a little, her mother would take her to church on Sundays because she could not be left alone at home. On other days she was left in the care of her grandmother when the mother went to the fields; but on this day there was no one to take care of her as everyone went to church. When the congregation sang together Apenyo would also join, though her little screams were not quite audible because of the group singing. But whenever there was a special number, trouble would begin; Apenyo would try to sing along, much to the embarrassment of the mother. After two or three such mortifying Sunday outings, the mother stopped going to church altogether until Apenyo became older and learnt how to behave in church.

At home too, Apenyo never kept quiet; she hummed or made up silly songs to sing by herself, which annoyed her mother at times but most often made her become pensive. She was by now convinced that her daughter had inherited the love of singing from her father who had died so unexpectedly away from home. The father, whose name was Zhamben, was a gifted singer both of traditional folk songs as well as of Christian hymns at church. Naga traditional songs consist of polyphonic notes and harmonising is the dominant feature of such community singing. Perhaps because of his experience and expertise in folk songs, Zhamben picked up the new tunes of hymns quite easily and soon became the lead male voice in the church choir. He was a schoolteacher in the village and at the time of his death was undergoing a teacher-training course in a town in Assam. He was suddenly taken ill and by the time the news reached the village, he was already dead. While his relatives were preparing to go and visit him, his friends from the training school brought his dead body home. Apenyo was only nine months old then. From that time on, it was a lonely struggle for the mother, trying to cultivate a field and bringing up a small child on her own. With occasional help from her in-laws and her own relatives, the widow called Libeni, was slowly building a future for her daughter and herself. Many of the relatives told her to get married again so that she and little Apenyo would have a man to protect and look after them. But Libeni would not listen and when they repeatedly told her to think about it seriously, she asked them never to bring up the subject again. So mother and daughter lived alone and survived mainly on what was grown in the field.

At the village school Apenyo did well and became the star pupil. When she was old enough to help her mother in spreading the thread on the loom, she would sit nearby and watch her weave the colourful shawls, which would be sold to bring in additional income. Libeni had the reputation of being one of the best weavers in the village and her shawls were in great demand. By and by Apenyo too learned the art from her mother and became an excellent weaver like her. In the meantime, her love for singing too was growing. People soon realised that not only did she love to sing but also that Apenyo had an exquisite singing voice. She was inducted into the church choir where she soon became the lead soprano. Every time the choir sang it was her voice that made even the commonest song sound heavenly. Alongwith her singing voice, her beauty also blossomed as Apenyo approached her eighteenth birthday. Her natural beauty seemed to be enhanced by her enchanting voice, which earned her the nickname 'singing beauty' of the village. Libeni's joy knew no bounds. She was happy that all those years of loneliness and hardship were well rewarded by God through her beautiful and talented daughter.

One particular year, the villagers were in a specially expectant mood because there was a big event coming up in the village church in about six months' time: the dedication of the new church building. Every member of the church had contributed towards the building fund by donating cash and kind and it had taken them nearly three years to complete the new structure of tin roof and wooden frames to replace the old one of bamboo and thatch. In every household the womenfolk were planning new clothes for the family, brand new shawls for the men and new skirts or 'lungis' for the women. The whole village was being spruced up for the occasion as some eminent pastors from neighbouring villages were being invited for the dedication service. Pigs earmarked for the feast were given special food to fatten them up. The service was planned for the first week of December, which would ensure that harvesting of the fields would be over and the special celebration would not interfere with the normal Christmas celebrations of the church. The villagers began the preparations with great enthusiasm, often joking among themselves that this year they would have a double Christmas!

These were, however, troubled times for the Nagas. The Independence movement was gaining momentum by the day and even the remotest villages were getting involved, if not directly in terms of its members joining the underground army, then certainly by paying 'taxes' to the underground 'government'. This particular village was no different. They had been compelled to pay their dues every year, the amount calculated on the number of households in the village. Curiously enough, the collections would be made just before the Christmas holidays, maybe because travel for the collectors was easier through the winter forests or maybe they too wanted to celebrate Christmas! In any case, the villagers were prepared for the annual visit from their brethren of the forests and the transaction was carried out without a hitch.

But this year, it was not as simple as in previous years. A recent raid of an underground hideout yielded records of all such collections of the area and the government forces were determined to 'teach' all those villages the consequences of 'supporting' the rebel cause by paying the 'taxes'. Unknown to them, a sinister plan was being hatched by the forces to demonstrate to the entire Naga people what happens when you 'betray' your own government. It was decided that the army would go to this particular village on the day when they were dedicating the new church building and arrest all the leaders for their 'crime' of paying taxes to the underground forces.

In the meanwhile, the villagers caught up in the hectic schedules prior to the appointed day, a Sunday, were happily busy in tidying up their own households, especially the ones where the guests would be lodged. The dedication Sunday dawned bright and cool, it was December after all, and every villager, attired in his or her best, assembled in front of the new church, which was on the same site as the old one. The villagers were undecided about what to do with the old one still standing near the new one. They had postponed any decision until after the dedication. That morning the choir was standing together in the front porch of the new church to lead the congregation in the singing before the formal inauguration, after which they would enter the new building. Apenyo, the lead singer, was standing in the middle of the front row, looking resplendent in her new lungi and shawl. She was going to perform a solo on the occasion after the group song of the choir. As the pastor lead the congregation in the invocatory prayer, a hush fell on the crowd as though in great expectation: the choir would sing their first number after the prayer. As the song the crowd was waiting to hear began, there was the sound of gunfire in the distance; it was an ominous sound which meant that the army would certainly disrupt the festivities. But the choir sang on unfazed, though uneasy shuffles could be heard from among the crowd. The pastor too began to look worried; he turned to a deacon and seemed to be consulting him about something. Just as the singing subsided, another sound reverberated throughout the length and breath of the village: a frightened Dobashi, with fear and trembling in his voice was telling the people to stay where they were and not to attempt to run away or fight. There was a stunned silence and the congregation froze in their places unable to believe that their dedication Sunday was going to be desecrated by the arrogant Indian army.

Very soon the approaching soldiers surrounded the crowd, and the pastor was commanded to come forward and identify himself along with the gaonburas. Before they could do anything, Apenyo burst into her solo number, and not to be outdone by the bravery or foolishness of this young girl, and not wishing to leave her thus exposed, the entire choir burst into song. The soldiers were incensed; it was an act of open defiance and proper retaliation had to be made. They pushed

and shoved the pastor and the gaonburas, prodding them
with the butts of their guns towards the waiting jeeps below
the steps of the church. Some of the villagers tried to argue
with the soldiers and they too were kicked and assaulted.
There was a feeble attempt by the accompanying Dobashi to
restore some semblance of order but no one was listening to
him and the crowd, by now overcome by fear and anger began
to disperse in every direction. Some members of the choir
left their singing and were seen trying to run away to safety.
Only Apenyo stood her ground. She sang on, oblivious of the
situation as if an unseen presence was guiding her. Her mother
standing with the congregation saw her daughter singing her
heart out as if to withstand the might of the guns with her
voice raised to God in heaven. She called out to her to stop
but Apenyo did not seem to hear or see anything. In
desperation, Libeni rushed forward to pull her daughter away
but the leader of the army was quicker. He grabbed Apenyo
by the hair and with a bemused look on his face dragged her
away from the crowd towards the old church building. All
this while, the girl was heard singing the chorus of her song
over and over again.

There was chaos everywhere. Villagers trying to flee the
scene were either shot at or kicked and clubbed by the soldiers
who seemed to be everywhere. The pastor and the gaonburas
were tied up securely for transportation to army headquarters
and whatever fate awaited them there. More people were seen
running away desperately, some seeking security in the old
church and some even entered the new one hoping that at
least the house of God would offer them safety from the
soldiers. Libeni was now frantic. Calling out her daughter's
name loudly, she began to search for her in the direction
where she was last seen being dragged away by the leader.
When she came upon the scene at last, what she saw turned
her stomach: the young Captain was raping Apenyo while a
few other soldiers were watching the act and seemed to be
waiting for their turn. The mother, crazed by what she was

witnessing, rushed forward with an animal-like growl as if to haul the man off her daughter's body but a soldier grabbed her and pinned her down on the ground. He too began to unzip his trousers and when Libeni realised what would follow next, she spat on the soldier's face and tried to twist herself free of his grasp. But this only further aroused him; he bashed her head on the hard ground several times knocking her unconscious and raped her limp body, using the woman's new lungi afterwards, which he had flung aside, to wipe himself. The small band of soldiers then took their turn even though by the time the fourth one mounted, the woman was already dead. Apenyo, though terribly bruised and dazed by what was happening to her was still alive, though barely so. Some of the villagers who had entered the old church saw what happened to mother and daughter and after the soldiers were seen going towards the village square, came to help them. As they were trying to lift the limp bodies, the Captain happened to look back and seeing that there were witnesses to their despicable act, turned to his soldiers and ordered them to open fire on the people who were now lifting up the bodies of the two women. Amid screams and yells the bodies were dropped as the helpless villagers once again tried to seek shelter inside the church.

Returning towards the scene of their recent orgy, the Captain saw the grotesque figures of the two women, both dead. He shouted an order to his men to dump them on the porch of the old church. He then ordered them to take positions around the church and at his signal they emptied their guns into the building. The cries of the wounded and the dying inside the church proved that even the house of God could not provide them security and save them from the bullets of the crazed soldiers. In the distance too, similar atrocities were taking place. But the savagery was not over yet. Seeing that it would be a waste of time and bullets to kill off all the witnesses inside the church, the order was given to set it on fire. Yelling at the top his voice, the Captain now appearing to have gone mad, snatched the box of matches from his Adjutant and set to work. But his hands were shaking; he thought that he could still hear the tune the young girl was humming as he was ramming himself into her virgin body, while all throughout, the girl's unseeing eyes were fixed on his face. He slumped down on the ground and the soldiers made as if to move away, but with renewed anger he once again gave the order and the old church soon burst into flames reducing the dead and the dying into an unrecognizable black mass. The new church too, standing not so far from the old one caught the blaze and was badly damaged. Elsewhere in the village too, the granaries were the first to go up in flames. The wind carried burning chunks from these structures and scattered them amidst the clusters of houses, which too burnt to the ground.

By the time the marauding soldiers left the village with their prisoners, it was dark and to compound the misery it rained the whole night. It was impossible to ascertain how many men and women were missing apart from the pastor and the four gaonburas. Mercifully, the visiting pastors were left alone when it became known that they did not belong to this village. But they were ordered to leave immediately and threatened in no uncertain terms that if they carried the news of what had happened to this village, their own villages would suffer the same fate. The search for the still missing persons began only the next morning. They found out that among the missing persons were Apenyo and her mother. When a general tally was taken, it was discovered that many villagers sustained bullet wounds as well as injuries from severe beatings. Also, six members of the choir were not accounted for. An old woman whose house was quite close to the church site told the search party that she saw some people running towards the old church.

When the villagers arrived at the burnt-out site of the old church building, their worst suspicions were confirmed. Among the rain-drenched ashes of the old church they found masses of human bones washed clean by the night's rain. And on what was once the porch of the old church, they found a separate mass and through a twist of fate a piece of Apenyo's new shawl was still intact beneath the pile of charred bones. Mother and daughter lay together in that pile. The villagers gathered all the bones of the six choir members and put them in a common coffin but those of the mother and daughter, they put in a separate one. After a sombre and song-less funeral service, the question arose as to where to bury them. Though the whole village had embraced Christianity long ago, some of the old superstitions and traditions had not been totally abandoned. The deaths of these unfortunate people were considered to be from unnatural causes and according to tradition they could not be buried in the village graveyard, Christianity or no Christianity. Some younger ones protested, 'How can you say that? They were members of our church and sang in the choir'. The old ones countered this by saying, 'So what, we are still Nagas aren't we? And for us some things never change'. The debate went on for sometime until a sort of compromise was reached: they would be buried just outside the boundary of the graveyard to show that their fellow villagers had not abandoned their remains to a remote forest site. But there was a stipulation: no headstones would be erected for any of them.

Today these gravesites are two tiny grassy knolls on the perimeter of the village graveyard and if one is not familiar with the history of the village, particularly about what happened on that dreadful Sunday thirty odd years ago, one can easily miss these two mounds trying to stay above ground level. The earth may one day swallow them up or rip them open to reveal the charred bones. No one knows what will happen to these graves without headstones or even to those with elaborately decorated concrete structures inside the hallowed ground of the proper graveyard, housing masses of bones of those who died 'natural' deaths. But the story of what happened to the ones beneath the grassy knolls without the headstones, especially of the young girl whose last song died with her last breath, lived on in the souls of those who survived the darkest day of the village.

And what about the Captain and his band of rapists who thought that they had burnt all the evidence of their crime? No one knows for sure. But the underground network, which seems able to ferret out the deadliest of secrets, especially of perpetrators of exceptional cruelty on innocent villagers, managed not only to piece together the events of that black Sunday, but also to ascertain the identity of the Captain. After several years of often frustrating intelligence gathering, he was traced to a military hospital in a big city in the country where he was kept in a maximum-security cell of an insane asylum.

P.S. It is a cold night in December and in a remote village, an old storyteller is sitting by the hearth-fire with a group of students who have come home for the winter holidays. They love visiting her to listen to her stories, but tonight granny is not her old chirpy self; she looks much older and seems to be agitated over something. One of the boys asks her whether she is not feeling well and tells her that if so, they can come back another night. But instead of answering the question, the old woman starts talking and tells them that on certain nights a peculiar wind blows through the village, which seems to start from the region of the graveyard and which sounds like a hymn. She also tells them that tonight is that kind of night. At first the youngsters are skeptical and tell her that they cannot hear anything and that such things are not possible, but the old woman rebukes them by saying that they are not paying attention to what is happening around them. She tells them that youngsters of today have forgotten how to listen to the voice of the earth and the wind. They feel chastised and make a show of straining their ears to listen more attentively and to their utter surprise, they hear the beginning of a low hum in the distance. They listen for some time and tell her, almost in triumph, that they can hear only an eerie sound. 'No', the storyteller almost shouts, 'Listen carefully. Tonight is the anniversary of that dreadful Sunday'. There is a death-like silence in the room and some of them begin to look uneasy because they too had heard vague rumours of army atrocities that took place in the village on a Sunday long before they were born. Storyteller and audience strain to listen more attentively and suddenly a strange thing happens: as the wind whirls past the house, it increases in volume and for the briefest of moments seems to hover above the house. Then it resumes its whirling as though hurrying away to other regions beyond human habitation. The young people are stunned because they hear the new element in the volume and a certain uncanny lilt lingers on in the wake of its departure. The old woman jumps up from her seat and looking at each one in turn asks, 'You heard it, didn't you? Didn't I tell you? It was Apenyo's last song' and she hums a tune softly, almost to herself. The youngsters cannot deny that they heard the note but are puzzled because they do not know what she is talking about. As the old woman stands apart humming the tune, they look at her with wonder. There is a peculiar glow on her face and she seems to have changed into a new self, more alive and animated than earlier. After a while a young girl timidly approached her and asks, 'Grandmother, what are you talking about? Whose last song?'

The old storyteller whips around and surveys the group as though seeing them for the first time. She then heaves a deep sigh and with infinite sadness in her voice spreads her arms wide and whispers, 'You have not heard about that song? You do not know about Apenyo? Then come and listen carefully ...'

Thus on a cold December night in a remote village, an old storyteller gathers the young of the land around the leaping flames of a hearth and squats on the bare earth

among them to pass on the story of that black Sunday when
a young and beautiful singer sang her last song even as one
more Naga village began weeping for her ravaged and ruined
children.

Stains

Manjula Padmanabhan

It was a tiny mark, barely visible. Yet Mrs. Kumar was holding the sheet between her thumb and forefinger as if she feared that merely to be in the presence of such a sheet might mean eternal damnation. Merely to know of the existence of such sheets.

She said, 'Blood.'

Sarah said, 'yes,' while wondering whether she should apologize. 'I'm sorry,' she heard her voice say, 'I – I'm sure it'll go away.' She could hear herself sounding one foot tall. 'I mean – I'll wash it –'

Mrs. Kumar said, 'Come. I will show you.' She turned and left the bedroom, still carrying the sheet.

They went down two floors and into the basement. There was a sink there, deep as a well, cold, cracked and forbidding. A pipe jutted out from the wall. A pressure-valve perched at the end of it. 'Here,' said Mrs. Kumar, 'here you will wash it.' She dropped the corner of the sheet that she had been holding into the sink. 'Wash now,' she said, 'it must not become ....' She searched for the word. 'Stain. It must not become stain.' There was an antique cake of laundry soap congealed into a tin soap dish on the rim of the sink. 'See – there is soap –'

She glanced up at Sarah, then turned again and left. What had the glance meant, wondered Sarah. There had been something there, something ... She shook her head and the bushy mass of her hair shifted on the back of her neck, feeling comfortingly warm and familiar. *Get this over with,* she thought, *just get it over with and don't let's think about it just now.*

She held down the release on the valve. A stream of liquid ice gushed out, biting straight through the tender flesh of her fingers and deep into the bone. She flinched, wondering whether there was any point to wetting the whole sheet. She picked it up and scrolled through it gingerly, looking for the stain.

It wasn't easy to find, what with the all-over floral print. Faux Monet. Ersatz Klimt. But it was a blue-based design and the stain was there, finally. A single pale petal of dried, graduate-student haemoglobin amidst the heaving water-lilies. Sarah positioned the spot under the outlet and pressed the release. More arctic water. She reached for the soap tray but it had become cemented to the rim of the sink. She hauled the stain-bearing area of the sheet over to the soap-dish and scrubbed the cloth into the soap, which was rock-hard with age. It was minutes before it grudgingly yielded up its suds.

Then she held the material between her numb fingers and scissored it back and forth rapidly, to work the soap into the stain. Wetted it again, just a little, enough to see that the petal was indeed fading. Scratched at it with her fingernail. Looked around for a brush, but there wasn't one. The fine scum from the soap was under her nail now. A faint blush of brown in the scum indicated that the stain was shifting. Minute particles of her being, her discarded corpuscles, were detaching themselves from the cotton fibres of the sheet, tearing free and riding up on the skins of soap bubbles so fine that she could only see them collectively, as scum.

She held the cloth under the stream of ice. The brown scum slid abruptly off the site of the stain onto that part of the sheet resting on the bottom of the sink. *Damn!* thought

Sarah. She held the release of the valve down with one hand and tried to hold the sheet up so that the flow of water washed the scum clear of the sheet.

It was absurdly difficult. The sheet filled quickly with water, becoming heavy and unmanageable. There was a moment when she considered holding the cloth in her teeth so that the frozen lump at the end of her left arm could smooth away the traces of soap from the sheet while she held the valve open with her other hand. But she decided against it, ultimately. It would have looked ridiculous. And besides, she wasn't sure that her teeth could support the weight of the sheet, now several pounds heavier as a result of the absorbed water.

Ultimately she draped the bulk of the cloth over her right shoulder, held the valve open with her left hand and used her right to smooth away the soap. The stain itself had faded to a memory, its edges slightly darker than its centre. But she rubbed it into the soap once more, flattened the cloth onto the palm of her left hand and scraped at it with the nail on her right thumb, scraped until it seemed to her that the blue of the underlying water lily was beginning to wear thin. Then, satisfied, she washed the scum away in the gelid water until all traces of soap had been obliterated from the sheet.

When she was done, she held the cloth up to look at it, stretching it between her two arms to do so. A film of water which had clung to the surface of the cotton gathered itself up into an icy rivulet which flowed straight into the warm space between her hair and her neck, down her back and into the divide of her bottom, resting only once it had reached right upto the threshold of her most private self. It was like a cold electric finger tracing the length of her flesh, invading her warmth, violating her with its icy impertinence. Then it fell away and dropped to the floor.

She shivered. Realized that her nightie had got soaked and that she was standing in a dark, unheated basement, half-swaddled in a wet bedsheet. There was something offensive

and illogical about it all which she would have to examine
and understand and file away. But not just now. Later.

She went to the laundry room by the kitchen. Mrs. Kumar
was already there, bending over, stuffing a damp and faintly
steaming wash into the round open mouth of the dryer.

'Uh,' said Sarah, ''scuse me?' Mrs. Kumar did not seem to
hear. 'Mrs. Kumar?' The old lady straightened up slowly. 'My
shee ...' said Sarah, indicating that she'd like to include it in
the load going into the dryer.

For a moment it seemed as if Mrs. Kumar hadn't
understood what Sarah was saying. Then she shook her head,
a quick bird-like movement. 'No,' she said, 'No! Not here!
Only down! In basement!'

Sarah said, 'There's no place in the basement –' But she
had been in a hurry to get away and it hadn't occurred to her
to look.

'There is place,' said Mrs. Kumar and bent once more to
her wash.

Sarah turned and went back the way she had come. Her
mind was blank. In the basement, she looked around and
saw that there was a light bulb with a dangling cord. She pulled
on it and in the resulting light, saw that a potential clothesline extended across the room.

She hung the sheet, turned off the light and went up two
floors to the bedroom. Shut the door. She was shivering. She
wrapped her arms around herself. *What's happening to me?* she
asked herself. She was shivering with anger, not cold. *What
am I doing here?* she thought. *What am I doing amongst ... these
people?* There. It was out. The words that had been hovering
at the edge of consciousness for three days now. These people.
Deep and his mother. Indians. Not-us. Foreigners. Aliens.

But not him, she thought. *Only his mother.*

Or was it? After all, he had lived with his mother these
many years. It had to have affected him. What would he say
about the sheet, for instance? Would he find some excuse,
some justification for his mother's behaviour? Or would he

see her, Sarah's, point of view? And if he didn't – wasn't that the thing which made his foreignness a problem? The fact that, instead of automatically seeing her point of view, he would flip it over onto its back and expose its soft underbelly, expose it for just another cultural blinker. 'Even you,' he would say, smiling with his beautiful teeth, 'have that Western bias which makes it difficult for you to see that there isn't anything intrinsically bizarre about being made to wash your bloodstain out of the bedsheet in a freezing basement sink!' And then he might cock his head to the side and say, 'Remember the horse-meat?'

She bit her lip. The argument had started innocently. On their way up to Deep's home from Cornell, they had driven past a meadow dotted about with Holstein-Friesians and she had nudged him. It had been a joke, nothing else. 'Wanna stop?' she had said. He had looked at her without comprehension. 'You know,' she had persevered, 'stop by and say a prayer or – or something –'. But he had still not understood. It had begun to seem too silly to explain. 'Never mind,' she had said, 'it's not worth going into.' He had insisted, however. So she had said. 'The cows, you know? We passed a meadow and it was full of cows and I thought ...' His expression had been so blank that she would have laughed except that she knew he got hurt easily. So she stammered painfully on. 'Well, you know – I thought – since Indians worship cows' But it had started to sound ghastly, even to her ears.

He had begun to nod in that quick tight way. 'You think it's funny, don't you?' he said, finally. Just one more laugh-riot from the cosmic joke book – the joke book in which everyone who isn't a Bible-thumping, beef-eating, baseball player is treated like a court jester. Everything we do, whatever we find sacred, is hilariously funny just because it's different –' And then the final rebuke. 'I thought you, at least, would understand.'

'Deep,' she had said, distressed. 'You've got it wrong –'

'What else can it mean?' said. 'We've talked about this. I've explained it before.' He paused and she could see the muscle in his jaw tensing. 'About cows.'

She said, 'Deep – it's just that I saw them grazing and, and I –' She stopped. What had she thought? 'I thought of a cathedral. I thought that maybe for someone who worships cows, a big barn must be like a cathedral is for us –' Was that really such an insulting thought?

He had said, 'We discussed it just the other day. Didn't you hear me? When I told you that it isn't just any cows? That it is *specifically* the Indian cows?'

It had been her turn to look blank. 'You mean, one breed?' she had asked, astonished.

His face convulsed with annoyance. 'Don't be stupid!' he said. His face worked, as he tried to compose an answer which would make sense to her. 'It's not a question of breed,' he said, eventually, in a calmer voice, 'it's more subtle than that. In an Indian village, cattle are the foundation of life, an integral part of the family. Here? They're just beasts! Milk dispensers! Meat!'

Sarah could feel a charge building up inside herself. *Why are we talking about cows,* she thought. *Why aren't we talking about you and me?*

'Do you understand any of this?' he had said. 'I mean – you look into the eyes of one of these animals there and you see nothing. Just a dull, stupid, unreflecting stare!' His upper lip had lifted in scorn. Sarah couldn't understand why or how it could matter so much to him. Then his expression had softened. 'But –' he said, 'you look into the eyes of an Indian cow and there – you see it. Consciousness! An Indian cow is a developed being. She has a mind, she has a life, she is a person – no, better than a person. A sort of living manifestation of the, uh, bounty, the giving spirit of nature.' He looked at her, glancingly, as if expecting very little. 'For the Indian villager, the cow's milk provides food and income, its dung is used as fuel and the bullocks are a major source of draught energy.

And on top of all that, they eat almost anything – they're part of the garbage disposal system!' He smiled slightly now. 'Does it make sense now? Do you understand the difference?'

Sarah had nodded. 'Yes,' she had said, uncertainly, 'yes, I think I can relate to what you're saying.' She had grown up on a farm, till she was eight. She fought down a vague irritation she felt at the way he had described American cows. *How dare you insult our cows!* She had wanted to say. But instead she had said, 'We have that kind of relationship too, with horses –'

That's when he had said, scornfully, 'Oh yes! Horses! During the war, you used to eat horsemeat! A truly nourishing relationship, wouldn't you say?'

'That's not true!' The words had whipped out of her. It was only the French who ate horsemeat!! Not Americans!! Never Americans!!! But the force of his contempt had drained her confidence. He was so often right about things like that. He seemed to store up tiny scraps of information just so that he could produce them at crucial points in an argument. 'It – it's not typical behaviour, what we did during the war –' Even as she said the words, there had appeared in her head a question mark. '*We?*'

He said, smoothly arrogant, 'In India, there used to be terrible famines. But even at the depth of the famine, even when children were dying in their mothers' arms, there was never any report of cows being eaten. People were willing to die rather than eat their animals!'

'Well –' she had said, 'well – I think that's stupid! It's just stupid to die rather than to eat what's there –'

He had said, 'Oh? So – in a famine you'd eat your sister's flesh?'

'That's different!' But she had felt so helpless. He was implacable, when he had his teeth into an argument. 'It isn't normal to eat one's own species –'

'But we've agreed that wars and famines aren't normal times – !'

It had gone on and on and on. There had been no
resolution. He had grown increasingly cool and confident
while she had felt her cheeks radiating a black light and had
heard her voice grow shrill and incoherent. Towards the end
of it, she had found herself saying that she couldn't respect a
people, a culture which didn't have the sense to avoid famines.
He said that a few famines were inconsequential in the face
of five thousand years of civilization. She said that the ethical
system to which she belonged could not view famines as
inconsequential. Whereupon he had replied that he couldn't
place much confidence in an ethical system which used, as its
central icon, the tortured corpse of its religious prophet.

It had taken her a few seconds to understand what he had
meant by that remark and when she did, it upset her so
profoundly that her eyes stung with sudden tears. So she had
turned her face towards the window. She didn't know what
had bothered her more – that description of Christ or her
reaction to hearing it. She didn't think of herself as a believing
Christian, yet it hurt her to hear that description.

They drove the last fifty miles in silence.

Deep's mother lived alone in an old two-storey building
surrounded by majestic elms. She had probably been standing
at the window looking out for the car, because the front door
opened even as the tyres purred up the driveway. Deep turned
to Sarah and said, 'Will you be all right?' She was relieved to
see that the sarcastic stranger with whom she had been arguing
had reverted to being the familiar friend and lover of the last
five months. She had nodded and got down from the car.

And yet ... Standing at the window three days later, she
knew that it hadn't been all right. That stranger, that alien,
who had been at the wheel of the car dressed in Deep's body,
hadn't vanished entirely after all. Having once appeared, he
had continued to lurk, just at the outer margin of Deep's
personality. Had he been there all along?

She hugged herself tighter. Why had Deep's mother
wanted her to wash her bedsheet in the basement? What could

possibly be the point of it? Then she thought of something. She thought of something she had heard her own mother and aunt talking about, laughing. A long time ago. She tried to focus on it, but couldn't. It had been too long ago and she had been a child at the time. She hadn't understood what they'd been talking about. But it triggered another area of thought. In primitive communities, menstruating women sat separately, sometimes in a special hut.

Is that what she's doing with me? Thought Sarah. Avoiding contamination. Avoiding the unclean magic of a bleeding woman. *Unclean.* Sarah felt a current of power course through her. *That reminds me,* she thought. *Time to change.*

She went to the bathroom and pulled down her panties. A scarlet streak told her that she was just in time. She reached for the kit-bag in which she stored her tampons, while in the same movement sitting down on the toilet. She reached with her right hand under herself to find the string of the tampon, wound it around her finger and tugged, feeling all the while curiously self-conscious of all her movements. As if she were performing for some invisible camera crew. Twentieth Century Woman Removing Vaginal Insert. The tampon came out with a silky squish, and she released it, letting it drop into the toilet. Then stopped.

Why am I looking away at nothingness? she thought. *Why don't I ever look down when I do this? Why are all my movements so automatic?* And even as these thoughts appeared in her mind, a gush of simultaneous thoughts: *I shouldn't be thinking this way!* It was unseemly to look at one's menstrual products. It was unnecessary to think about what one was doing when one removed tampons. It wasn't proper. And yet ... why not?

She wiped herself with toilet paper. Then made herself look at the results. *It's a beautiful colour,* she thought, *red and warm, like – like Burgundy.* She wanted to giggle. *Imagine being caught sitting on the toilet and looking at my own blood!* She thought, then added, with surprise. *Why do I feel so guilty? Why? Even when I'm just alone with myself?*

As if to augment this thought, she heard, from the bedroom, the door open and Deep's voice. 'Sarah?' he called. 'Are you in there?'

'Yes!' She answered and quickly dropped the toilet paper out of sight.

He opened the door and said, 'You're not dressed yet?' Then he caught sight of the kit bag with the tampons in it. 'Oh,' he said, 'oh. Sorry.' And shut the door. Sarah narrowed her eyes and smiled to herself. *Powerful magic, this blood!* she thought. *It can make a man apologize at ten paces, just at the sight of the equipment!*

By the time she was through with her bath Deep had already gone down. She found them, him and his mother, in the sunlit kitchen nook, with the remnants of breakfast on the Formica-top table. She didn't feel like eating anything and said so, pouring herself a mug of coffee. She could feel Deep's eyes on her but didn't look at him. He was encouraging her to eat what his mother had made, because, as he had already told her once before, it was rude to sit at the table and refuse food. *Too bad,* thought Sarah. *I'm not going to perform for him, for either of them.* If his mother could make all her meals without consulting her guests, then she, Sarah, could refuse to eat those meals without consulting anyone.

Mrs. Kumar started to speak to Deep, in Indian. Deep responded, muttering. He seemed to be arguing with her, but it was hard to tell. The language sounded that way. *A bit like Klingon,* thought Sarah. Full of explosive consonants. Deep said, in English, 'My mother says, it's not safe to go hungry in ... your condition. She says she prepared this –' he pointed to a disgusting looking mush '– especially for you. To build you up.'

Sarah turned what she hoped was a blank look in his direction. 'What "condition"?' she asked.

The corners of his mouth were twitched inward in irritation. 'You are bleeding heavily, she tells me. Apparently you stained the sheets.'

Sarah said, 'Sheet. It was one sheet. And a very small stain.' She turned to Mrs. Kumar. 'Mrs. Kumar, I'm sorry, but I'm not hungry just now.' She spoke distinctly and slowly. 'Thank you for making something special, but I really don't need it.' Turned back to Deep. 'If it's all right with you, I'm going for a walk just now.' She smiled tightly and got up from the table, taking her mug of coffee with her and went out, walking slowly.

The front yard was fenced in with wooden palings. Sarah walked down the driveway and onto the road. There was no sidewalk. Deep's father had been a surgeon with a good practise in this small rural community in northern Pennsylvania. He had died four years ago, leaving the property and a fortune in investments for his widow and son to live on in comfort for the rest of their lives.

Sarah's breath, augmented by the heat of the coffee, steamed busily out onto the crisp air. *They do well here for themselves,* she thought to herself. *These Indians, these aliens.* She was trying to see that it felt like to view a minority group with race-hostility. She was mildly amused to see that she couldn't do it easily, that she felt guilty thinking thoughts like that. Even though, going by the typical logic of race-hostility, she had reason to feel embittered about the soft life that Deep's father had afforded for his family.

Her own childhood hadn't been easy. Her father had grown up on a farm and later managed to buy himself a garage. He had struggled to put his five children through school. Only she and her sister had gone to college. Two brothers were still in school and one brother had died at eighteen, in a car accident caused by his own drunkenness. *Aliens! Aliens!* she thought, *But isn't it funny that I can't even think up a cuss-word for them?* Maybe they hadn't been around for long enough to be absorbed into the vocabulary of racial abuse.

She hadn't been walking for long before she heard quick footsteps behind her. It was Deep. 'What's the matter with you?' he said, panting slightly. He never wasted time with preliminaries. 'You've been acting strange since this morning.'

'It's your mother,' said Sarah. 'It's the bedsheet. I don't understand why she made me wash it like that.' She would have liked to add that it was more than that. It was the horsemeat, it was the prophet-corpse, it was the revelation that there were chasms between them, which would never be bridged. She didn't think that the visit was working. She would rather leave right away and not stay for Christmas.

'You're so hung-up,' said Deep, calmly, his face showing no sign of any emotion, his voice flat. 'She's just an old lady. Why is it so difficult to do something different for a change? To bend yourself just a little?'

'Deep – she wanted me to wash the bedsheet in a sink, in the basement, in sub-zero water! It's not just something different! It's something so stupid and unreasonable I don't know what to do with it! I mean, I thought we'd agreed that there's enough illogic in the world without having to add crazy out-dated customs to it!'

'What I don't understand is why you stained the sheets at all,' said Deep.

Sarah said, 'One sheet.'

'All right, one sheet, then. But why did you have to do it? It's not as if you don't know how to ... be careful! I don't think it's at all ... polite to do that sort of thing.'

'Polite! ...' She laughed, gusting a thunderhead of white breath. 'What's polite got to do with anything! It's not polite for your mother to sneak around looking at our sheets either, you know!'

'It's your fault for not having made the bed in time.'

Sarah turned on Deep. 'I don't get it! Why does she have to come into our room at all? We're grown up, aren't we? I was still in my nightie, I hadn't even left the room and she was in there and making the bed!'

'Sarah –' he sighed. 'My mother's just a lonely old lady. She has no-one to talk to or fuss over when I'm not here. I don't think you can see how important it is for her to be able to do things for us –'

'– for you, you mean!' said Sarah. 'It's not for me she's doing it, it's for you! Her little son!'

He shrugged. 'Okay, for me, then. But she's lonely – don't you see that? She needs to be needed. She needs to feel useful. Why do you make such a big deal about it? Why does it matter so much?' He was affecting to sound tired of it all. The weary male worn out by the bickering of females around him. 'You're a feminist when it comes to young women and to women of your culture. But when it's my mother, who doesn't speak much English and isn't sophisticated, she's suddenly the enemy, the oppressor –'

'Deep, she's playing a power game,' said Sarah. 'Anyone can play it – you don't have to be a man or – or – white, or American. You won't see it like that, because she's your mother and the game works in your favour. But all these little things – the making of the beds, the not letting anyone else wash dishes or cook, she doesn't let anyone touch any of it – it's her way of maintaining control. Don't you see that?' She drew in a breath, sharply, the cold air hurting her throat. It was a hopeless discussion, because the knew he would never be able to see it her way. But she tried nevertheless. 'It's clear enough to you, when it comes to world events, when it's Russia controlling the flow of arms to Uzbekhistan – or the US controlling patents in the Third World. But when it's your mother controlling the flow of my blood onto our sheet? Oh no! Then it's tradition! It's being polite!'

He said nothing for a few moments. They were talking on the grassy verge along a large street now, up a slight incline. The cars coming over the crest of the low hill seemed to respond to the sight of the two of them by swerving sideways, like skittish horses. Sarah wondered idly what the drivers thought. *Do they see a couple walking along,* she wondered, *or do they see a racial statement?*

Deep said, in a quiet voice, 'I thought we had something special.'

Sarah waited a space before saying, 'We did. We still do – I think – but –'

'But you've moved out of my reach. You're seeing me as a foreigner, as an alien.'

Sarah's head was swaying from side to side. 'No, Deep, no! It's not like that! Really!' Even though it was.

He said, 'I'm not stupid, you know. I mean, it's interesting to me. I thought you'd be different, but you're not, really.'

Don't react, thought Sarah to herself. *Be still now. He's going to say something. Hurtful. Brace yourself.*

He said, 'I thought being black must mean that you're more sensitive – but that was stupid of me, huh? Another kind of racism. When it comes to the important things, you're just an American. Just a Westerner.' His face was expressionless and his voice was perfectly bland. He could have been reciting the multiplication tables, for all the emotion he showed. But that was just his inscrutable-Oriental way. 'I thought you of all people would understand what it means to be an outsider. To be excluded from the mainstream – but obviously I was wrong.'

He continued for a short while, during which they were passed in succession by two Corvettes, a Datsun and three battered-looking station wagons filled with dogs and children. Sarah felt like a guest at a stranger's cocktail party, listening to the conversation with comprehension but no involvement. *I should feel insulted,* she thought, *why don't I feel insulted?*

They had reached the crest of the hill now and had stopped. Deep said 'What are you thinking?'

Sarah said, 'I want to go back. I need to change my tampon.'

* * *

During lunch, the dull ache in Sarah's lower abdomen became a concentrated mass of pain so fierce that she found herself gasping softly to herself, hoping that she couldn't be heard. As soon as she could, she excused herself to the bedroom and lay down. It felt good to be on her back, but the pain didn't let up. It was a small hard fist of pressure, a living presence. *It's just got to do its thing,* thought Sarah, *it's not actually malicious.* She thought of the lightless inner world of her pelvis and the mute scream making its inexorable way out of the avocado-shaped muscle in which it had been held captive. *Come out,* she spoke to it, in her mind. *Don't be afraid. I won't deny your presence.* Instead of running away from the pain, she would disarm it with attention. *Come,* she thought at it, *let me look at you, let me understand your structure.*

It was dark, she decided, and glossy. A glossy pain. A deep, rich blue, royal in its own way Forceful. Powerful. She could see it as a male entity, a strong, husky bellow. *But I don't resent you,* she thought, *isn't that interesting?* It was possible to look steadily into the centre of the pain and in some undefined way, celebrate it. It was a trial by strength, a specialized type of wrestling match between her body and itself. There was no victor or loser, the struggle itself was everything. *You fill me,* she thought. *Here I lie, supine, while you, confined as you are to a passage no thicker than a pencil's lead, no longer than an AA battery, are able to irradiate my entire being so that I feel your heat from the farthest limit of my toes to the root of my hair.* She thought of the sparking network of nerves which moment to moment, sent in their bulletins of sensation from locations around the multiple dimensions of her existence, yet none of them could drown out the roar being broadcast from her uterus, from her cervix.

She smiled, her eyes shut, concentrating on fashioning something positive out of her pain. She didn't see Deep enter the room, walk silently around the queen-size bed and stop when he was by her side.

She opened her eyes.

'Why are you smiling?' he asked in a whisper.

She paused before she answered, not certain that it was wise to share her secret. Then she relented. 'Because,' she whispered back, 'I'm in pain.'

'Pain?' His face puckered immediately in concern. He sat down, causing the edge of the mattress to buckle under his sudden weight. 'Is it serious? Have you taken anything for it?' His voice was suddenly loud.

'No!' She whispered, lifting her head off the pillow in her earnestness, 'no! I'm sort of ... enjoying it ...' She relaxed once more, taking his hand in hers.

Deep stared at her, frowing. 'I don't understand you any more,' he said. He had the kind of expression on his face that men get when they start to ask themselves whether the woman in front of them is experiencing a mind-altering hormonal storm. 'How can you enjoy pain?'

She said, 'I'm trying it out. You know, an experiment. I can visualize it, I can sort of imagine it as a – a – kind of –'

He said, 'How do you know you're not seriously unwell?'

'I'm just bleeding. It's a normal, natural event.'

He continued to look suspicious and unconvinced.

She shifted to her side. 'I don't know why, but it's different this time. It's not just blood coming out, but sort of *chunks* of stuff. So – of course it hurts. The pain is from expelling solid matter, from pushing it through the narrow passage –' She saw the expression of distaste on his face and stopped. 'What's the matter?' she said. 'You look as if you're going to be sick!'

He turned his face away. 'In India,' he said, 'we don't talk about such things. Women's blood. We just don't talk about it'

She allowed a spasm to pass through her before answering. 'But Deep,' she said. 'This isn't India, this is here.' She paused. 'I don't mean America, either. I mean, this is Here!' She patted the surface of the bed. 'The special space we make between us, the space of just our own reality! No immigration officers, no bureaucrats to tell us what to say or how to sit and stand! We're the authorities here, we're the ones who decide what we want to talk about!'

His head was moving about, he was hunching his shoulders in discomfort. 'It's not realistic,' he said, 'to think that way. We're private individuals as well as social entities, affected by and affecting the realities within which we live.' He looked at her. 'You're not just Sarah, my girlfriend. You're also – an American black, you have your history and your separate destiny. If I took you back with me to India, people would stare at you, they'd stare at your hair and your different race and my own relatives would reject you. Reject my choice of you – even though we're almost the same colour.' He looked at her now. 'I've told you this before but I don't know whether you've really understood it. I'd never be able to take you there. I'd never want to expose you to that kind of ... humiliation.'

Sarah said, 'Deep, is that how you think of me? As a Black Woman?'

He shrugged, trying to wriggle away from the simple trap she had laid for him. 'I see you as Sarah. And as a woman. And as an African American.' Then he turned it around. 'You do it too! You see me as a foreigner, as an Indian! Admit it – the novelty is part of what attracts you!' He shook his head wearily. 'We can't wipe away our colours and our bone-structures! When we try to, we risk losing things which are important, we risk becoming cultural zombies –' He swept his arms wide, indicating the whole country, perhaps the whole western hemisphere. 'Isn't that what the West is suffering from? A loss of meaningful tradition?'

Sarah turned her face into the pillow and breathed a few times to suppress the giggle which she knew would upset him if he could hear it. She had had an irreverent thought and wasn't sure whether she had the energy to express it or not. Then she looked up. 'We have TV,' she said. 'We have K Marts and Hollywood –' But he was already shaking his head. 'We have Star Trek and Superman. Freeways and credit cards –'

'No!' He exploded. 'It isn't the same! It isn't the same at all!'

She said, '– the only difference is, it's not old, it's not gilded with time –'

He said, 'This just shows how impoverished you are!'

Sarah said, '– and we haven't had generations of historians to show us how unique and precious what we have is – because we still have it! It's not lost under some ocean or sunk under centuries of poverty! It's in the coke bottles and in the chewing gum and the neon lights and – and – all the things that you sneer at so much!'

He paused a moment. 'And anyway,' he said, 'where do *you* fit, in this world of Superman and Star Trek? Those are the white man's myths – you can't claim them as your own!'

Sarah tucked a pillow into her belly and curled around it. A new fist of pain had begun to form and was forcing its way down and out of her. She would have liked to moan softly, but it would have created too much of a response in Deep. She didn't want to give him that satisfaction. She wanted to end the discussion. She closed her eyes and made her voice sleepy. 'Sure I can claim them!' she said. 'I'm American, right? They're part of me ... even when I'm not a part of them.' She patted his hand away 'Now leave me to sleep.'

He waited a few moments to see if she meant it, then got up and left, saying nothing. She continued lying on her side for a while, thinking about their talk and about the pain inside her, wondering whether it was abnormal after all and at what point she should seek medical help. She asked herself what she had liked about Deep in all these months. He had seemed gentle, she decided, that was what had attracted her. He wasn't a big burly jock. He didn't come on strong. He was cool, soft-spoken and always thoughtful. His colour was ... well it was there, an added factor, but it was only colour, nothing else. It didn't go Deep. She smiled at the pun on his nickname. Deep short for Deepak. He said his name meant 'light'. A tiny flickering flame. When he had asked her what her name meant, she had said she didn't know. He had teased her and at the time she had thought nothing about it. But now she realized, it must have been of consequence to him, one more sign of her inferiority on the scale of traditional value.

Something he had told her long ago returned to her mind. He had been speaking about his parents, how his father had come to the US. He had come as a student, stayed to become a citizen, set up his practice and then, when he had a respectable income, had gone home to India to have a bride selected for him. He had married Deep's mother after having met her once, formally, surrounded by all their relatives, unable to exchange more than two words of conversation. 'Tea?' She had asked him and he had answered, 'Yes.'

It had bothered Sarah, that story. She had asked Deep what he thought about it, whether he thought it was right for two complete strangers to get married. He had shrugged and said that they weren't really strangers. They both came from similar families, with similar customs and similar food. Aside from the detail of personality, they were very much alike.

Sarah had laughed at that phrase 'detail of personality' – 'But personality's *everything*!' She had exclaimed, 'not just a detail!' Deep had got offended then and said that every culture had its traditions and it wasn't right to laugh at his. She had asked him if he would get married like that. And he had said, shuddering, 'No! Never!'

But she wondered about that now. He's American, she thought to herself, he's a citizen and yet it's only on the surface. Inside, he's this other thing. He had explained once that to be born into a strong tradition was to know the steps to an intricate dance which started with birth and ended with death. 'When you know all the steps by heart, you don't have to think any more – you are the dancer and the dance,' he had said and she had loved the mystery, the poetry of it. It hadn't occurred to her to ask him what happened when a dancer found himself alone on the floor of a different tradition. Could the steps of one dance fit the music of another? Could classical ballet perform to rap?

The pain, having reached a peak, began to subside. She fell into a light sleep, awakening to dampness which demanded immediate attention. She rolled over the side of the bed to avoid bringing her bottom into contact with the bed and went to the bathroom. Blood darkened the crotch surfaces of her panties, her panty-hose, her jeans. It took her twenty minutes to wash away all traces of it. She started to hang the clothes up in the bathroom, then stopped.

Deep's mother might well come in here and find the clothes. She'd know at once what they meant. It was highly likely that she would demand that all Sarah's clothes be washed by hand, by Sarah, in the basement. *Once you entered the logic of clean and unclean blood, you could find your way around the maze fairly easily,* thought Sarah. The bleeding woman is penalized for being in that 'state': the correct condition, of course, is to be pregnant or nursing. Older women, like Deep's mother, had the loss of their own fertility as an added reason for wanting to punish younger women.

Sarah wrung her clothes out carefully and packed them into plastic bags. She started packing the bags into her backpack and then, without really thinking about it or planning anything, packed her other stuff as well.

Downstairs, the house was silent. Deep's car was not in the driveway. Maybe he had gone shopping with his mother. Sarah let herself out the front door, checking behind her to make sure that it was locked. Then she set off. Overhead the sky was grey. There were random snowflakes gusting about, but no storm had been forecast. Within an hour she had boarded a bus and was on her way back to Cornell.

It was evening by the time she got back to the apartment she shared with three other women. There was a message on the answering machine for her from Deep. 'Call me,' he said, 'As soon as you hear this. I need to speak to you. Are you all right?'

So she called him.

'Why did you leave?' he asked in his direct way. 'My mother was very upset. She said it was bad for you to travel while you were bleeding like that. She says you might get very sick. You don't understand her at all. She's really concerned for you.'

'Tell her,' said Sarah, 'that I'm all right. Tell her I like to bleed and that I especially like to travel when I'm bleeding. Tell her that I got stains all over the seat of the bus and that everyone knew, by the end of the trip, that I was bleeding because I had to stop so often to get off and change my tampon. Will you tell her all of that?'

Deep said, 'She asked me if I was going to marry you.'

Sarah said, 'Oh yeah?' and there was a silence.

Deep said, 'She told me that it was all right if I wanted to, that she liked you, that she felt you were right for me.' There was another silence. 'Sarah,' he said, 'what's the matter with you? Did I say something wrong?'

'No,' said Sarah, shutting her eyes.

'Look, Sarah –' said Deep. 'You know what I said? About not taking you to India? Well, I was thinking about it, you know and I can see now that it could be all right too. I mean things have changed, even in India. My mother accepts you and that's a big thing. I think it could be different. It *would* be, I'm sure of that, perhaps.'

Sarah said, 'Do they wear tampons there? In India?'

There was a pause before deep said, 'Sarah, I don't think you realize yet what a powerful statement we can make by being together –'

Sarah said, 'You didn't answer my question.'

He asked her to repeat her question and she did. He said, his voice sounding stiff, 'I don't know. I don't know about those things.'

Sarah said, 'Well, how about your mother then: did she wear tampons?'

Deep said, 'Sarah, I don't think these are proper questions.'

Sarah said, '... or Maxi Pads? You could tell her that I'm thinking of changing from tampons to pads because I no longer want to hide my blood from myself.'

Deep said, 'Sarah, you *know* these are not proper subjects for discussion.'

'I don't know anything,' said Sarah, 'just now, except that it matters very much to me to have answers to these very things. Because – you know what? I've decided that the only level of culture I care about is the kind which makes my own life reasonable and intelligent. Listening to music and hanging paintings on the wall is all very well, but if at the end of the day someone wants me to hide my blood underground and to behave like an invalid – forget it, you know? If that's what tradition means, then I say, take it off the shelf. Leave it out. My packet of ultrathin, E-Z wrap pads and what it represents to me about the journey my generation of women has made, is all the tradition I need.'

'Sarah,' said Deep, 'are you comparing five thousand years of civilization to ...' he choked on the words '... feminine hygiene products?'

'Yes,' said Sarah and put the phone down.

The Valley in Shadow

Shashi Deshpande

Green forests covered the slopes of the two hills, leaving identical bare crowns on top. At the base, too, the lush growth gave way with a shocking abruptness, so that the valley in between was stony and arid as if a giant hand had scooped all the greenery out of it. I had thought it a beautiful view on the first morning. Now, as I stood alone on the verandah of our room for the fourth day in succession, the view was already stale, tainted, as it were, by my vision. I avoided it and looked instead at the garden that lay before me, the usual hotel garden with potted bougainvilleas and cemented walks bordered by wilting flowers. There were all the appurtenances of a holiday spot in it ... swings, sandpits, and at this time of the day, the men who made their living out of the hotel guests. The man who sold curios and picture postcards was moving purposefully from room to room, while the one with ponies squatted patiently for the children to come out and claim their ponies. The monkey man had settled down with his rattle, and the monkey, off duty as yet gazed round in a kind of bewilderment. Sounds and sights already as familiar to me as the cries of hawkers on the road outside our home. Now the children gathered round the monkey and the man's voice rose, speaking to the monkey in a peculiar sing-song tone, a tone that never varied in volume even by a decibel.

And then, everything else receded. For a moment, the world narrowed to a pair of hands. The hands that now appeared on the wooden railing of the verandah of the next room. 'Hi', the voice greeted me, 'and how are you this morning?' I smiled, then realized he couldn't see my smile. The thin partition wall was between us. He could see me only if I leaned forward as he was doing, with my elbows resting of the railing, my face propped on my hands. Stealthily I felt my elbows. Roughened. It was reassuring, like a symbol of our intimacy. Rub cream gently into your elbows each night, the beauty tips advised. Never again for me, I thought. I will never do that.

'Family out?'

'Yes.'

I moved my gaze once again to the valley which the sun resolutely refused to brighten. All day it remained untouched by the sunshine, while the peaks on either side glowed triumphantly.

'Family out?' ... that was what he had said the very first morning. 'Family out?'

'Yes.'

'Cute little fellow you have.'

'Yes.'

'You haven't gone with them?'

'No.'

'Oh good,' he had said, 'you do know another word apart from "Yes".'

He had laughed. I had already noticed that his voice was deep and resonant, but that laughter, however, had been high pitched. I had laughed too, but hesitantly, nervously. My uneasiness encompassing the question ... why was he talking to me? For me, communication with a man is like exploring foreign territory. A woman's responses I can guess at, her mind I can follow, whichever way it goes. But with a man it is always a groping in the dark. As we stood there and talked, I had looked at our hands resting on the wooden railings in front of us and they had emphasized the difference between us. Was that why, I had wondered, he was talking to me?

Now I could see he had just had his bath for his wet towel lay on the railing – a bright orange and black striped one. The whiff of soap and after-shave lotion came to me. Suddenly I wished I was bathed and dressed and ... No, that wish I had abandoned long back.

'Don't you ever go out?' he asked me.

'No.'

'You don't like to walk?'

'No. I don't.'

It was not a lie. And yet it was not the whole truth, either. The truth, the whole truth and nothing but the truth, so help me God ... But this was not a court, and I was not a criminal or a witness. And we would soon part, this man and I, going our different ways, and he would never know that I had not told him the whole truth. Why, then, did it matter so much? Why did I feel ashamed to keep the truth from him? The thing is.' I blurted out awkwardly and shamefacedly, my speech and words, I thought bitterly, as awkward as my walk, 'I can't really walk very much. I had polio when I was a child. I'm crippled.'

I used the worst possible word. The word I hated above all, a word which seemed to have nothing to do with the real me. Now he would be silent, uncomfortable; he would say a word or two to me from that height on which he stood as a normal human being. And I would continue to sit here watching the sunshine take over everything, leaving only the valley in darkness, until I saw them returning, my husband and child. My child would run to me, laughing, clamouring for my attention, wanting me to share his excitement with him, and I would forget what I was for a while. But he would soon run away from me and I could not follow him, and the thought of what I was would be forced on me once again. It's my fault, I thought. I should not have agreed to come here. What would I do on a holiday ... I who could neither walk, run, nor enjoy like the others? I carried my inability to enjoy with me wherever I went.

Even as a child I had noticed how people looked at my legs first and then, very perfunctorily, at the rest of me. 'Who will marry her?' my mother had moaned as I grew up. But my father had gone on doggedly with his proposals to young men, never hiding my disability, so that each time the matter ended there. When one young man had consented to meet me I had thought ... perhaps he will see me and not my legs. When he agreed to marry me I had thought ... he has seen me.

'Well, if you can't walk, why don't you ride then?'

This man spoke in a voice so matter-of-fact, so devoid of any awkwardness, sympathy or condescension that I was startled. I leaned forward and looked at him. He was looking at me too. It gave me a strange feeling, as if I was flooded with sunshine. I thought of the valley and of how, if the sunshine ever illuminated it, its ugliness and aridity would be emphasized. And for some reason my thoughts went back to that night, six months after the birth of my son.

Six months now, I had wondered, and still he avoids me. I had not known how to tell him that there was nothing to keep us apart any longer. Each night I had rehearsed the words in which I would say this to him and each night shame and some kind of a fear had held the words back. That night I had gone to him and tried to tell him without using words. Gently, and yet very firmly he had put me away from him and said, 'It's better we don't.' 'Why?' I had asked him stupidly. And he had said, 'After all, we have a son.' And all at once I had known that the sight of me was distasteful to him. He had put up with me because of his desire for a son. But why, I had thought in a last spurt of anger, had he married me at all? But I had known the answer to that one as well. I had known it from the first few days of our marriage. He had married me for the usual reason ... money. Not just the money my father gave us, but the money I earned each month. And even if I was earning more than he did, the fact of my being crippled leveled out the difference between us so that he did not have to feel humiliated as he would have with any other woman. That night I had shut out forever all hopes of any human contact.

And yet now the morning after my confession I had my bath early. I dressed myself in a soft cotton sari, one that I knew I liked. I went out, and seeing the two towels hanging there ... the child's gay and colourful and my husband's, a sober gray ... I savagely whisked them off the railing and took them in, telling myself they were dry anyway. When I came out I noticed that his feet were on the railings now, two feet, clean, naked and somehow vulnerable. As I sat down the feet disappeared and the hands appeared. I put my own in front of me.

'Hi, you smell nice today,' he said.

'Sandal soap,' I said boldly and despised myself for being unable to accept anything gracefully.

The monkey man now came up to us, started his rattling and said to the monkey, '*Saab ko salaam karo.*' The monkey obeyed and the spectators tittered appreciatively. I felt sick. '*Memsaab ko salaam karo,*' he now said and I uttered a strangled protest.

'Would memsaab like the poor little monkey to go away?' the voice said to me across the wall and over the monkey man's rattle.

'Yes,' I said emphatically and immediately he called the man over, I saw some money pass from hand to hand and the man went away leading the monkey which walked with a sort of hideous coquetry emphasized by the skirt it wore.

'Okay?' the voice said.

'Fine,' I replied and even to me my voice sounded different.

'Memsaab seems to be enjoying her holiday at last,' the voice went on. And I wondered ... had I got away at last from the bitter woman who dragged her resentment with her like the monkey its skirt? I imagined how the monkey would look without that skirt, leaping agilely from branch to branch ... But I was no monkey, was I? I laughed suddenly and he said, 'What's the joke?'

'I was thinking of those scientists who work on monkeys, guinea pigs and rabbits and apply the results to humans.'

'I know. Give a monkey coffee to drink and when it gets some kind of carcinoma, they tell you ... drink too much coffee and you'll get carcinoma too.'

We laughed and I said, 'Imagine, I didn't want to come here for a holiday.'

'Where did you want to go?'

'I don't know. Nowhere. I just wanted to go on working, I suppose.'

'Absorbing work?

'What! Working in a government office?'

Now the feet came up again. I heard the sound of a match scraping. The smell of a cigarette. 'You make me feel an idler.' The smoke drifted languidly towards me and in an instant was nothing.

'I must have a few days off each year. I can't go on if I don't.'

'And where will you go next year?' I waited with painful eagerness for his reply. A small pause. Then he said, 'Depends. It's something I don't plan too early. And you?'

'I don't know, either. I don't dare to look beyond today. Sometimes it frightens me, the thought that I have to keep going. I don't know where, or what for. So I stop thinking about it and just drift.'

Silence. It doesn't do to be too serious. People aren't interested in your miseries. 'How are you?' Fine, thank you.' What if you say ... 'I'm wretched, I'm absolutely miserable'? Nobody will ever ask you that question again.

The feet disappeared again. I heard his voice say, 'Shall I come over there? We've had enough of the Pyramus-Thisbe stuff, I think. Though that doesn't really apply here, does it? All right by you if I come over?

I panicked. 'No,' I said. 'Please don't.'

I heard him settle back in his chair. I cursed myself for my cowardice. Why did it matter so much that he would see me, see how clumsy and graceless I was?

'You make too much of it, you know,' the voice came to me remote, all expression carefully kept out of it. 'It doesn't matter all that much really.'

Doesn't matter? To whom? To you? A group of youngsters ran out into the garden. A boy playfully pulled at a girl's arm and she shrieked, shrieks that turned into laughter. I smiled. I could have laughed. And then I saw the valley again, dark, brooding and barren. I shivered.

'Can I come out with you?' I asked my husband the next morning.

'What, for a walk?' The disbelief could have been insulting but somehow wasn't.

'We could ride.'

'You couldn't.'

'No, I couldn't.'

'Of course, if you're bored with being alone, we'll stay here with you.'

'Daddy, let's go, I want to go.'

'No, you go on, both of you. I'm all right.'

'Do you have something to read?'

'Yes.'

'Sure you don't mind?'

'No, you go.'

Go, please go. At last they went. And I sat in the room telling myself ... I won't go out, no. I won't. And you, each time there was a knock at the door, I was aflame with hope. Once it was the dhobi to take away our dirty clothes. Once the boy who came to polish shoes. And I wondered whether I would be able to identify his steps if he came. Maybe I would.

And then there would be the knock at the door, my gruff, 'Come in.'

'Are you all right?' he would ask.

'Fine,' I would reply.

'You didn't come out today.'

'No.'

'I was a little worried. I thought ...'

My heart would be pounding ... surely he would hear it ... my hands trembling. He would see them and say, 'What's the matter? Why are you so scared?' He would hold both my hands in his and ...

I came out of it with a start and stared stupidly about me. The fantasy had been so strong I could almost feel the taste of his lips on mine, the smell of his cigarette in my nostrils. For a moment, revulsion against my own self filled me; until the thought came ... what the hell is wrong with me, a thirty-year-old woman with a responsible job, that I should behave like a hysterical adolescent? The words steadied me somewhat, giving me a kind of spurious courage that pushed me out of the room. I went and stood at my usual place, staring ahead of me. Clouds today so that one of the hills was dark and shadowy, while the other gleamed brightly. The valley in shadow, as usual, as always.

And then I saw the hands. Hands on the railing beside me. Hands like mine. A woman's hands, but the nails shaped and painted so that the hands had an edge of sophistication. I stared at them as they lay on the orange and black towel in a kind of caressing intimacy. And then I heard the voice from inside, 'Mamata ...'

'What?'

'What are you doing out there? Come on in.'

I went in myself and lay rigid on the bed. I imagined the voices next door. I imagined even more and was engulfed with shame to think of the fantasies I had woven round him. Me with my crippled body.

I was still lying there when they came back ... my husband
and child. The child was whining and came running towards
me. I thought he was tired and cradled him, I found his body
hot.

'He has fever,' I said accusingly. 'You shouldn't have taken
him ᴏut.'

'I wish to God I hadn't,' he said moodily, throwing himself
into a chair.

'Let's go back,' I said suddenly. 'Let's go home.'

'Yes, let's.' he agreed instantly to my astonishment. 'I'm
tired of this place.'

You too? I wondered, but I didn't want to know anything
more. Since the day he had turned his back on me I had
closed my mind to him. And yet, now, as I looked at him,
compassion flowed into me. And, momentarily, it was as if
the shadows had lifted. So that, somehow, it suddenly seemed
possible to talk to him. And perhaps in the evening I would
meet the other man as well. 'Hi,' he would say, as friendly as
always, 'come and meet Mamata.' And I would get up and
walk towards them smiling, uncaring of how I looked.

And now, I had a feeling that if the valley was in shadow
no longer, if the sunshine fell on it, perhaps even its bareness
and aridity would look beautiful.

The Tree of the Century

Mridula Garg

The tree had no idea that the twenty- first century was upon us. What have trees to do with centuries and millennia? It had never occurred to him to find out whether it was the 19th or the 20th century when he had first taken root and begun to grow. Hundred years are just a blink to a tree. However old a tree may grow, its daily routine remains the same. Whoever heard of trees retiring! Young or old, their work remains the same. Housing birds, giving shelter to the weary, shedding leaves to enrich the topsoil, manufacturing seeds for the future greenery and contributing to the arts. Yes sir. The trees make music by letting their branches and leaves play on the breeze. A veritable orchestra, playing different ragas at different times of the day and seasons. Some of them are excellent perfumeries too. Correction. Not some; all of them are perfumeries but not all fragrances reach the cussed humans. The fault lies not with the fragrance but our bewildered senses, afflicted by the stench of over consumption.

Our tree was a veteran, centuries old. Throughout the day, he practiced yogic deep breathing. The breath, he exhaled from the recesses of his lungs, was called oxygen by human scientists. But the practice of Yoga did not prevent him from keeping a careful note of all the human antics that went around and beneath; after all deep breathing was second nature to him. At nightfall, he recalled the funny, weird doings of humans as he rested and laughed to himself. The tepid breath he then exhaled was termed carbon dioxide.

The tree grew in girth and height as he grew in age but his feet remained firmly rooted in one place. He could not go gallivanting around and above like the birds which came to rest on his luxuriant boughs. But they more than made up for his immobility by their journeys, whose tales they told with gusto as they homed to the branches at eventide. What gossips the little birds were, worse than chattering old men and women. The tree knew, not all their tales were true. He also knew that gossip soon gets out of hand and takes wing soaring to an ever-widening orbit. And these were birds after all, used to soaring high. The tree might not have traveled in space but had traversed enough in time to sift the real from the imagined. So at nightfall, after the birds fell silent, he recalled the spicy details of their chatter and chuckled to himself.

In the winter months, the stories grew spicier as the migratory birds made their rounds. God knows where they flew to in the summer months but they never forgot to return in the winter. That is how it is with nomads; however far they go, they do not lose the yearning to return; a nomad is not a mendicant, you see. The stories, the birds from far away lands related, were sometimes so strange, that the shock made him forget to laugh for a while. When he finally did, late at night, the chuckle turned into a fierce guffaw. No wonder, there were sudden spurts in the quantity of carbon dioxide in the air during the sharp winter nights.

Not that the birds always brought distressing or comic news; there were times when their reporting brought solace to the tree's distressed heart. Like the time the cuckoo returned in March from a three-month sojourn in the South of India. It told of wide roads being laid without a single tree being cut.

Also of four floor houses leaving space for tall trees to go over the top through holes cut in the balconies. The tree felt so good that night that he forbore to laugh and even took a short nap to the beat of the music the breeze was playing on the branches. But he did not stop breathing; not for a split second. That would have been catastrophic. In fact the tree's forbearing to laugh had a salubrious effect. The scientists, the world over, were bemused into thinking that some trees produced oxygen even at night.

Time passed. The tree continued to do his work; it was time that turned treacherous. It turned footpath into lane; lane into road; road into highway; highway into flyover. Trees were pushed from the center to the margins. But their nature did not change. They carried on regardless. A tree, you see, is a little like God. With a beginning maybe, but definitely without an end. Trees do not die unless uprooted. As for that, even God would find it difficult to survive if cast out from the roots.

As the roads grew wider and the buildings higher, an altogether unfamiliar smell had come to pervade the atmosphere, the stench of loneliness. Had anyone talked of loneliness at the turn of the century, the tree would have immediately retorted, how can a tree be lonely? There are trees upon trees far into the horizon. But now, he was not so sure. Sometimes there was no companion tree to be seen for a great distance. Our tree turned to the human beings passing below for company. Some walked, some ran, jogging they called it, and some just sat in the shade to rest their weary bodies. A new raga could be heard composed of the jugalbandi between people breathing at different beats and the breeze passing overhead.

What the tree liked best were the old folks out on a walk with little children hanging on to their fingers. The older the guardian, the smaller the toddler he had in tow. The tree felt quite maternal when he saw the old folks bent double to suit the stature of the infants. He gave expression to the mother

love the only way he knew how. By inhaling deep, deep and
exhaling a waft of cool, cool breeze from the recesses of his
lungs. The weather's suddenly improved, they exclaimed. The
tree felt happy and exhaled with more gusto. In no time, he
found that the toddlers had grown into youths and then into
old folks, who had new infants in tow.

Time was passing at its usual pace when one day, a bird
from far away China landed on the tree. The story she told!
She was the only bird left in the whole of China, and that too
by pure chance, with the pellet from a catapult landing a hair-
breadth away. She managed to fly out of the country by hiding
in wide leafed trees at night and entered India.

'What about the other birds? Why were they killed?' the
tree tried to revive her with the oxygen from his lungs as he
wondered at the annihilation of birds. The bird had the answer
ready as soon as she got her breath back. 'The rulers of China
decreed that as the birds ate up grain, it was the duty of every
Chinese citizen to kill as many as he could. The citizens obeyed
the orders without question. They began to kill birds with
such zeal that soon they were annihilated. But I managed to
survive.' Suddenly she chortled with glee.

Why the laughter, thought the tree and she again had the
answer ready.

'We took our revenge soon enough. One year went well
without the birds but after that, the burgeoning population
of worms and pests paid put to the harvest. There were no
birds to control their numbers by making a meal of them.
Everyone knows birds prefer worms to grain any day.'

Everyone except the rulers. Such stupid rulers! Not stupid,
vain, the bird explained. Vanity draws a thick curtain between
the distant future and the eyes of he who must be instantly
obeyed, however idiotic his orders. The greater the
compliance, the thicker the curtain grows. Megalomaniacs
cannot see further than their noses, so full are they of
themselves. The despot said kill birds. Everyone ran helter-
skelter, doing just that. He grew vainer and more shortsighted

with each kill, forgetting the natural order, which was bound to strike back at the hour of its choosing.

Wow, thought the tree, you are the wise one. He vowed to take special care of her, even refraining from laughing at night when she was safely tucked under the leaves, just in case she fluttered down and was hit by the carbon dioxide drifting down. He fervently hoped she would soon learn to philosophize; not forget the tragedy, no one does that, but she could learn to make a shrine for her grief and move on. If only she could find a mate, not be alone; no one should ever be left alone. Why if she nested here, she might start a whole new breed of birds

But the bird did not mate or nest. Wise she might have been, but not equal to her grief. She willed herself to live on for some more time; then quietly one day, willed herself out of life and became one with the earth in the new land.

The tree grew afraid.

Had the bird found the courage to go on and start a new life and breed, he would have geared himself to fight any bestiality. But why call it bestiality? Beasts can never be as devastating in their tyranny as humans. They do not have the wherewithal. Even when housed in the biggest of forests, the sphere of their influence is limited. Only humans can increase it enough to destroy whole cities and forests at one stroke. Save us from future humanism, God, not bestiality. But they say God is dead. No, he cannot be. That is a canard spread by the humans. God must not die. He has to live for the sake of the trees. Then only can they unite against the inexorable march of humanism.

The fear of God being dead added to the fear that had taken hold of his heart with the death of the bird so that he forgot to let out the last intake of breath. Trees are not allowed to be afraid. If they are, the disgruntled souls of the disinherited of the earth grow over assertive. They suck the oxygen from the air and then, anything can happen, even the unthinkable As it did then.

The wind turned into a whirlwind for a while, for a brief moment when the tree, steeped in fear, was holding its breathing in limbo. As if it was the disconsolate soul of the dead bird, which had whirled it up. The stunned elder tree saw to his utter mortification that the lofty and robust young tree, which had stood by his side for years, lay uprooted on the ground.

Dear God, that young one was like his own son. How could this happen! The storm was hardly anything to speak of. The wind just a trifle swifter than normal breeze, though full of poignant gloom. They had both weathered much wilder storms. What happened today? Such an irrational death! Oh my son, my very own beloved, my young one! You who were so full of the zest for life and the hauteur of youth; so brave and fearless, eager to reach the sky; how could you be struck down by a mere wisp of a wind?

How often had I tried to tell you, do not let your height go out of hand. Concentrate more on building the strength of the trunk. But you were bent upon competing with the sky. Whenever I repeated, what is the point of growing tall like the date palm, if the fruit remains out of reach, you laughed saying, have you lost your memory, old one? I am not a fruit-bearing tree, remember? What about offering shade to the travelers, my insistence made you break into guffaws. Am I not giving it to the denizens of the fifth floor house? See, the ground has climbed to the fifth floor; the travelers now pace on the roof-tops. Do not laugh so much; never laugh during the day, I warned you, it pollutes the air. You paid no heed, muttering, save me from the sermons of the old. I wanted to tell you that trees do not grow old but I did not want to offend you or did I just grow impatient? I did tell you a few times, if you must laugh, do so at night when everyone and everything is at rest and your sarcastic air do them no harm. But when you paid no attention, I stopped preaching. I stopped chiding you about your unnecessary height too. I was wrong. I should have continued to offer advice; after all I had the benefit of the traditional knowledge of centuries; I should have continued to warn you. If only I had not given up so easily! You might have heeded me at last and not grown quite so spindly and tall. With a stout trunk, you might have withstood the onslaught of the grieving wind, eager to transport the distressed soul of the bird quickly to paradise.

The storm abated. The breeze stopped its wailing and began to sob. Had the bird regained paradise? And the young one? Was he there with her, nestling in eternal peace and serenity? Or ... no one knows for sure. The ancient tree found no solace in his reflections. All he could do was to turn his grief into benediction by exhaling more and more oxygen into the environment through deep breathing.

When the birds homed to the tree that evening, they forbore from chattering in deference to his loss. The birds, which used to nest in the branches of the young dead tree, also flew to the old one and joined in the mourning. Some time passed in silence. Two deaths, coming close together had struck them dumb. Then, as happens in common expressions of grief, the birds started consoling each other, in muted tones, as they looked down on the corpse of the young tree, cradling the alien bird in his arms.

The tree heard them tell each other, it is horrible how so many young trees have fallen foul of the wind lately. It is all the doing of the myopic rulers. Roads have gained precedence upon trees to such an extent that they forget to leave enough breathing space around their roots, when laying the concrete slabs. Without mother earth to sustain them, they can barely breathe what to say of growing robust trunks. The urban trees are like consumptives now; untimely death claiming them for its own with each whiff of a storm. Seems the rulers here are as megalomaniac as the ones in China.

Oh my God, the tree sighed in remorse, how obtuse of him to have blamed the lad for not heeding his advice. With exemplary fortitude, he had overcome the deficiency of his lungs to rise above the killing fields and invent his own oxygenated breeze. What could he do but laugh at the irony. So many have succumbed to the callous indifference of vain officials and a slothful public, so many more will, in the days to come, he lamented and keened to himself.

It was not yet fully dawn, when the tree was surprised to see a whole gang of men and women descend on the dead lad and set to tearing his limbs apart. He well knew that this was how the last rites of trees were performed but surely not with such callousness? Could they not pause a while to mourn the death of one, felled in the prime of youth before attending to their needs of firewood? Did they not have even one little dirge to sing for him? Ah, such a lusty, strapping, beauteous tree to meet such an untimely death! Why oh why? Was it an accident or just the fumbling of a blind fate! Could it be a fate of our making? There was no guilt, no sympathy; not even a sigh to mark the loss of a thing of beauty.

The night was over. The day was upon them. The time had come for the tree to take deep breaths and breathe out oxygen. But his agony had reached a point, where it becomes impossible to breathe in. All he could was to let out dismal sighs. He realized that in the wake of the deaths of the young of the tribe, there was not much time left for him. The all encompassing noise and plastic garbage of the consuming rich along with the concrete of the incompetent town planners held his roots captive in their asphyxiating grip. The slightest rise in the breeze was enough to fell him. But there was no breeze anywhere. Only noise and a stifling stink from the mounds of rotting garbage. Should he try to conjure up a breeze, the way his lad had done or should he give up? He was still ruminating when suddenly the noise took shape in words. They were everywhere, reverberating in the graveyard of trees.

Save the Environment! Grow more Trees!

The irony of the slogans made him forgot all about breathing. He burst out laughing and laughed through the day, holding his breath as if he would never ever breathe again.

It so happened that when the tree laughed for the first time in living memory during the day, it was the dawn of the much touted twenty- first century.

Translated from the Hindi (Ikeesveen Sadi Ka Ped) by the author

Mayadevi's London Yatra

Bulbul Sharma

The day Mayadevi turned 68, 70 or 75 years old (her date of birth was an ever-changing event linked to her moods) she decided to go to London. Everyone in the family was stunned when she announced this, but no one dared to speak out because the old lady ruled over the entire three-storied house with a quiet reign of terror. Whenever she decided to do something, her three sons and their wives quickly agreed, since they had learnt slowly and bitterly, over the years, that no one questioned the old lady's whims. Though there was no need for Mayadevi to give an explanation to her submissive and docile family, she still called her sons and gave her reasons for undertaking such an unusual journey at her age. 'I want to see Amit before I die.' This eldest son of hers had gone to England to study when he was eighteen years old and had never returned to India since then. He wrote to his mother on the fifteenth of every month and sent her money regularly, along with many expensive but useless presents, but did not come home to see her, because he had an acute phobia of flying. He had travelled to England by ship in 1948 and once he had landed there after a traumatic and unpleasant journey, he never stepped out of the safety of the island during the last 40 years. There had been a few short, tension-filled holiday trips to France and to Italy, but these were either by train or by boat. Around every October as the Puja season approached, he promised his mother that this year he would take the plunge and get into an aircraft and come to Calcutta, but his nerve failed him with reassuring regularity each time. 'The wretched boy was always a sissy. He could never cross the road if a cow was standing in the middle. Lizards frightened him and rats made him scream even when he was fifteen years old. I will shame him by going to London – to his very doorstep, even if I have to bathe in the Ganga a hundred times after I return,' the old lady declared and the sons, who thought it a very foolish idea, nodded their agreement as they had done all their lives. Once the momentous decision had been taken, Mayadevi began planning for her journey on a warlike footing. She first applied for a passport and visa but filled in the forms with a lot of arguments and protests because she did not like the impertinent questions the government dared ask her. Once that was over, she bought a big register and wrote down her plan of action step by step.

Now she decided to attack the English language. Though Mayadevi had never been to school she could read and write Bengali fluently and was far better read than her graduate, accountant sons. She could understand simple sentences in English but had never spoken the language to anyone in her entire life, since the occasion had never risen. Now she hunted out a tattered old English primer which belonged to one of her grandchildren and every morning after she had finished her puja, folded her *Gita* away safely, and distributed the sanctified sweets, she sat down to study this jam-stained old book. The household, usually peaceful and quiet in the mornings, was now filled with Mayadevi's strange rendering of the English primer. Sitting cross-legged on the floor and rocking herself backwards and forwards, she read each line over and over again in a musical singsong as if she were chanting a sacred verse. Then she would suddenly stop and ask herself questions. 'Did Jack fetch the bucket?' she would ask in an accusing tone, and then reply, 'No, Jane fetched the bucket.' She would get up once in a while, adjust her spectacles and take a short walk around the room, holding the closed book near her chest as she had seen her grandson do when he was memorizing a text. The servants did not dare come near the study area but watched her nervously from the kitchen doorway. They were sure she was learning English only to terrorize them more effectively. 'At her age she should be only reading the *Gita*, not repeating jack-jack-jack like a parrot', they said, but only when within the safety of the servants quarters. The lesson unnerved the cook so much that he stopped fiddling with the marketing accc ınts and turned honest, in case the old lady, armed with the English language, caught him out. The daughters-in-law too found the lessons very odd and giggled quietly in their bedrooms but they were careful to put on a serious face when they came anywhere near the vicinity of the English lessons. The sons too kept their distance from their mother after their eager efforts to help her with her English pronunciation had met with a cold rebuff. 'For 60 years I had managed this house and my life without any help from you or your late father. I do not have any wish to start now,' she said, dismissing them with a regal wave of the tattered book.

So she carried on learning the primer and the household not only got used to the strange sounds, but caught the infectious tone too and the servants began humming, 'Jack and Jill' as they went about their chores. Within a few weeks Mayadevi had finished the primer and graduated to more difficult books. She now carried on long conversations with herself to air her newly acquired knowledge of English and as the days went by the characters from the primer, the *Teach Yourself English in 21 Days* and other books got mixed up with each other in the most unfortunate, tangled relationships. 'Did Jane go to the grocer's shop alone? No, Mr. Smith went too.' 'Mrs. Smith is sitting on the bench in the garden with Jack. She is smoking a pipe. How are you Jack? Quite well, thank you. Where is the tramway?' her voice would drone endlessly till she had learnt all the words in each and every book by heart and so had the rest of the household. Now there were only three months left for the date of departure and Mayadevi went into the next stage of her travel preparations for the great journey which had been named London Yatra by her family, though, of course, behind her back. 'Now I am going to wear shoes', she announced and ordered one of her sons to get her a pair of black canvas shoes and six pairs of white cotton socks. Mayadevi had always walked barefoot in the house and worn slippers on the rare occasions she went out to visit. The no.3 blue rubber slippers lasted her for five years at least and though they hardly ever stepped on the road, they were washed every day with soap. But in England these faithful slippers would not do, and so Mayadevi reluctantly and with a martyred air forced her thin, arthritic feet into her first pair of shoes. For one hour in the morning, after the English lessons, and then another hour after her evening tea, the old lady practised walking in her new shoes. Like an egret stepping out on clumsy, mud-covered feet, the white-clad figure paced up and down the house, accompanied by a rhythmic squeaking of rubber. Soon there were large blisters on her feet, but Mayadevi carried on the struggle like a seasoned warrior and no one heard her expel a single sigh ever. Her sons admired her from a distance, but did not dare to praise her, since they knew she distrusted flattery of any kind and always said, 'Say what you want from me and leave out the butter.' So no one ever praised her, and came straight to the point when asking for favours.

When there was only one month left for the departure, Mayadevi wrote to her son in England and informed him of her plans. He instantly went into a severe panic and telephoned her, which he had never done in the last 40 years. 'Ma. Please do not undertake such a dangerous journey.

Planes are crashing all the time. You can be hijacked to Libya.
Air travel is really unsafe now. You wait, I will definitely come
home by ship next Puja,' he screamed hysterically over the
bad line. Mayadevi listened to him patiently and then replied.
'I may be dead by next Puja. My ticket has been bought. You
will come and receive me at the airport and make sure you
come alone and not with that giant wife of yours,' she said
and put the phone down firmly though she could hear her
son's voice still cackling on the line. From then on there was
total silence from across the ocean but that did not bother
the old lady and she now moved into the final preparations
for the London Yatra. She started visiting her relatives one by
one and each one was informed of the travel plans personally
by her, just as if she was following the norm for issuing wedding
invitations. She did not sit for long in any house but just gave
a brief outline of why she was going to England and then left
without accepting any tea or even a glass of water. The relatives
were surprised not only by this flying visit like royalty, but
also by the fact that she chose to tell them why she was going.
'The old battle-axe is losing her strength. Getting soft in the
head now,' they said, but were secretly pleased that she had
condescended to visit them. After this came the most
important stage and one morning the old lady called her sons
and the family priest for meeting. The daughters-in-law and
the servants, not invited, took turns to listen at the door. 'In
case I die in that land, though God will never do such a thing
to me, bring my body back immediately before they
contaminate it. Then see that all the rituals of purification
are done properly,' she said, fixing the priest with such an
unblinking, cold look that he began to tremble with fear and
could not help thinking that the old lady had died already
and was watching him from heaven. Once the plans of how
to deal with her dead person had been discussed to her
satisfaction, Mayadevi gave them detailed instructions for the
purification rites she, if returned alive, would go through on
the very day she came back. 'There is a week–long penance

to be done, brahmins are to be fed and the entire house is to be washed with water from the Ganga. So see that you take leave from office, all of you,' she said to the sons who understood the importance of the occasion and readily nodded their heads, hoping the meeting had finally ended. Now only one week was left for the date of departure. A large, battered suitcase, which had been a part of Mayadevi's impressive dowry when she came to this house as a fifteen-year-old bride, was brought out from the dark corners of the store-room and Mayadevi began packing. Six white cotton sarees, six petticoats and an equal number of blouses, one white sweater and a grey shawl, along with a small red cloth bag for her *Gita* and her prayer beads, and a plastic box for her false teeth were the only items she packed.

'Everything except the *Gita* and my teeth, will be thrown away when I return, so why waste money?' she said. The suitcase was packed and ready five days in advance and left on top of the stairs like a coveted trophy. Everyone who came or left the house would trip over it but not a murmur of protest was heard. In fact the servant proudly dusted it every day and the children approached it with awe.

Then finally the day of departure arrived. Mayadevi got up before dawn, bathed, and went into her prayer room. She knelt before the gods and whispered, 'Give me strength to endure this ordeal and let me not die in that land. I promise to make you new ornaments of gold when I return. Please bring me back safely to you.' She sat for a long time in that small, incense-filled room and only when the light began to stream in through the windows, did she get up and go out to wake up her sons. Soon the entire household was rushing around, though there was nothing very much to do. The suitcase was dusted a few times and the children made to touch their grandmother's feet every time they passed her way. The sons kept clearing their throats and looking at their watches. 'Has she got everything?' they muttered but not too loudly, since none of them wanted to go and check. Mayadevi packed five large packets of puffed rice in a cloth bundle and filled up her grandson's plastic water bottle. This was all that Mayadevi was going to eat for the next twelve hours, because she was not going to touch any food 'that God knows who had touched.' The day passed quickly as visitors came to say goodbye. Each one admired the suitcase and, after bumping into it, remarked how light it was. The plane left at 12 o'clock at night, but Mayadevi and her sons were already at the airport four hours before that. They sat solemnly in a row and watched the clock now, instead of their wristwatches. They had never before spent such a concentrated and confined time with their mother and were finding it very difficult to sit so close to her on the plastic chairs. They took care to change places so that no one had to sit for too long near her and each brother could get some respite. Once in a while Mayadevi spoke to give some last-minute instructions. Her sons only nodded and cleared their throats once again. At last the flight was announced. The old lady lifted her head and listened carefully. Suddenly one of her sons got carried away by emotion and tried to give his mother a few travel tips, but she got up quietly and joined the long queue of passengers weaving their way to check in. One by one the sons, bending with difficulty under their middle-age spreads, touched their mother's feet. She blessed them with a rarely seen gentle smile and as they stood like orphans, she sailed out of their vision and into the gaping door of the security area. The sons were not worried about their aged mother. They only wondered how England would cope.

It was raining when the plane landed in London. A flicker of worry crossed Mayadevi's mind as she wondered whether her still uncertain shoe-walking ability would be able to manage the wet ground. 'It will have to be done', she said to herself looking down sternly at the shiny black shoes as if ordering them to obey her. She adjusted her saree, still crisp and starched after twelve hours and got ready to leave the plane.

Throughout the flight she had sat ramrod straight and when the air hostess had offered to adjust her seat to a more comfortable, reclining position, she had said, 'Why I sit like that? I am not sick,' in a sharp voice, freezing the pretty young hostess's smile before it could even begin. She ignored the old lady after that but could not help glancing at the odd white-covered head each time she passed her seat. Mayadevi's neighbour too had stopped talking to her before they had even crossed the Hindukush mountains and now pointedly looked the other way. She had tried to be friendly and helpful and had showed the old lady how to fasten her seat belt. Mayadevi at first did not say a word and the younger girl thought she was just shy about not being able to speak English and became even more friendly. 'Everyone was so kind to me in India. Even though the people are so poor, they have such large hearts,' she said, warming up to the subject, happily rehearsing what she was going to say many times over when she reached home, when suddenly Mayadevi opened her mouth for the first time and said, 'Why they not be kind? They lick white people's shoes two hundred years and now it become bad habit like drinking and smoking.' The girl was shocked. Never in her six months' stay in India, during which she had traveled the length and breadth of the country, staying only with families since one could get to know the 'real India' that way, and also hotels were so expensive, but she had never ever met with such rudeness. She was gathering her wits to say something sharp in reply, when Mayadevi shook her head firmly and also crossed her hands over her lap, in the traditional manner of refusing food at Bengali feasts, to doubly confirm her refusal. She then watched the young girl eat her meal and stared at her with an expression of such distaste that the poor girl left her food half-eaten, though she was enjoying the European meal, even a plastic covered airline one, after six months of endless dal and chappatis. Once in a while, Mayadevi would eat a handful of puffed rice and take a few sips of water from her plastic bottle. The bundle containing the rice and the water bottle had been carried close to her body throughout the journey and when the security men at the airport had asked her to send it through the X-ray machine she had clung to the bundle like a lioness to her cubs and said, 'Touch it and I shall throw it in your face. I will starve for the next twelve hours and if I die, you and your next fourteen generations will have the sin of an old woman's death on your heads.' The security men, trained to deal with terrorists, did not know how to handle this and allowed the old lady and her clumsy bundle to pass without any checking. Actually Mayadevi did not really need the rice and could easily have stayed without food for many hours at a stretch, since she had been fasting for some auspicious day or the other from the time she was a young girl and her stomach was quite used to stern starvation regimes. But now that the plane was about to land, it suddenly gave a loud rumble of protest, startling Mayadevi by this uncharacteristic rebellion. The young girl heard the grumblings too and allowed herself a small mean smile. 'Old cow, hope she has a bad time here,' she thought but then immediately felt guilty and filled up Mayadevi's landing form for her. Mayadevi never said 'thank you' and as soon as the plane came to a halt she shot up from her seat. She marched down the aisle clutching her food bundle close to her body so that no one could contaminate it by touching it and was the first passenger to get out of the aircraft. She then slowed down and attached herself to a group of Indian passengers who had also just come off the plane. She followed them closely but when they reached the immigration area and began queuing up, she walked past them and planted herself firmly at the head of the line. No one could ask an old lady to move back and even if someone had, Mayadevi had her steely look ready. The young blond man at the immigration smiled at her kindly, even though it was against his principles to smile at immigrants or visitors of any hue. In return for the rare grin he received the famous dead fish stare, under which innumerable men and women of Calcutta, young and old had quelled. The young official felt sheepish for no reason at all and quickly called for an interpreter, an almost SOS urgency creeping into his voice. 'I speak English. You speak English with me', Mayadevi said clearly. The immigration official cleared his throat and said, 'How long do you plan to stay in UK?' and when Mayadevi said nothing, he repeated the question, adding a 'Madam' this time. 'No need to say again, again. I answer you. I stay in this land one week only. Not a day longer. You can tell your Queen Victoria', said Mayadevi. The stunned official stamped her passport with a resounding thump and waved her on as fast as he could. 'This is one old bird who is not lying to me. Won't ever catch her working at Selfridges, for sure,' he said and laughed nervously as if some ordeal had been passed.

Mayadevi again followed the passengers she had marked out and made sure they collected her suitcase and carried it for her in their trolley. Her son was waiting for her outside when she finally emerged, but even though she saw him at once she gave no sign that she recognised him. The 50-year-old extremely successful dentist, member of the Royal College of Dentists and a very old London club, did not dare raise his arm and wave to his mother. She walked towards him slowly and after she reached him, stood staring at him as if he were a total stranger. The son lurched forward and made an awkward, half-bending movement to touch his mother's feet but at the same time surreptitiously tried to look as if he was tying his shoelaces. Mayadevi, who was on full alert, her eyes carefully scrutinizing her son for faults, pounced like an eagle on the first wrong move. 'Ashamed to touch your mother's feet, now are you? A mother who has not long to live but even then has traveled such a great distance, fasting for twelve hours, sitting with all kinds of half-castes so that she can see her son,' she hissed. Amit, who was well known in the dentists' circles for his dry, sharp wit, was about to defend himself with a few crisp, well chosen words, but before he could speak something clicked inside him. As he looked into that old lined face, an irrational fear jolted his memory and he said in a whining, childish voice, 'No, Ma, ... I ... so many people here,' he stammered helplessly. Now that she had established the old family hierarchy in the correct order, Mayadevi told her son to pick up her suitcase and take her to his home. Though the mother and son had not seen each other for more than thirty years, they drove to the semi-detached house in the beautiful, green, tree-lined suburbs in unbroken, stony silence. The mother asked no questions and the son offered no explanations, because he somehow felt that she knew everything about him already, and disapproved strongly. When they reached home Mayadevi got out of the car in a suspicious, stealthy manner as if she was expecting hidden traps in the neatly laid out garden. Mother and son entered the house like two mourners and when his wife came out of the kitchen to greet them, Amit almost burst into tears with relief.

'Welcome to England, Mrs. Banerjee. Hope you had a nice flight,' Martha, Amit's wife, said cheerfully. Mayadevi looked up at her tall, large-boned daughter-in-law through the top of her spectacles for a few long, uncomfortable seconds and then said, 'I want to wash hands. Everything so dirty.' Martha's plain, good-natured face showed a brief flicker of surprise but she beamed at her mother-in-law and said, 'Come and see your room and then we will have a nice cup of tea. Hope you like the new curtains we put up for you, Amit did not know what your favourite colour was, so I chose blue,' she prattled on, her voice full of genuine affection for the old lady she had never met before. Amit crept up to shelter behind his wife's ample frame, as his mother examined the room and cringed each time Martha went too close to her. He knew what would happen if Martha touched her by mistake. 'Are you feeling cold? Shall I turn up the central heating?' asked Martha, suddenly feeling the cold herself. Though Mayadevi was shivering in her thin cotton saree, she said, 'Not cold, only wash hands, so much dirty,' Martha quickly led her to the bathroom, gaily decorated with trailing plants and fluffy rugs. Mayadevi slammed the door shut on Martha's smiling face and began to wash her hands. First she washed the taps thoroughly and then she began rinsing the soap, though it was a brand new one. Then she finally washed her hands meticulously four times in a row. When she had finished, she turned the tap off with her elbow, so as not to touch the tap again. She dried her hands by shaking them about in the air, looking scornfully, as she did so, at the pretty, flowered hand towels Martha had put out for her. Then she went out to search for her son. 'How will I bathe in that jungle you call bathroom? Why has she put carpets in the bathroom? To hide the dirty floor?' she charged full force, happy to have found something to complain about so quickly, 'Ma, she will hear you,' said Amit, glancing nervously at the kitchen door, even though they were speaking in Bengali. 'You must be tired. Why don't you eat the rice I have made for you and go to sleep now,' he said, desperately hoping she would agree. Surprisingly she did. 'If you are telling the truth that she did not make it,' was the only half-hearted resistance she put up and followed him to the kitchen. 'I cooked it, Ma, she did not even touch it. I am not lying to you.' He said and flushed when he saw Martha watching him even though he knew she could not understand what he had said. But Mayadevi made sure that the message had got through by giving her a triumphant look. She took out her false teeth with a sharp, satisfied click and sat down to eat. The meal, a bowl of overcooked rice and a muddy brown dal, was consumed quickly and noisily as Mayadevi chewed with her gums and when she had finished she took her plate to the sink and washed it carefully twice. She shook it dry by waving it in the air and then kept it as far away as possible from the other plates and dishes. Martha's friendly smile had by now faded to a bewildered, confused look and she stood silently, watching the water from the plate drip all over her hospital-like, sparkling clean kitchen floor. But she did not know what to do or say. Amit stood next to her, wearing the expression of a sad, unhappy man, expecting even worse times ahead.

Mayadevi, quite content now, with the way things had gone so far, left them both and went to her room. She dragged the bed cover off the bed, spread it on the floor and then after saying her prayers, fell fast asleep at once. She woke up in the middle of the night and sat bolt upright. The grayish yellow streetlight streamed in through the window and the sky outside was a lighter shade than she had ever seen. Calcutta seemed very far away. 'God forgive me, I will return soon,' said Mayadevi feeling lonely for the first time in her long, solitary life.

The next day passed very much like the first one, only Mayadevi cooked the food for herself and Amit. He felt guilty about not eating with Martha but his mother's contemptuous, 'Ha! A slave to his wife,' plus the delicious fragrance of long-forgotten, favourite dishes, compelled him to sit down and eat with his mother every evening, as he came back from work. Martha never complained and he did not dare to ask her what they both did during the day, but he got the answer anyway judging by the new, unhappy lines on his wife's forever cheerful face. Like two boxing champions trapped in a ring, Martha and Mayadevi circled around the house, avoiding each other but at the same time keeping a wary eye on what the other person was doing. The old lady would listen as her daughter-in-law went about doing her housework and then she would tiptoe out, her eyes gleaming like a fault-finding laser beam, to check out her work. She opened drawers, peered under the beds and ran her fingers over the window panes. But she could not find any dust or cobwebs as she did on her weekly checking rounds in her house in Calcutta. Angry and bored, Mayadevi took to sitting in her bedroom in sullen silence for the entire day. Martha did try from time to time to make friendly overtures but each time she met a solid wall of silent rebuff. Mayadevi would shut her eyes tightly and pretend to chant her prayers every time her daughter-in-law looked into her room. She never wanted to go out to look at the shops, watch television or drink tea, and Martha could not think of anything else to cajole the old lady out of the room. Slowly the six days of unspoken tension passed, and Mayadevi happily began packing her bag once more.

'Thank God, it is over, the wretched trip,' she muttered. The last day of the visit was a Saturday, and Amit had taken the day off from his clinic. He had been hoping that some emergency would crop up and he would have to rush to the clinic, but he knew very well that it was a foolish thought and a dentist had no crisis of broken molars or sudden cavities in his career. He decided bravely to face the situation and take his mother out shopping. Martha, her good-natured spirit still alive, offered to come along too but Amit said in a courageous voice, 'No, you rest, dear. I will take her alone', as if he was going off to slay some dreaded dragon. But Martha insisted on coming along to give him unspoken support. They drove to the large shopping centre near by, Mayadevi sitting at the back, spurning all friendly remarks and efforts at showing her the sights of London. When they reached the huge, glittering building, there was an embarrassing tussle in the car park. Mayadevi did not want to get out from the car. 'Why should I go to this big shop? What do I want to buy from here?' she asked her son, facing him squarely. Amit stared helplessly at the giant shopping complex with ten floors of the world's best merchandise, but he could not think of a single thing his mother could buy there. 'Well, now that we are here let us go in. You can tell everyone at home what you saw, can't you?' he said with a wide, foolish grin, as if he was talking to a child. Mayadevi's saree got stuck in the gap between the steps and she, thinking Amit had stepped on it, kept scolding loudly. They disentangled her and then walked straight into the fairyland of lights, cosmetics, perfume and lingerie department. Mayadevi suddenly stood still. She felt as if she had been struck by lightning. In her entire 75-odd years, she had never seen a world like this. Hundreds of bright lights gleamed everywhere she looked. Dazzling blinding mirrors as tall as trees and walls that had solid gold lamps on them. There were countless mysterious, colourful objects she could not recognize on every glossy surface. Silken bits of lace were draped all over glass shelves and though they had an odd shape like two cups, Mayadevi, who had never worn any undergarments like most other women of her age, thought they were the most beautiful lace decorations. She could smell the fragrance drifting up from the glittering glass bottles filled with magical potions. It was the most powerful and sweet incense she had ever smelt. There were jewels as big as eggs in boxes that shone with silver and gold threads. Mayadevi felt that she had died and come to heaven, only the people were wrong. 'There should have been our gods and goddesses in this paradise, not these pale humans,' she said softly to herself, not moving in case it was a dream. Her daughter-in-law suddenly understood what had happened to the old lady. She took her arm and gently guided her through the mazelike, narrow lanes of the department store, overflowing with gleaming merchandise. For once Mayadevi did not flinch at her touch and followed Martha meekly as if she was a celestial maiden guiding her in paradise. 'I think we should get her nice warm jumper, Amit,' Martha said to her husband who had not yet noticed the sudden change in his mother. They went to the women's department and Martha picked up a pale blue cardigan. 'No, no, only white', whispered Mayadevi still in a trance. Martha found a fluffy white one quickly and also a lacy white shawl to go with it. She presented them both to the old lady with a friendly smile. But this gift was a greater shock for Mayadevi than seeing the big department store, in all its glory, for the first time. Her late husband, her many children, and countless relatives had always given her what she had asked for, but no one had ever given her a present. Her steely eyes unused to crying became almost blind with tears, and through the blur she took Martha's hand and shook it as she had seen people in her phrasebook do. 'Good girl, very well, thank you', she said to her daughter-in-law, showering her with all the polite words she knew in English. By the time they reached home Mayadevi's brief moment of weakness had passed and the vision had cleared. She was her old iron self again, but there was a certain change in her demeanour. She did not actually smile but her eyes had lost that old freezing glance and she called Martha by her name. The next day, before she left for the airport, she let Martha make her tea and though she did not thank her when she placed the cup in front of her, Martha little knew how much sacrifice and giving it meant for the old lady. The journey to the airport was silent this time too, but not an unhappy, uncomfortable one. When the time came for Mayadevi to leave she patted Martha's hand and said, 'When I die, you come to Calcutta for funeral. Let my fool of a son be. You come.' Then after making sure that her son had touched her feet properly, she walked into the 'passengers only' area. She did not turn around to wave at them though she knew she would probably never see her son again. She was content that she had done her duty and now she looked forward to the year-long penance, purification and sacrificial rituals she would have to do to wash away the sins of the London Yatra.

Portrait of a Childhood

Shama Futehally

From the beginning we knew that our home was different. It was, of course, indefinably different from the homes of our school friends, as we saw whenever we went on visits. There seemed to be some uncomprehended gap between our home and the blue walls, stainless steel pans, and mothers barefoot in the kitchen, which is what we saw in the homes of our friends. There were other friends whose houses were somewhat like our own – where the table was laid with linen and there were potted plants and cut flowers and a clean servant bringing refreshments on a tray. Nonetheless it was true that our home and garden were uniquely beautiful, and this was clear even to a child. The front door opened on to a sitting room, mute but gay, in dark blues and browns with a low stone wall and french windows in front. These led on to a verandah which had low, cool benches made of large slabs of smooth stone; and beyond that was a garden so exquisite, so genuine, as to be hardly believable. In the evening especially, as the long rays of the sun brought into focus its smooth surfaces of lawn, its dark and light patches, its thick clumps and light stone paths, its pond with the lilies and the kingfisher, my ten-year-old heart used to suffer at the sight of it.

And beyond the garden were fields with toddy palms, with not another house in sight except that of our cousins where we would go to play. A mud road led around the fields, and there was also a mud path through them which was our 'short-cut'. Both roads seemed very much our own, there was hardly ever anyone else using them. In a way the fields seemed our own too, they went with the house and the garden, as the right kind of setting. But as we grew older we heard more and more frequently that there were 'squatters' in the fields. The grown-ups used to joke about it, about sitting in the garden with their backs to the fields because of the 'squatters'; and figures carrying rusty kerosene tins and disappearing behind the toddy palms became a common sight. When we had visitors we felt very ashamed. The little alcove in the sitting room where we had breakfast looked directly out on to the fields; sometimes the scene was bad and if we had a guest staying we had to apologise with charm. By the time I was twelve or so, I had learnt to do so myself in case my mother was not around.

Nevertheless, it has never occurred to us that the fields might disappear, that somebody else might want them and take them. When we first began to hear that 'buildings' were going to be put up in the fields, a sort of dread made itself felt in the conversation, and nobody said very much about it. For my twelve-year-old self and my ten-year-old sister, it meant a first stirring of awareness that things which ought to be in our hands were not so, that fields which we wanted and liked, and which we ought to have, could be so completely outside our control. That other people were taking them over, that they were going to cut off our lovely view and put up buildings, was something I hardly allowed myself to imagine. But whenever I did think of 'buildings', I had at the back of my mind large, clean buildings with marble fronts, like the ones in town. The truth was still to be learnt.

Meanwhile, our lives revolved very largely around our Ayah, to whom we clung, literally, all through our early years. She was large and fat and unchangeable, in her white sari. It was only slowly that I realised that she was a small bent woman, and not even particularly fat. She had a smooth fair face with a thick ugly nose which always bothered me; I felt that if only I could take it away and put another nose in its place she would be perfect. That Ayah was only human, and therefore subject to change, became apparent on the day she was mysteriously taken somewhere in a car and brought back wearing spectacles, which gave her a funny little squirrel face like an illustration in a children's book. 'Now you won't get headaches any more,' said my mother. But we looked at Ayah, giggling and ashamed and feeling that the world was not quite the place it used to be; and, to our dismay, Ayah looked rather sheepish herself.

In any case a sort of change had begun. One day I saw with surprise, while drinking my afternoon glass of milk, that my head came up to Ayah's shoulder and that I would soon be as tall as her; it was as if a little block in my mind had suddenly fallen into an empty slot with a bump. Because, as I had explained seriously to my cousin at the age of four, my parents were as tall as the toddy palms and Ayah was nearly as tall, but not quite. And now all at once I was nearly as high myself. Also, I was slowly beginning to see that there were curry stains on her saris, they were not really white, and the blouses were always torn under the armpits. And there was a peculiar smell whenever Ayah hugged us, and I began to wish that she wouldn't.

Now Ayah was the aunty of Paul, who cooked and chauffered. Paul was a hero to end all heroes. He could carry us on his shoulder all the way to our cousins'. He could play gulli-danda as no one else could. He used to buy us sweets while driving us to school, and his jokes were the best in the world. 'Bas!' we used to say, as he ladled food onto our plates. 'No bus here,' said Paul, 'bus at the bus stop.' And he would whisk away the dish on his palm, leaving us paralysed with admiration. He was usually in a vest and khaki shorts and had a little silver cross tied on a black thread round his neck. He had a shadowy string of brothers and sisters, nine or ten of them, and he would forget all their names as none of us would ever have dared to do. We were never tired of asking the name of his youngest sister, and hearing in reply, 'Lora, or Phlora, some such.'

'And where does she live?'

'Oh, somewhere good.'

When the great Ayah Disaster took place, we minded more because of Paul than because of Ayah.

It happened like this. We had a visitor staying with us, an awesome intellectual English lady who nonetheless had beautiful leather bags, soft high-heeled shoes and a pink frilly thing to wear round her shoulders while she put on her make-up. I used to watch her mutely from a distance and wonder what it would be like to be her. One day I heard her saying to my mother, in the sort of English which belonged to another world, 'I'm terribly sorry to have to say this, but I think one of your servants may be dishonest.' Then there was a huddled conversation between them and I crept away. And about half an hour later we heard unusual screams and shouts in the backyard and ran there to see a dreadful sight. There was Ayah, hair dishevelled, standing small and alone on the gravel, throwing her arms about and shouting. Everyone else had gone away. Paul, in the kitchen, was looking miserable and pretending not to hear. 'After fifteen years! Just because a foreign memsaab says something!' shouted ayah. And we, who had always been on Ayah's side, we stood there dumb, on the wrong side of the battle. There was a moment when Ayah's red wet eyes met mine, and neither of us knew what to do. Ayah and I, who had always been the best of pals! My sister and I went away, leaving her shouting in the empty backyard. We never saw her again.

Meantime, the buildings were going up. I had assumed that one day we would just wake up and find large cool buildings around our house, with potted palms, a chowkidar, and shiny cars in front, but slowly the terrible truth began to dawn. It all began with a fat paan-chewing man wearing a blue nylon shirt and dark glasses, who arrived in a jeep one day, while two other people measured the ground with a tape and wrote things in a book. Rapidly, trenches were dug, they filled up with rain water in the monsoon, and an assortment of cement-coloured men, women and children arrived with their pots and pans and began to live under small pieces of coloured plastic or strung-up sacking. Green and pink saris were hung up to dry on the large water pipes in one corner of the field. I still thought that after it was all over the buildings would be beautiful, like those in the clean haven of 'town', twenty miles away. But one day my father said casually, 'Well, this is hardly worse than what it will be once it's finished,' and at once I knew that the buildings, too, were not in our hands, that they would be like the other buildings in the neighbourhood, with three or four grimy floors each, large black patches caused by the monsoon, and with clothes hanging all over them. And I felt sick with despair. I was slowly learning that it was no use expecting other people to be like us, that they were inexcusably different, that one had to twist and turn one's way through them in search of others who were proper people like we were. And so for the wonderful world which existed in book – the Famous Five and their adventures, the 'smashing' fun they had at their 'super' school – of that I could only dream, whenever I managed to take myself off to the swing at the bottom of the garden, to get away from the world in which I had to live.

And that happened more and more often, and for longer and longer periods. One day we were sitting in the garden in the evening, which we resolutely did in spite of the skeletal structures that were coming up all around us. Suddenly there was a barrage of little stones from the air – we turned to look

– and there, laughing away, were half a dozen little labourers'
boys sitting on the unfinished balcony of one of the buildings,
with their fists obviously full of pebbles, all sniggering. Our
anger and horror are hardly to be described. Somebody
spluttered, 'This is what happens when you lift them out of
their proper station.' I went off to the swing to forget not just
that scene, but also what the future would bring.

Yes, that swing, on which I learnt to swing rhythmically so
and so dangerously fast was becoming more and more
necessary. Whenever anything happened which I wanted to
drive out of my mind I rushed to the swing. There was, for
instance, the day when I saw Mr. Ghote having his lunch.

Mr. Ghote was my father's typist, which means that he sat
in a small room in the factory premises which were not far
from us. He was a tall, morose-looking man who was kind to
me, giving me a sweet occasionally or letting me have
sharpened pencils with rubbers attached. One day I went there
at lunchtime with my father and saw Mri Ghote huddled
among his papers with his tiffin carrier – one of those with
several small round boxes. As we came in he looked
embarrassed and tried to hide the carrier behind his desk. It
seemed to contain a brownish vegetable and two thick
chappatis; and it was so clear that he was ashamed of them
that I wanted to run away. At such time the swing was my only
refuge ... I would run to it, begin to swing, and hurriedly
remind myself that Mr. Ghote probably had quite a lot of
happiness in his life after all. Indeed I was becoming quite
adept at doing this – anything I wanted out of my mind – and
it was done like the pressing of a button. Increasingly, there
were sights or episodes which caused a helpless mixture of
feelings. If I saw a young woman from among the labourers
holding a howling baby, and crying to herself, I would hardly
know what I was feeling, but whatever it was I wanted it out of
my mind at once. If I couldn't get it out I would feel angry.
This anger, to tell the truth, interfered a great deal with my
peace of mind which, in any case, was hardly peace of mind

any longer. Quite often I didn't know exactly what I was angry about. If someone were scolding a servant, I would be angry with them for being angry and angry with the servant for looking so miserable. And it took me hours to recover.

One year we were taken to Kashmir on a holiday. By this time, aged fourteen, I did not expect much enjoyment from life, it seemed to consist mostly of things which one had to avoid. But such enjoyment as was possible was surely all compounded in such an event as going to Kashmir. We were to fly there, another glamorous prospect. On the morning we were to leave I got up especially early so as to squeeze all possible enjoyment out of the day.

We left for the airport by seven. But my father had made a most unfortunate remark just as we were leaving. 'What we are spending on this holiday would feed several families for a year,' he said. I was trying to get this out of my mind as Paul chauffered us out of the lane, and there in front of us was a queue at the milk booth, and Mr. Ghote standing in it. He had his empty bottles in a blue and white striped cotton bag. I told myself hurriedly that Mr. Ghote could not be allowed to interfere with this occasion of all occasions and I resolutely prepared to enjoy myself to the full. But somehow the enjoyment had become very elusive. There we were, as dreamed of for several days, waiting in the airport lounge to go by plane to Kashmir. But in some way I felt dreary about it, the airport was too dusty and the plastic of the seats too red. On the flight, too, I waited unrewarded for some pleasure to emerge from the fact of the grey-blue seats, the complimentary sweet, the meal all wrapped up in plastic. And that evening I was looking out of our hotel window in Srinagar at the Dal Lake lit by fairy lights and feeling unmistakably dead, as I was to do for many years to come.

Life Sublime

Anita Agnihotri

$\mathbf{B}$oth her feet in water from the melting ice block, Malini tries to recall. When was it that she saw Arunabha alive for the last time, which day, at what time? In an effort to remember, she closes her eyes for an instant, standing straight, with the garland in her hands. She lowers her aching neck, her head. Yes, of course, it can't really be called seeing. Malini was the one who saw him for a few seconds, he did not see her.

It was yesterday morning. Seven or just before; the morning light breaking out of the clouds all of a sudden had touched Malini's balcony railing. Rain was forecast. Malini had tossed and turned a bit in her sleep at the sound of thunder, of rain falling in her dream. Now, she didn't feel like leaving the bed, and felt a slight back pain after getting up, a sort of cold. All just tricks of the body not wanting to make the effort to bathe.

Skipping a bath would be an indulgence. Then the laziness would drag on into the office as well. This thought propelled Malini into the bathroom even earlier than on other days. She had long ago stopped oiling her hair, her shoulder-length curly unslicked hair quite a headful even in her mid-forties.

Latching the door, letting her sari palla fall off her shoulder, she hummed the second stanza of a song that was going around in her mind. 'In the sky ahead, in realms moving and motionless ... lit by this light eager and fresh ...' as she checked automatically for the things she needed, and when she was on the third stanza, she realized the towel wasn't there. She quickly came out onto the balcony to fetch the towel off the clothesline, on her lips the lyrics 'The earth here keeps gazing she waits ...' her humming gave way to a luminous smile, of which she herself was completely unaware.

Arunabha was in front of his house, going out.

Whenever she steps out there in the balcony, her eyes are bound to land on the house on the left, the one with the madhabi vines up and over the verandah blooming their heads off in pink and white bunches. Arunabha was out of the gate, on the road, and from there he was signalling to Rina, that's his wife, about something. Rina didn't seem to understand, so then Arunabha cupped his hands around his mouth and said loudly, 'The bag.' The bag of light blue plastic leapt down and Arunabha caught it from below. He was headed for the market. A straight tall figure, a pinstriped shirt and a lock of hair carelessly tumbling over the forehead, he looked much younger than his fifty-three years.

She came back to the bathroom with the towel. The smile still lingering on her lips. Out of habit, a habit of twenty-five years at least, whenever she thinks of Arunabha or sees him from a distance, this smile comes to her lips without her being aware of it.

How come, then, that people talk of intuition? That danger for a loved one casts its advance shadow in your mind! Is all that just made-up stuff? Malini had no premonition, not the slightest. After she'd bathed, she quickly applied light makeup to her face – eyeliner, but no bindi – and did up her hair. Dressed in a blue-dotted print sari and blue blouse, she finished breakfast, eating like a bird, and at exactly nine was off to office in her Maruti. It's a private office; you must arrive on the dot. The day at the office went like other days. A meeting of the sales advisory group, laughing and joking in the lunch break, then in the afternoon she and Amrito Tripathi sat down to finalise the note for the upcoming annual general body meeting. She also brought home a printout of the note for minor corrections, a practice that goes against her grain. She never brings office work home, and because it was so contrary, she didn't even touch it after she came home. At six-thirty in the evening Taramoni brought her tea, neatly arranged on a steel tray covered in embroidered cloth. And right then, Amarnathbabu, the gentleman who lived in the first house of their street at the crossing of the big road, came to return a few English magazines he had borrowed from her. Calling out to Taramoni to bring another cup of tea, she remembered that Amarnathbabu had given up drinking tea, and she said instead, 'There may not be any lemon at home, but some lemonade –'

Amar-babu got up to go, 'No, no, why don't you have your tea. I dropped by on my way home after seeing how Arunabha is.'

'How Arunabha is, meaning?'

'Oh, you don't know, Arunabha is in the intensive care unit since this afternoon! You didn't know? Really?'

Dumbstruck, Malini shook her head. Giving her a brief outline of what had happened, Amar-babu wheeled his scooter out in the dark. 'Want to come with me? Come along then.'

'No,' Malini was calm. In her mind, an old hurt feeling was smarting. Just a telephone call, Rina couldn't even call her to tell her! Malini would've dropped everything and gone over, she would've cared about nothing else.

It took Malini a little while to go out. Taramoni came to ask about dinner, she responded absently. She wasn't sure if she should rush to the hospital right now. If Arunabha were present here, she could've asked him about the condition Rina was in, ought she to go prepared to spend the night there; now that's not an option. Malini felt paralysed. Just as a long time ago at age twenty four, while turning in her hand an invitation letter with a dot of turmeric on it, she simply could not make out what was written in it. A very dear and familiar name, Arunabha Basu was, with no prior notice at all, going somewhere, hand in hand, with an unfamiliar name, Rina Choudhury. Now where was Malini to go and what was she going to do? Thinking of this, her ears seemed to go deaf from the drumming of her own heartbeat. Had these two situations grown from the same root, from Arunabha's absolute centrality to her existence. The thought of taking the car didn't occur to her. Walking through the drizzle, her hair wet as if with drew drops, she reached the suburban town hospital.

She had never had to be there in such an unpleasant state. Actually, in the last two and a half years since she first came to this town, no sense of loneliness had ever touched Malini. Arunabha himself had found her the rented place. His own house had just been built; the plaster still to get a coat of colour; its plumbing and woodwork still going on. Malini's landlord lived in Delhi, he came once in a while to sign a contract with a new tenant, then went back. For about a year Malini felt a little alone, though in that period the Arunabha-Rina family came and went all the time in preparation for their moving in, and naturally whenever they were here, they all spent a lot of time together in her drawing room, because the new house was still without an electricity connection. After that time, seeing Arunabha once each weekend, calling him on the phone when necessary and, most of all, knowing that he was right next door the sensation of these kept Malini's cup filled to the brim. Arunabha knew where to get the indoor plants; he found the tiny little bookstore on the fourth floor of the new shopping centre; his hunter's nose sniffed out the new vegetarian restaurant before it was even opened. And in all these adventures Malini's unfailing companion was Abhi, Arunabha and Rina's only child. Abhi now studies chemical engineering, stays in the hostel, comes home during the vacations. Abhi's hero is his father though when they disagreed, he would come stomping to his Mala-mashi.

In front of the hospital haphazardly parked were two-wheelers of all kinds, the car parking a bit farther up to the right. Malini followed the shabby corridor, past the emergency room. She had come here a few time to see those friends and colleagues who don't easily go to a private nursing home, but the possibility of her coming here to see Arunabha had never entered her mind. Scattered knots of people were waiting in front of the intensive care unit; some of them glanced at her but didn't make way for her. The doctor wasn't there in the duty room outside. No question of going in without permission, so she waited. With a slight leftward turn of her head she would have seen Arunabha, perhaps sleeping or unconscious, but Malini did not feel like looking. She decided rather to wait there for now. No matter how long it took.

And just then, Rina came out of the door. Her hair crumpled at the back of her neck, dark circles under her eyes, the bindi on her forehead smudged, she wore infinite exhaustion on her entire body, as though she had been through a sandstorm from that morning to the evening. Rina took Malini's hand in hers and uttered in a tearful voice, 'He's sleeping. They've sedated him. Want to look?' Malini wasn't ready for the pressure on her fingers that came with the last sentence. Her unprepared body was pulled to one side of the glass.

And just then Malini's body shivered from a sense of desolation, a feeling of terror. They had sedated him, he's sleeping. Can anybody be so still in sleep? His chest not even rising and falling? The hands on his chest seemed as though they had been still for centuries. The wrist bare, the familiar Titan quartz watch not there. In this half a day it seemed as though someone had infused his faced with ink. Would this man get up again, would he ever talk and smile?

'Is Abhi informed ... I mean ... has he been called?' That was all Malini could say, turning away from the door.

Before Rina could say anything, one of Arunabha's colleagues spoke up, 'Yes, Boudi has had a word with Khoka. He's in the middle of his exams, so he hasn't been asked to come. As it is, the condition is quite stable ...'

That colleague's wife put her arms around Rina and gently led her out, saying, 'You've been sitting here so long, have something to eat, I brought some tea from home.'

Rina turned, said faintly, 'Mala, go home. It'll get late, may be in the morning ...'

'Why don't I stay the night here ...' Malini said, like a stubborn child.

The crowd make noises of disagreement ... 'No-no, no need for you take the trouble, we're all here, taking turns, you've office so early in the morning.'

Rina nodded tiredly in agreement. Malini felt a piercing pain.

Rina, Arunabha's colleagues, their wives – they are all so together, and the intimacy of their relationship so impenetrable. There's no room here for Malini. For a long time after she got home, she couldn't sleep. Around twelve-thirty, eyelids dropping, she let her body drop onto the bed. Amidst the sound of hard rain, of the loud patter on the corrugated awning over the windows, and of wind blowing, she woke up two or three times and stood by the window, looking at the deep night outside. Was Arunabha opening his eyes now, the sedation wearing off? What was Rina doing? She kept remembering Rina's harried, dishevelled, bindi-wiped forehead. Had Malini stayed on there tonight, Rina could've slept a little. Malini looked at her watch. It was two-thirty.

Would Malini ever know of this? She would, if a long time after that night, sitting in the soft sun of a winter day and slowly picking up the ball of wool from her lap, Rina would tell her. 'At two-thirty, he opened his eyes.'

'Really?'

'Yes, I leaned over his face, asking "How do you feel?" His voice was so weak, so scared, uncertain! He said. "Where are you going again and again?" I said: I've been sitting right here, only went to the toilet a little while ago. "How many times to the toilet! Why can't you keep sitting near me!" He closed his eyes again. Then, with eyes still closed, he said, "Mala ... didn't come?" I said: she did in the evening, you were sleeping then, the doctor did not allow people to go in, but she'll be back early in the morning, for sure ... Arunabha said "Yes," and then drifted back into the haze.'

No, this little detail Malini could not have known at the time.

Close to the morning, before the light of daybreak touched her lovely forehead, Malini, Arunabha's Mala, passed through a dream. Every time, on waking, she feels as if she had had this dream before, and yet that sense doesn't stay with her during the waking hours. The dream is really the wrong side of her own life ... The rustle of a new sari, the garland of white tuberoses around her neck, Malini is being married. Arunabha's silhouette is in the distance, beyond a dark corridor, where he's standing by a pillar.

A terrible pain tears up within her, Malini is trembling from the pain. 'I'm being married, Arun-da, I'm leaving,' she's saying it aloud, but no sound comes out. 'Just one life it is, only one life,' some such expression flows from the shadowy Arunabha to Malini, but he's absolutely still, his lips not moving at all ...

Then the birdsong woke her up. Her limbs reluctant to move, she still managed to bathe early. Had a cup of tea, thought of telling Tara to fill a flask with tea, to take to the hospital, then thought Arunabha's friends would be bringing tea. Thinking it might look bad, her going there so early, she got there at eight-thirty. Found solid emptiness in front of the intensive care unit, only a few crows on the porch farther away. A sweeper passed by with his bucket-and-rag. No one else there. Where did they all go?

Spotting a sister, Malini went up to her and asked. 'He has been shifted to Bikramnagar early his morning. We don't have the equipment here, the heart condition couldn't be monitored.'

'But after such a major attack ... can be take the journey?'

'That I don't know. The doctor must have been aware of everything when he gave the instruction.' With this, the sister hurried off towards the operation theatre.

In that state of directionlessness, Malini came to the office. To put her mind into work, she brought quite a few projects down from the shelves. Yet she simply could not concentrate, the threads kept breaking. She felt like running all the way to Bikramnagar, but told herself that she'd go, she'd ask for leave to start off early once she got some work done.

At ten minutes past twelve, the red telephone on the Deputy G.M.'s desk screamed. Khanna listened for half a minute. 'Yes. All right,' and lifting his brows, asked for Malini.

And at that moment something snapped with a crack within her chest. She went to the phone the way one goes into a totally dark tunnel. Arup, Arunabha's friend, was on the other side.

Malini picked up her bag and got up from the chair. Khanna smiled kindly, though it wasn't a time for smiling, and said, 'Take it easy. Don't come back to office today. Do you have money with you?'

The red Maruti raced through the damp sunshine to Bikramnagar. Forty kilometres from Birpur to Bikramnagar. An hour's drive if there's no traffic. Once past the town's bends, crowds and signals, the placid length of the state highway pulls like a magnet. Blue skies and the shade of eucalyptus on both sides. This route is Malini's favourite at other times. Today, her hands mechanically on the steering wheel, the car streaks spell-bound through the noon hour. While in her mind rise and fall the lines from a poem she read a long time ago. On the book's cover, a young Pablo Neruda's reflective, preoccupied face in sepia.

Tonight I can write the saddest lines.
Through nights like this one I held her in my arms.
I kissed her again and again under the endless sky.
Tonight I can write the saddest lines.
To think that I do not have her. To feel that I have lost her.
To hear the immense night, still more immense without her.
And the verse falls to the soul like dew to the pasture.

In a short time, Arunabha's life will scatter like fine pollen in the sky, the clouds, the air. Maybe it already has, Malini won't even know that. Such a rush to leave the body that was so dear for so long. Just as one day he couldn't brook any delay in leaving one loved woman for another.

Bikramnagar's hospital is much bigger than Birpur's. Inside, all kinds of departments, wards, research labs. Sounds of sobbing and muffled weeping on the way upstairs. The intensive care unit there too. Many pairs of sandals and shoes lying outside, their owners inside in bare feet.

Her back to the wall, Rina sits on a high stool, her hands on her lap. No tears in her eyes, her hair undone, thick with grief. Malini's eyes go to Rina first, then to Arunabha. His head bent to one side, eyes closed, glasses removed. After the long continuous suffering, the whole body in soothing quietude. Fresh blood on the sheet near his left heel. Why the blood? With a shiver Malini clasped Rina. And at once, Malini's body shook from tears flowing uncontrollably like muddy water after rain. The people around her turning at her, staring, and she oblivious, crying as if she had lost control over herself. It was quite some time later that Malini became aware of what she had said at the time. Clasping Rina's head in both hands to her own chest, stroking her hair, she kept saying, ... 'why did this happen, why this, what will happen to me now ...'

And, looking at Malini's face with her deep-set eyes, Rina said through her tears, 'We've to go a long way, a very long way ... a lot of suffering is written ... this is nothing at all ... a lot of crying to be done on the road ahead ...'

* * *

Her feet in the pool of melted ice on the floor, Malini remembers yesterday morning when she saw Arunabha for the last time. Full of life, straight and tall, the rebellious lock of hair on his forehead. Adroitly catching the shopping bag as it sails through the air from above. And of Muzaffarpur thirty years ago, when she saw Arunabha for the first time. The wall around the rail colony, its red buildings, the edge of the high well, and Arunabha. He had just graduated from engineering college, dressed in yellow shirt and white trousers, almost boiling over with fresh youth. The wild-haired tenth-grader Mala produced absolutely no romance in his mind; every time he saw her he pulled her hair or slapped the back of her head. Mala was twenty when Arunabha changed jobs and went away, first to Patna, and then to Calcutta. Before leaving, the acknowledgement he left with a burning pair of lips on her forehead, eyes and lips, the heat of which Mala followed with letter after letter, softening its fierceness with coats of smooth clay. No, there was no promise of marriage from him. Still the ongoing game between the two of them had given her no inkling that a six-month silence would be followed by an invitation card for his wedding. And how was Mala to know that Arunabha's mother's friend's daughter Rina would be hidden in the wings somewhere?

Holding the burning coals in, Mala came for the wedding. She couldn't keep herself from coming. Nor could she, standing in the pantry, ignoring its stuffy heat and the cockroaches, keep from getting the new bridegroom's kurta wet with her tears.

The slabs of ice are melting very slowly. Arunabha lies on the huge bedstead, flowers all around him, deadweight of flowers atop his chest. Abhi is mid-way he hasn't reached yet, and it's very important to wait for him. Still, the ice keeps melting.

Stupid girl, you just couldn't do it, could you? In this life, to lift your face up to another face decorated with sandalwood paste! Her parents, her aunt, they tried and tried, but failed. No groom passed Malini's standard, Some too tall, some too short, some stubby-fingered, some spoke English in an American accent. At the office, so many Abhijits, Siddharthas and Parthapratims tried and tried, but failed. Malini remains single. This strange game of hide-and-seek between her and Arunabha – it seemed to be moved by some invisible signals, as if sent out by the antennae of a huge butterfly, its wings spanning the Milky Way! They'd lived in the same neighbourhood for so long, yet why did they keep apart? Why did all that love not find a way? What held Malini to Birpur for two-and-a-half years despite the stings of pain? And if she was held here, why wasn't she given a signal of danger yesterday morning? And if not that, then why that glimpse through glass of his stilled face, and why did she come back home after that, why then go over to Bikramnagar ... and now, why is she holding the garland with her feet in a pool of melting ice? What can it mean, this hide-and-seek through life and death?

Abhi is on his way. It's late at night. The boy is coming all the way in a rented station wagon with two friends. The ice must not all melt before he's here.

For a long time Rina lay on the drawing-room floor, on her face. Now she has sat up. The sofa and the chairs are pushed away everywhere to make room for the people moving in and out. In the midst of all that, Rina sits up on the floor leaning on her hands; the housewomen, wives, unmarried girls, women of all ages have sat themselves down around her.

A momentary glance that way, it suddenly occurs to Malini that this scene is the same as of the wedding night all over again. On that night the bride was surrounded by her friends, talking about Arunabha, giggling while giving accounts; and Rina's blushing face gleaming, a slight smile on her lips. Tonight also, sitting amidst her friends, Rina is talking softly of Arunabha and they're all listening intently. Tears in Rina's eyes, mist in the others'. '... Suffered a lot, you know, ... the tearing pain in his chest, he kept calling me from inside that unit, sometimes for Abhi, for Mala ... I kept running in there ... they wouldn't let me inside ... with so many doctors beside him. .... Finally they slit his leg, hoping to bring the pressure down from bleeding ... he bled so much, they hurt him so, ... still they couldn't! ... His screams of pain ... ah, the pain he suffered!'

A gentleman from Arunabha's office walked hurriedly past Malini and places the flowers; he hasn't noticed the icewater on the floor, so his socks get wet, and his face shows discomfort.

This time, Malini slowly lays the garland at Arunabha's feet. She really wishes to touch his forehead, but restrains herself. It's too late in this life, she had waited too long. In a strange way she doesn't understand, everything has got left behind.

The night gradually tilts towards dawn.

Two-thirty.

Last night at this time in Birpur hospital, Arunabha opened his eyes with difficulty, asking, 'Mala ... hasn't come ...'

Mala was then standing at her window and looking at the rain-soaked night-world.

This night once again the clock hands point close to two-thirty.

The humming, the restlessness subsided once Abhi arrived. Only a young boy, yet how he lowered his head quickly onto the mother's shoulder, how he quickly put his arms around her and called, 'Ma!' How he said to her, 'But I'm here. Look at me.'

'Mashi!' Abhi's call ends Malini's trance. 'You've been standing for a long time, now go into the bedroom and sit with Ma. Try to sleep a little if you can. It will be late in the day before we're back.'

The truck is going to leave now. Arunabha is in it, countless flowers, a few people. Other friends and acquaintances in the vehicle behind. They will return after cremating him by the sea.

From tomorrow Abhi will begin the son's social rites of bereavement. For Rina, widowhood has already begun today. Malini too has lost everything, yet she has nothing to master except the art of being discreet about the expression of her grief.

The truck rattles with the roar of the engine. Their old watchman is opening up the iron gate, Arunabha will leave now. Abhi walks to the truck, he climbs on it and takes his place.

Glancing once at her own darkened, lonely house next door, Malini turns to look for Rina. Rina is standing quietly at a window upstairs, one hand on the railing. Does Arunabha know that at the time of his departure, the two of them have silently, tearlessly made way for his soul to rise up, the woman who wanted Arunabha all her life and the one who had him, both! Now that Arunabha is no more, can't Rina and Malini merge together and become one? The light at the window above and the darkness at the doorway below; this house and the next?

Poor Abhi is to stay up all night. He has just arrived after seven hours of road travel. Let him not get sick. About to touch her own forehead Malini realizes that she is becoming unconsciously merged with Rina, reposited in her.

Translated from the original Bengali by Kalpana Bardhan

Martand

Nayantara Sahgal

ഉ ഏ

Martand took his lean length out of the comfortable depths of our best armchair and said reluctantly, 'I'd better be going.'

Naresh, my husband, did not reply.

I looked up at Martand but he was not looking at me. He never did, eye-to-eye, except when we were alone, and then hungrily, as if each time were going to be the last – as it easily might have been.

I got up, too. I wanted to cry out every time he left me, to hear my own voice wailing like a lost child's. We had been talking politics, if the chaos caving into everyday life could be called that. Strain and suspense had become part of office and home. There was no getting away from it. Crying would have been a release from that as well.

Refugees glutted the district, and more and more kept straggling in. Not one big flood with an end to it. This was an endless, haggard human sea of people who knew with profound instinct that there was no going back. They were here to stay. And here, food and medicine were short. Space was getting harder to squeeze out. There had been little enough before. And time was running out.

'In other countries men can dream,' Martand had said earlier in the evening, 'but our dreams remain food and shelter, shelter and food, year after year. We've never had enough for ourselves and now we have to provide for these extra God knows how many.'

'We *know* how many,' said Naresh bitterly, 'Millions. Why beat about the bush? It's going to get desperate, wait and see, unless the refugees ease off.'

It was clear that a serious crisis, the worst yet, might soon be upon us. Martand had agreed.

'It already is,' Naresh had said with harsh finality, 'We should have sealed the frontier long ago.'

'And let them die,' lay unspoken between us.

'Well, it's not our problem,' Naresh threw at us defiantly, as though either of us had protested.

'Isn't it?'

Martand had looked at my husband consideringly, compassionately as he said it, and I at the wall. I was caught between fact and vision, between the two men, belonging mind and body to each. I loved and believed in them both, but Martand, I knew, was trying to do the more difficult thing. He kept trying to hold a tide at bay, to turn it off its dreadful course, if he could, with the tone of his voice, the look in his eyes – such instruments as human beings are left with when hardly any other resource remains. Inner religion pitted against destruction. For Martand still had visions of a good world. For months Naresh and I had shared them, here in this very room till late into the night. Now, only I did.

We had talked all evening about the refugee crisis, but what a nerve-racking thing our own three-cornered companionship had become. What a lot of gaiety I needed simply to get through each day without continual mention of disaster. Disaster was always there. Was there ever a time it had not been? But now ordinary everyday happiness had become part of it. I felt happy only when I was near Martand and then I would have to be careful not to let it show. That was how it had become, the once easy natural give and take between the three of us. Now only its outer crust remained, a paper-thin but sheltering wall that hid my private torment. I had lived inside it these six months, ever since we had met Martand soon after our Kashmir holiday.

Martand is the Kashmiri name for the sun god and there is a temple to him in Kashmir – miles of drive past brilliant young green rice, in the earth's most beautiful valley flanked with tall, straight poplars, fringed with feathery willows, under serene expanses of sky. I had needed to go to Kashmir, quite apart from the pilgrimage I wanted to make to the temple. I had longed to get away from the frantic, teeming district in Naresh's charge to clean open space; Kashmiri space. There were other nearer hill stations but I couldn't bear the thought of any other. And then, incredibly, Naresh had got his leave. With every Government officer so heavily overworked, we had hardly expected it.

Naresh had grumbled goodnaturedly about the distance. 'What a prejudiced lot you Kashmiris are, convinced there's no place like Kashmir.' But he had given in.

There isn't, of course. Kashmir is unique. I did not want the rationed beauty of other places, a glimpse of hill and cloud. I wanted a pageant of it, the immense incomparable valley unravelling as we drove through it. I wanted to surrender to something bigger than necessity, and I had to visit the Martand shrine. Where science had failed, faith might work.

The temple was off the motor road. It was thirteen hundred years old, a massive burnt-out saga of ruined glory with a broken Grecian colonnade surrounding it. When we got there, it seemed afire under the late afternoon sun, a tiger gold, its energy rippled visibly through its carvings. Then the light changed and softened before our eyes, sinking deeply into the stone, leaving it flesh-warm and pulsating. I put the flat of my hand on a lovely broken column, leaned my forehead against it and felt it all taken into me.

'Have you had enough?' Naresh asked indulgently.

He was sitting against one of the columns smoking his pipe.

'How's that going to get you a child, granted Martand is the fount of fertility?' asked.

Reluctantly I gave up my hand's contact with the stone and came to him with my answer.

'Now? Here?' he protested.

'Why not,' I pleaded, 'there's no one for miles around.'

'But the village is less than a mile away. Anyone could come along.'

'Please, we're wasting time.'

And we wasted no more. The gold fire in me caught up with Naresh as he pulled me down beside him.

Martand, when we first met him just after that holiday, reminded me of that ruined splendour. He looked descended from an ancient, princely lineage. I felt a shock of recognition and betrayal.

'You look frightened,' were the first personal words he said to me.

I was. I should have waited for him. But I couldn't tell him that. Instead I told him he had an unusual name and asked him about his ancestry, and Martand laughed.

'If I tried awfully hard,' he said, 'I suppose I could find out my great-grandfather's name.'

I must have looked scandalized.

'Is that very dreadful?' he had teased. 'No, there's no blue blood in my veins. I come from solid middle class stock. Scholarships all through medical college. But there's romance in the ordinary. Romance isn't the heights. It's what a passing stranger recognizes. It could even be in working in an inferno like this, and learning to love it.'

Naresh saw Martand out to his car and came back into the room. He was bone tired and irritable.

'He never knows when to leave. I've got an early meeting tomorrow. He probably has to be up at the crack of dawn too.'

I said, to take his mind off Martand, 'When do you think this refugee business will let up?'

'On Doomsday,' he said violently. 'That's when any problem in this country is going to let up.'

He went into the bedroom to put away the whisky bottle while I rinsed out the glasses. A lot of whisky got drunk whenever Martand came.

Naresh came back. 'He drinks like a fish, too,' he said, helping me with the glasses.

Naresh was angry, but not about the drinking. He was angry with Martand for still having dreams, and with me for being enmeshed in them.

When we were in bed he said, 'How long are we going to make excuses for not being able to meet targets, not having enough to feed and clothe people and make life livable for them? And now with this ghastly deluge going on and on, we'll never have enough of anything in our lifetime. Have you thought of that? I want to get out of this hell-hole and live a decent life somewhere where people have *enough* of everything. It doesn't seem too much to ask. Let's get out for a year or so.'

I felt paralysed.

'I'm making some enquiries,' he went on, 'I could ask for a temporary posting at one of our missions abroad. Just for a breath of fresh air. I've had a bellyful here.'

I lay in bed, trying to empty my mind of all thoughts. A lot of whisky had got drunk – by all of us. Martand had once said, 'It helps to numb feelings. One can't watch all this unprotected and remain human.' It was one of the few times he had admitted to strain.

'Do you agree we should get out then, darling?' Naresh mumbled.

And he fell asleep without waiting for an answer.

There was a crowd as usual outside Martand's clinic next morning, looking torpidly, dully at me as I walked through.

Flies, dust, heavy, hopeless heat. Another day of learning to love it, I thought, and another minute till I open that door to Martand.

He was sitting at his desk, his sleeves rolled up, his feet in slippers, his stethoscope still around his neck. He had forgotten to take it off, like he sometimes forgot to eat, and continually forgot the huge dishevelment around him. He asked his assistant to bring some coffee.

'Sorry the cup isn't very elegant,' he said when it came.

He was always saying things like that. Sorry, when he repaid a debt, about handing me grubby-looking change or a tattered note. Sorry that we could not see the hills from his window – there were none to see.

There was only a grim growing mass of humanity, almost machine-like in its menacing immobility as it waited. I couldn't see these people as individuals any more. It was it. Waiting for cholera shots, for rations, for clothes, for space, for air, for life, for hope, as if It could do nothing, nothing for Itself. A monster robot seeking succour, devouring the pitifully little we had.

'Do you think the kingdom of heaven is a germ-free place?' asked Martand, giving me his smile over his coffee cup.

I put mine noisily down spilling coffee. I felt a rush of hysteria and horror at all the sights and smell of suffering interminably around us. How could he stay so untarnished at the heart of them?

'Who cares? It's here is this mess we have to live. Oh Martand, I can't bear to stay or to go away. I can't bear anything any more.'

'You must,' he warned, no longer smiling. 'There's a very long road ahead of us yet. Don't lose your nerve now.'

He meant the refugee crisis, as well as the time span left to him and me to find our way to each other on the dangerous, joyful, heartbreaking road we were travelling together. He got up to go into the dispensary and carry on his work, and I remembered why I had come.

'I found these peaches in the bazaar. There hasn't been any good fruit for such a long time. I had to bring them for you. I'm taking some home for us, too.'

'Then take these with you. I'll come and eat them at your house. I'll come to dinner,' he said.

'No, don't. Naresh won't like it. He was very irritable last night.'

'Was he? Why?'

There was that untouched innocence about Martand, a purity without which I could no longer live. That was why I couldn't give him up, however long we had to wait for this to work out. There was so little time to talk about personal problems, and when we were alone together we did not talk.

At the door to the dispensary Martand turned around to say, 'Let me speak to Naresh about us.' It was not the first time he had urged this.

'No!' I cried.

'He is too good a man to deceive.'

'Don't you know anything about human nature?' Panic made me shrill.

'All right, all right,' said Martand softly. 'I must go now, my love. Take care, won't you, as you drive home. It's a bad day today. Some of my staff are giving trouble and refusing to work. And thank you for the peaches.' I left his share on the table. For my cheap ideas of safety – my safety – I would deprive myself of the sight of him and the sound of his voice this evening. Safety in a mad world did not make much sense, and I was not made for living a double life. My endurance was wearing thin. One of these days I would throw myself on Naresh's mercy and tell him. One of these days, but not today.

At home I washed the peaches and put them on the dining table. When I went back into the dining room with plates and cutlery, Naresh was standing there staring at them.

'You're home early,' I said and I knew in a flash it was time – if at once – to tell him about Martand.

Naresh was waiting, a queer stricken look on his face of half-knowing, fearing, unbelieving, and the tension grew intolerable. I went up to him and he put his arms around me.

'Then you hadn't heard,' he said. 'That's why I came – to tell you.'

I looked up at him, all my terrors realized.

'Martand was stabbed,' he said, 'less than half an hour ago. Not by a refugee, by one of his own assistants. They sent for me immediatcly. I was with him when he died.'

Naresh sobbed while I stood holding him, deadly calm, as if I had known this would happen. I still had my sight and hearing, but that was all. Nothing could move me any more.

'We'll go away,' he wept, 'we'll go away.'

Yes, I thought, to a place where there was enough of everything and charity could be a virtue, not a crime. We would go where my child could be born in safety, and where a man would not be murdered for loving mankind. As we clung together I knew we had both changed invisibly beyond recall. Naresh, mourning Martand, had found his faith in goodness again, while I, surely as I breathed, knew that everywhere within hand's reach was evil.

The Rainmaker

Githa Hariharan

When I got to the end of the chapter, I shut the book and looked out of the window. I saw a familiar figure, untidily wrapped in a drab sari, sitting under the peepal tree.

It was raining. The rain was stubborn but toothless, the half-hearted kind that falls towards the end of the season. There was a damp, soggy feel to the air, like the inescapable smell of something greasy left unwashed for days.

Through the fragile, transparent screen of rain, I saw my mother from the window of my room. She looked exactly as she did nine years ago; like the framed photograph that went up on our living-room wall then. The spineless rain, my mother under the tree, and I at the window. For a moment, everything shrank, and was reduced to the three sole visible parts of an intriguing, irresistible picture. It was like opening the door of a forgotten, unused room by accident, and stumbling on a mysterious discovery.

My mother sat on the ground under the large, shady peepal tree, doing nothing. She did not stare blankly into space, a look I could not easily separate from her face. Instead she sat quietly absorbed, thinking the kind of normal thoughts a woman might think, resting briefly under a tree in her own backyard.

I quickly picked up the book and forced myself to begin the next chapter. The final exam, for those who did not take it in May, and for those who did and failed, is in October after the rains. Some people say you sit for an exam, and others say you take one; or you read for one. You also appear for an exam. I did not appear.

My younger sister Gouri, who has always needed me to mother her, held me in her arms when I buried my face in her neck, crying weakly. She sent home the doctor's report and packed my suitcase in our hostel room.

How long could I keep myself from looking out of the window so close to my desk? I took a quick look and saw that she was still there. She now looked up at the tapering leaves that dripped a second rain on her, a measured drip-drop that slipped down the tips of the leaves.

If Gouri had been at home, perhaps we would have gone down together, called our mother and brought her into the house, out of the rain. But I was alone upstairs. In the living-room downstairs, my father, who opted for early retirement, would be seated before his chessboard, trying out the moves he had memorized the night before. On the table beside him, the game of patience he had earlier laid out would be ready for his mid-morning break from chess. In the sick-room next door, my mother's mother, matriarch, would be napping, snoring like a baby after the ayah had given her a sponge bath.

I didn't go down to take a closer look at my mother. Nor did I wonder why she had come. Instead I watched her through the brittle rain, wondering why she had chosen the peepal tree, and not the gulmohar that in a way owed its life to her. I thought it would have made her happy to see the gulmohar still surviving, even flourishing, in spite of its yearly invasion by caterpillars.

I must have been about eight I think, when the gulmohar was first attacked by a horde of furry, black caterpillars. The large tree was covered overnight with hairy inches of movement. Just looking at them made Gouri and me itch all over. The caterpillars didn't remain on the tree either. Some fell off the leaves when the wind blew, and they crawled all over the backyard. The wall behind the house looked diseased, with ugly strips of black plastered here and there, like bristly eruptions.

The tree was close to the wall that divided our backyard from the neighbour's. Many of its large branches overhung the wall, sweeping it, shading a corner of the yard next door.

The neighbour, an avuncular old man who liked to keep his yard tidy, complained about the caterpillars. He wanted us to cut down the gulmohar, or at least prune its branches severely. He was polite and apologetic at first, but as the weeks went by, and both tree and caterpillars remained untouched, we often heard my grandmother and the neighbour screaming insults at each other across the wall. There was not much else the poor old man could do. My grandmother looked different now, but then she was a woman with a large, purposeful body. Her face was stunning, like a Kathakali mask. Against a very dark skin, her wiry, curly hair was completely silvery-white; and she had a pair of cruelly thick and mobile, ash-coloured eyebrows.

My grandmother never let a challenge escape her. She chose, for instance, two perfect sons-in-law. She, like my mother, had two daughters. The elder one, as fat as my mother but less shadowy and withdrawn, married young and produced six children, four of them boys.

For her timid younger daughter, my grandmother drew in an unbelievable catch. My father was a fair, slim young man with ridiculously even features; and as quiet and soft-spoken as his bride-to-be. I don't know how they arrived at the agreement, but it was all very convenient. My grandmother had the house; her daughter, a harmless, docile girl given to sudden bouts of weeping, needed looking after as much as she needed a husband; and my father moved into the house as if a pliable, obedient son had been acquired, not the usual autocratic son-in-law.

In the pictures I had in my head, my parents looked strange together. He, so smooth and beautiful, and she, squat, muddy-complexioned, with untidily meeting eyebrows and oily hair. I couldn't recall a raised voice, a single angry word between them. They yielded to my grandmother on all things, both large and small, but in a sense it made no difference to either of them. There was something self-contained about the two of them – his quiet hours at solitary games, her endless hours lying down on the bed in that room, still and staring.

A few years after my mother died, my father decided to retire. He now spent all day at his chessboard, learning mastergames by heart. He still played alone, or with some alter ego we had not met, taking hours over every move; planning strategy.

No one went to the backyard now. In any case it was never a real garden. No one bothered with it and it was just there, a space that belonged to us, merely two trees, overgrown patches of shrubs and weeds. Not one of us had thought of either nurturing or beautifying this bit of land. It was just property. After the briefly absorbing quarrel over the gulmohar tree, the yard went back to being neglected and forgotten. The caterpillars came and went every year, but we never heard from the neighbour after the surprising visit my shy, tongue-tied mother paid him one day.

My mother had always been different from other mothers – I dimly recognized this as a child does – but the year of the caterpillar-stricken gulmohar, it sank in with all its weight. I acknowledged the fact to myself, though not in words I could recall.

Between the spells of rain, the sky was tainted by a foreboding grey, like a visible absence of clear light. Then the rain came back and so did my mother, to her now regular post under the peepal tree.

The rain dampened everything and left its tearful imprint wherever it fell. It no longer poured; but though it was soft-spoken and insubstantial, the rain pervaded every corner of the house, the sky and the backyard. Everything was stale and overripe, but also shadowy, as if it was the right season for ghosts.

When Gouri and I were children, we used to make up ghost stories to scare each other. Night after night, we huddled close together in bed and took turns at recounting grotesque true stories of a bloody arm that stuck out of a concrete wall, and an old, old woman with no teeth, just a pair of fangs, who waited for us behind the door of a closed room.

But our best stories were about another pair of ghosts. One rose from a pond, bloated with slushy water, dripping and shapeless, for a brief view of the world above. We had decided this ghost could not leave the swampy pond. Condemned to an eternal life in the muddy water, the ghost could push itself to the surface slowly, inch by inch, and emerge up to its waist once a year.

The other one was a tree-spirit, a ghost who possessed a tree. This was harder to see or describe. Like the pond-ghost, the tree-spirit was also a damp ghost, but it was not loaded down with mud or submerged in water. You knew a tree was possessed if it suddenly turned wet and weepy. It dripped a rain like pathetic, pointless tears.

I had got used to seeing the woman under the tree often. She was there several times a week, always in broad daylight, thought only when it rained. A few times she looked up and our eyes met. There was no recognition in hers, but she gave me, once or twice, a pleasant, neighbourly smile so that I couldn't help responding.

Only once she came into the house. This was much later, when she no longer smiled at me or sat still and absorbed. By this time she looked puzzled, a little more like she used to when she was alive.

When I saw her get up one rainy afternoon and walk towards the house, moving out of my view, I went downstairs. I went to the sick-room where she used to be, and where her mother now sat propped up by pillows in bed all day. I saw the old woman sitting there, completely senile, a cabbage, or a caterpillar, chewing and chewing though her false teeth lay in a box by her bed, and her mouth was full of nothing but spit.

I ignored her, as we all did now. Since she had arranged a hired help for herself before she got sick, no one ever went into the room if they could help it. I opened a cupboard, though I was not sure what I was looking for. The empty cupboard was like a dark room, and I stood outside where it was lit, looking in.

Then I smelt the stale scent of coconut oil that has been left on unwashed hair for days. I turned around and saw her standing behind me.

The day she died I had come to the room like this, almost accidentally, looking for nothing in particular. She lay on her bed as usual, but she gave me a long, searching look.

She called me to her and said, I am so tired. I just can't go on any more. She spoke calmly, so rationally that even when she told me about the pills and where the empty bottle was in the cupboard, I didn't really think there was anything wrong. I was eleven then. I could only believe in a momentous event – life or death – if it was loud and dramatic; something big enough to be real.

About a month after she died, Gouri and I stopped our storytelling of ghosts. I never imagined for a moment that my mother now belonged to that border world of half-existence, or that she was a source of terror to those still living.

I looked at her as she stood in that room, and it was impossible to feel fear or love for this domesticated ghost that shuffled behind me gently, looking at me each time I turned around with the bewildered longing I had seen on her face before.

She followed me upstairs, and alone in my room, I tried to talk to her. I couldn't bring myself to ask her about herself, so I told her little bits of recent news: that Gouri and I were in college, in the hostel, that my father had retired, I had been sick, and that her mother would probably soon die.

She smiled and nodded, and sat on my bed. After a while, I changed and got into bed, and though I could not see her with the light off, I felt her presence sitting by me. I heard the rain pattering outside, over and over like an endless refrain.

In the morning when I woke up, she was gone. She never came into the house again. She had gone, it seemed, a second time; escaped not only my earlier, childish need for her, but now even my stale grief, or my guilt that I had not, could not have understood. How can a silent ghost, a vulnerable tree-spirit, console or forgive?

Looking at the rain before I went back to my books, I remembered a nonsensical chant Gouri and I had made up long ago. A rain of frogs, a rain of pearls, a rain of fire, a rain of ashes, a rain of kisses. Now I caught myself adding, flowers rained from her hands, tears rained down her cheeks, blows rained upon her. Then, it has rained itself out.

A few days later, she was back under the tree. She sat there, looking up at the shiny, dripping leaves with an incredible yearning. I looked at her and the leaves together, like two objects so inseparable that they had to be seen in the same frame.

This is the last rain of the season, I suddenly though to myself, as if I knew it for a fact. And at that exact moment, like a piece of perfect timing, she turned her head and looked up at my face.

She was smiling, not her polite, neighbourly smile, but something full-fledged and glorious. I gasped and moved away from the window, shocked at last.

Then the peepal tree, now that it was no longer raining, shook off its sparkling costume with ease. It looked banal somehow, like an ordinary shade-giving backyard tree. And though I did not see her again, though I did not as yet know if anything had changed, I felt the child in me leave that room forever.

Menaka Tells Her Story

Priya Sarukkai Chabria

Listen: Nothing was happening in Indralok. The rakshasas had been subdued, the Naag kings, jewelled hoods folded, were slumbering over their treasures, Lord Indra had laid aside his weapons; his attributes, the thunderbolts lay docilely at his feet over a pile of snoozing storm clouds. He yawned. Lord Indra had been winning at dice for a thousand years and He was hugely bored. That's when Narada Muni materialized and asked, 'God, who among your celestial nymphs is the best dancer?'

Lord Indra devised a competition. His nightly routine was to quaff nine jars of soma, then crash. He decided the apsara who kept Him awake with her dancing till He finished the last drop of the tenth jar would be declared the winner. Since I, Menaka had just returned from a dance sabbatical my colleagues requested me to win; they were tired of dancing for Him. So it was that Tillotama and Rambha dropped out early while Urvashi gamely kept on till the ninth round. 'Menaka is Best Apasaraaaa!' Lord Indra announced, and snored, the tenth jar rolling dry.

Down on earth, Sage Vishwamitra was in deep meditation. It was his four hundred and ninetieth year. The heat of his tapas was scorching the lowest of Lord Indra's Seven Heavens; we heard the denizens there were scampering on tiptoe. It was reported that Sage Vishwamitra would soon gain enough power to rocket into Lord Indra's throne and topple Him.

Lord Indra decided on damage control: Despatch an apsara. It's a barbaric practice. Sages are at their most corruptible when poised to gain power over the Gods. But if they see us, they blow their minds on pleasure and forget Heaven. So the myth goes. None can imagine how demeaning it is for us apsaras – sky-crossing nymphs who devote our immortality to the arts – to be dangled as bait. Besides, we face blazing heat, the lust of ancient sages, their dragon breath. Some haven't brushed their teeth for eight hundred years.

Pause, and think about it, will you? I, Menaka, and my colleagues, the apsaras, lustrous with the beauty of creativity, were offered as entertainment for pleasure seekers; our supple artistry bent to serve as distractions; our bodies, filled with the play of fecund energies were reduced to goods. This is why we are flippant; changeling creatures, bright and more frivolous than can be suspected by mortal minds for we guard deep secrets. Our work is dangerous and free. We use our laser-sharp minds to conceal ourselves; we pass off as our disguises.

In the bad old days before globalization we dancing girls didn't have career options. There was only one sponsor for our art – Lord Indra. Having 'won ' the dance contest I was chosen for the job. I borrowed from the rainbow its colours for my robes, acquired the patter of raindrops for footsteps, arrayed my hair like monsoon clouds and presented myself to Lord Indra. When I left Indralok I was in disarray.

I homed in on blistering heat, towards a huge anthill shining white-hot. That had to be Vishwamitra! I conjured fragrant dew from my body the way mortals sweat. My dew-sweat washed away the anthill. O the disappointment! But I'm a professional. I stamped my feet and a garden bloomed.

I summoned mist and light, I was softly backlit to perfection.
I began singing seductively and low so that the tune snaked
into his mind like a recurrent dream. His eyelids fluttered. I
began my dance, trailing my shimmering veils over his limbs,
dropping them; I began the Air Tumbling Siren Sequence.
It's the last part of the routine. I tumbled before his closed
eyes, limbs splayed and circling, for five years, non-stop. I was
dizzy.

I thought: One last effort before I rest. I leapt into a 360-
degree pirouette in the air while breaking my garlands and
showering petals on him, I somersaulted in slow motion. I
was upside down, hair streaming, hip bells slipping on my
breast, skirt on my face when he awoke. He looked, stretched
one arm to grab mine dangling above his face; one tug and I
was below him. That was it.

He wasn't good. Even ... but that's another story. Vish came
instantly; but what can you expect from a sage who's been
planning to usurp the power of the Gods? After a decade his
body temperature fell to 300 degrees centigrade so I knew all
but the Lower Heavens should have cooled to egg-cooking
heat. Another twenty years passed in singing, dancing and
sex. Vish said he felt hungry – for food. This meant he had
lost most of his supra-natural powers. I was delighted for I
could now plan to return home and seek solace, solitude,
through my art. I became a food gatherer for him like archaic
mortal tribeswomen. I diligently gathered fruits and berries,
de-stoned and de-pipped each one before popping these into
his open mouth. An artist, reduced to this!

At this point in my story I must inform you that we apsaras
aren't like mortal women who are routinely raped but still
get pregnant; we need the touch of tenderness to become
fecund. He was tender with me once and I conceived. I told
Vish he *must* be a good father, I needed him to bond with his
child. I remember he rolled his eyes.

One day as he was resting his head on my growing middle
and munching red berries the inevitable happened. I had

forgotten to de-pip one berry. The pip lodged in a cavity in his teeth. He tried to dislodge it with his tongue. He failed. He tried to poke it out with a twig; he failed. With his remaining powers he roared out a mantra. The pip shot out of his mouth. 'Menaka,' Vish cursed, 'you are like this berry. Sweet and luscious on the outside but stony inside. I realize Lord Indra sent you to snare me! I reject you through all Time, Space, and Meaning. I return to my austerities.' He turned to the pip. 'O little pip, you have led me back into awareness. For this flourish!' Immediately a great tree grew between us.

'Vish,' I shouted, 'think of your innocent child! Wait for her birth! Don't you desert her!' But Sage Vishwamitra was storming into the forest without a backward glance.

A famous painting by Raja Ravi Varma 'illustrates' this momentous event. It shows Vish as tall and handsome turning his face away from me, who, contrite in white garments is offering my little Sakuntala to him for acceptance. I contest this. Vish was never any woman's dream and he abandoned me *before* I gave birth. The painter even got the colour of my garments wrong: These were sapphire with sadness, ruby with rage, amethyst with anxiety for my child. But this is the way my story is told. I've been misrepresented all through time, and that too in the arts that I so love.

I gave birth to my daughter in a sacred grove and placed her near the Sakuntala birds that I knew make good foster mothers. Only once could I let her suckle before I was vaporized back to Indralok, sucked up to my crystal palace in the Seventh Heaven.

Mine was the first girl-child to be abandoned; I, Menaka, am remembered throughout history as the first mother to have abandoned her daughter. The truth is my Sakuntala wouldn't have survived the passage back to Heaven for she was half mortal. I flung myself on the brilliant encrusted floor of my aerial chamber. And wept. Raged and wept.

I didn't attend the celebrations Lord Indra commanded in my honour. I didn't hear the conch and drums; I only heard my daughter's weak cries. 'Menaka is weeping for her daughter,' Lord Indra was informed. 'Menaka will be rewarded when she is ready', He graciously announced. Once a month low-ranking nymphs would ferry my sparkling teardrops in their palms as proof of my grief.

Lord Indra didn't know I'd never be ready. He didn't know I'd never forget Sakuntala's small hands on me, her wee mouth at my nipple, her little red face, her wet crinkled ears, her tiny feet that had kicked me in the womb. There's insufficient time in the universe to forget such moments.

I continued to weep. Being a water nymph I can weep endlessly, and I float on water, gathering it towards me. My tears piled beneath me, couching me in their sad rocking. I had twelve feet of tear-bed under me when the Chief of Security – an odious giant I had once spurned – dropped by to check me out. He peered down to hear me murmur, 'Sakuntala, how I wish, I wish, wish ...' Twisting his moustache he roared with pleasure, 'I'll report you!'

'What!' Lord Indra's voice boomed through the heavenly halls, 'You say she still weeps for Vish – wamitra!' Silence flooded Indralok. Then His voice boomed in laughter. 'Impossible! How can she desire anyone after being with Me!'

The only person I wished to be with was my infant daughter, back on earth. But I knew if *I* asked for the boon of mortality Lord Indra never would have granted it. My desire had to be camouflaged and strike Him as His Own Brilliant Idea. So I continued weeping. It was a risky plan I devised, but what option did I have in those primitive patriarchal times?

Years passed. Emissaries came and went; my tear-bed was a tower almost two hundred feet high when the Chief of Security paid another visit. He was a dot way below. He shouted up to me, 'How dare you be so high-and mighty, nymph?' I didn't bother to reply. He stomped out.

'Impossible, but true!' Lord Indra materialized in a flash of lightning. 'Menaka has dared to build herself a throne higher than Mine!' Thunder swept through my chambers, lightning fell like rain on the floating balconies; squalls twisted my towering tear-bed. 'Menaka, you've become arrogant. You must be punished!'

At last! I flew down, flung myself at His feet and agreed, 'Yes, Highest of Gods, I deserve the worst punishment! Change me into a mortal.' 'Ha, I will,' He roared. Space blackened and I waited, but nothing was happening. I opened my eyes to redness; Lord Indra was red with rage.

'Do you think I, Lord Of The Universe, don't have ideas of My Own?' He stormed. I couldn't see for the lightning. I heard the roar of thunder, His Voice. 'Hear My Curse. You will continue to dance till the end of Time.' Lord Indra paused; lightening quaked but did not fall. With a crash He resumed, 'Henceforth you will dance in every man's heart - but with a difference. He might lust and assault your ilk. Yet he will not be blamed nor need hold himself responsible for the violence he inflicts, for you, Menaka, most foul temptress, will be charged, each time, with robbing him of virtue. You will be held liable.'

'Great God,' I cried, 'Do not make me wreck frail humanity, nor become a symbol of shame to my own sex. Remember I once saved Indralok! It was I who saved Your throne!'

Those were classical times; even Gods had to heed certain rules. Lord Indra stroked His beard, tickled His chin, He burped. This meant He was thinking. 'A curse cannot be revoked,' He finally proclaimed, 'but it can be modified. To hide your shame you will be invisible to all but the last man you slept with. Now you're banished.' Even as I saw my form begin to disappear I shouted, 'Embedded in every curse is a ray of hope. Where's mine? I demand it!' Lord Indra chuckled. 'Menaka, for your quick wit We grant you this: If ever a mortal you have bewitched regrets his actions you will be released

from your Curse. Then you can die.' Only my throat and head
were visible when I shouted, 'Great God, Your victory over
Sage Vishwamitra is recorded in imperishable myth. You owe
my story more. I too need a hearing!' As my ears were
evaporating I heard Lord Indra thunder, 'Menaka, nymph
wild in beauty and intelligence, hear Me. You'll get to tell
your story once. This doesn't mean you'll get a hearing,
though. Ha! Thought you could outsmart me? Ha Ha Haaa ...'

Thus began my wandering over skies and centuries. First
of all I realized that I 'became' all sexual urge, the passion of
its fragrance, the very pull. I did not mind this in itself, for as
an apsara I know the pleasures of the Gods beggar the
imagination of the most voluptuous and the most perverse of
mortals. Why, I remember the time – and it wasn't even the
best – when I was turned into an octopus-like creature, every
inch of my skin covered with scented sexual suckers and ... .
But let me not detract from my story. Cast out from Heaven I
apprehended the full import of Lord Indra's Curse. On earth,
the free erotic play that was customary with the Gods had lost
much of its charm, its mutual delights. Instead the dark, violent
side of passion gained prominence, raked as if with its talons.
Whenever I spotted a man lacking in tenderness The Curse
came into play, so I believed. Like an automate or a zombie
rising, my transparent bells would start tinkling in his heart;
my invisible feet would start pulsing their rhythms through
his blood ...

Thus it happened that a zillion crimes against women went
unpunished for the blame was solely placed on me: Menaka
was goading them on, glittering Menaka, the rampant desire
that sings in every body, was egging them on ... But pause for
a moment and think of me. As the erotic impulse descended
into that of assault there was no escape for me screaming
soundlessly, trapped within the violator's body, pounding to
be free. You hadn't thought of me, had you?

But I'm never passive. Through befuddling pain I analyzed:
In no Time or Space or Meaning could such acts – where I

am the cause, perpetrator, violence, victim and repercussion
– be my doing even though cursed. Responsibility lies with
each human being. I set to revoke The Curse.

Revolting against this use of my substance I slid petition
after petition through spiralling warm wind currents into Lord
Indra's Lowest Heaven. Without resting I encoded my protest
on each spy satellite: Not in my name! I sent it out on deep
space probes, I swirled noxious factory fume to spell: Not in
my name! In reply I heard silence. This made eternity lonelier.

This went on eon after eon. I had raged so incessantly that
my curly tresses changed to dreadlocks, my golden
complexion changed to the shine of clotted blood, my
diaphanous garments changed to shreds of trailing smoke, I
thought I was more Apparition than Vision. Though vision is
what I possess: Created to birth lyrics that harmonize the
Three Worlds into One; through my presence to bring forth
impossible dreams and sing of the everyday sacred. For I am
that which rages with fires unquenchable, that beauty without
rules, that flow irredeemable. I range beyond the horizons of
dawn skies, and of eclipses; I could fill ocean depths with light
were I but acknowledged. I could create love like glitter bombs
that show the expanse of sky.

I ask: Can anyone understand my anguish? Do you even
dare?

I've skipped centuries in my storytelling. Let's undo them
for there's one point I wish to clear. Yes, I'm aware of a certain
recorded literary discrepancy: If I were invisible, how did I
put up a sudden appearance on Earth as evidenced in
Kalidasa's lyrical play, *Abhijanasakuntalam*? I admire Kalidasa's
command over language but that's about it. Let me tell you
the famed poet-playwright got most of it wrong – though I
did appear.

Hear my version: My child Sakuntala grew up in a forest
ashram; she was a loving, strong-willed girl. My daughter was
a minor when King Dushyanta – who was hunting in the
vicinity – spotted her. He awakened her sexuality and seduced

her with promises of eternal admiration. As a mother I know Shakuntala fell more for the storybook idea of romance embedded in that encounter than him, *per se*. Come on, he, a powerful king lay at the feet of this bare-foot girl from a hermitage; he wrote love poems to her on lotus leaves and slid them downstream to her; he even gave her, as a promise of undying love, his signet ring – which my child lost one day, splashing about in the river.

As you know he abandoned her soon after saying he had pressing official matters; my daughter believed his every word. She spoke truths like the day brings light and thought no less of anyone else. As her pregnancy advanced she grew impatient and constrained by imminent motherhood. She was told not to climb the trees she so loved, she couldn't chase deer nor was allowed to go boating though she was a strong rower. Besides she was an adolescent who like all others of her age wanted to reap the benefits of being adult, she chose to go to 'her' man.

My doe-eyed Sakuntala presented herself at her husband's court. Big bellied, trusting, she stood in his throne room – and was rejected. Can't remember who she is, my son-in-law-to-be blandly stated to his court; not the faintest memory, he said. It was the same old story.

Sakuntala was weeping with rage, tearing at her bark garments, demanding Dushyanta remember her body, she was the focus of a hundred censorious eyes, and helpless; she screamed she'd rather kill the child than give birth to a lie. My Sakuntala was declared mad.

This is when I turned visible. For I, Menaka, am a mother first. It's common knowledge that there's a wee loophole in every curse and law, income tax *et al.* The loophole in mine was that only once in an eternity could I show up in a shadowy form. I, water nymph, summoned the powers of dew, mist and rainbow to coalesce around me and give me shape. Semi-translucent I descended from the skies to vindicate my daughter and carry her away to another forest ashram. I sang comfort to her in my divine tongue; she wept the coarse tears of mortals.

My Sakuntala, she flowered there, she invented herbal dyes with which she painted the ashram walls, she also grew to be a bard of the forests, of its silences and cries and its rustling lights; the first of her compositions she sang to her newborn son, Bharata. He grew up surrounded by solitude and song. No wonder he became Bharata the wise king of this splendid and sad geography.

I have changed; my flippancy flipped out of me for there is no longer any need for disguise. My heart is like a water balloon waiting to burst. Indralok is now more remote than a faded dream. I tried to maintain contact with my colleagues Rambha, Tillotama and Urvashi. No response from them, for millennia, though garbled versions of their adventures leaked through the stratosphere. I tried reaching Lord Indra thinking he must have deliberately ignored my petitions. But even He has disappeared, His powers usurped by a succession of Gods in a series of avatars.

During the Mahabharata era Lord Indra's power struggle was with Lord Krishna, though more recently it is Lord Rama who is often construed as being on the warpath. But I have different memories of Lord Rama while He was an avatar on earth. He was an exceptional God. Of course He took His duties extremely seriously, but He was mild-mannered, and a keen ecologist, as was His wife, Sita Devi. They spent no less than fourteen years in the forests. In fact, as I recall, She loved the wilderness so much that soon after Their return to Ayodhya for His Coronation She opted to return to the forests to bring up Their twins, Lav and Kush, in this environment rather than the palace with its intrigues. The Twins grew to be fine, curious adolescents. That's when Sita Devi decided She'd done Her duty and wished for Her space; She chose to return home to Earth. Her mother, the Earth, received Her as all mothers should their daughters: Earth tore Herself open to surround Sita Devi. I remember still the fragrance that flowed from the Earth at that moment.

All this happened long, long ago. I'm flying low in altitude and emotion. I gaze at multi-coloured mountains, sigh and rise to skim the Himalayan snow peaks. Suddenly I spot a man tottering out of an icy cave in high fashion Indralok apparel. I dive and do a slow fly past, disbelieving my eyes. 'Hey you apsara,' the decrepit mortal commands, 'come down.' 'I'm visible to the naked eye! What was that Lord Indra said – about the last man I slept with etc.? This relic must be Vish, father of my Sakuntala, she of the pearly ear lobes, long dead. 'Nymph, come down instantly to pleasure me,' he bellows, as if I were instant coffee. Vish has survived, but has forgotten.

I remember Lord Indra's last words: Should any mortal regret his action and take responsibility after feeling my dance – this Curse will end. Or I will. Maybe at the beginning of yet another millennium humankind is finally capable of being true to its name – being both human and kind. It's a slim chance.

There's no way am I going to entrust this chance to Vish. I've to do it by myself. For I'm doing this out of my belief that tenderness is the groundwater of our existence. 'Dance,' he snorts, trembling, 'I'm an impatient man.'

Who knows of my impatience?

I'm going to Air Tumble, pirouette 360 degrees in space and circumscribe the earth like a rainbow on fire. I'm going to flame with dreams and scents sacred. I'm ancient, and determined. I'll dance like never before, with my love embodied in every gesture, my caring in every glance; my sorrow a secret.

And this too: I, Menaka, have decided to throw my story to the winds, for the winds to gather in their laps and let it there grow and spread with dew and mist and rain. Maybe my story will cover the earth as speaking dew that spreads without distinction, touching all; and as mist that dissolves the distance between heaven and earth, wrapping us in its soft hands, letting us into the secret that we see little and so must be loving with each step we take. Maybe my story will fall to earth through the rain, each raindrop holding a fragment, a word, which will release on falling, redolent with truths. Maybe the time is propitious; maybe my story will be heard at last.

I, Menaka, desperate and hopeful, am going to take a deep breath and leap into dance.

The Story of a Poem

Chandrika B.

Sushma is writing a poem. The first two lines form themselves very easily on a sheet of paper.

A tear-drop sways my lashes
as I think of you – even now.

These are very ordinary lines that can be written by any romantic or post-modern poet. If they deserve any special attention, it is only because they are written by a woman. You know, our society – which incidentally includes Sushama's husband Reghuraman too – always go out of the way to find out the latent autobiographical similarities in women's writings. If Reghuraman reads these lines he may not eye Sushama without any suspicion, for he is very particular that his wife, like Caesar's, should be above any suspicion.

Sushama's poems are thus born in a hostile and suspicious world. Look at her, writing the poem at the kitchen table on which lie scattered some white sheets of paper, a broken pencil, a knife, vegetables sliced and otherwise and a few plates. The rings of ladies fingers may be for frying or for making a kichdi. The unripe bananas, drumsticks, tomatoes etc., foretell the possibility of an aviyal. Sushama: Just watch her. She leaves the half-sliced vegetables on the table to write the first two lines of the poem, then leaves the poem and comes back to the vegetables. Now she has sliced a whole lot of ladies fingers into beautiful rings. Her lips are mumbling something inaudibly as she puts them away and turns to the unripe bananas. See her peeling them easily with the tip of her knife. Suddenly she stops and picks up the pencil and we can see four lines of the poem being born effortlessly:

> I remember –
> how we walked huddled under an umbrella,
> how the torrential downpour drenched the lonely street,
> how you put your hand on my left shoulder,
> how my whole body shivered at your touch,

Sushma's eyes brighten up very slowly. The movement of her hands slow down as if she is falling asleep. She is going off – into another world that has rain, the rhythm of rain and electrical finger-tips. Let us leave her there and go to meet Reghuraman.

Reghuraman is standing at the school bus-stop waiting for the bus to take him to the office. Usually he goes on his bike, but today the bike refused to move. So he dropped the children at school in an autorickshaw and is now waiting at the bus-stop. The bus must come soon, for Reghuraman has to reach his office before the red question-mark appears against his name in the attendance register.

Reghuraman's seat in the office is near Shriranjini's. Reghuraman likes Shriranjini. He has fantasised on several parts of her body as belonging to Sushama; but, strangly, he has never wished to have Shriranjini as his wife. As wife he prefers only women like Sushama – who is quiet, who does not talk much, who does all the chores without ever complaining and who is excellent in culinary arts. Shriranjini is good – but only as a friend. A good friend to talk to when your mind feels dry. Someone good enough to be taken to the Indian Coffee House to argue over a cup of tea and masala-dosa about Borges or Aravindan or Deconstruction. If she objects not, he is willing to explore a bit further – but only upto the point from where he can turn and walk back. No, he would never wish to have Shriranjini as wife; let feminists be the wives of other men.

As Reghuraman thus reflects on Shriranjini a bus stops before him. Children in school uniform clamber down leaving the bus almost empty. Reghuraman sits comfortably near a window and continues thinking of Shriranjini. Now he wishes that she comes to office today clad in red silk. As he entertains these simple thoughts the conversation of two self-styled critics from the back fall upon his ears.

A: Did you read E.'s latest story in the magazine?

B: Yes, I did. I think the dissatisfied wife in the story is the author herself.

A: I too thought so. But how can you say with certainty?

B: You see, a colleague of mine lives near her house. He told me that ... er ... there are certain problems in her marriage. Haven't you noticed – all her heroines go in for extramarital affairs. They hate marriage.

A: You're absolutely right. So the affair of the girl in the story –

B : ... is of course, the author's.

Reghuraman who knows E ... the author, and her happy married life, listens with curiosity to the yarn of stories about her. He feels relived that Sushama is not a writer. Or, this rough society would have peeped into his bedroom too. As it is, people will only say that Reghuraman is a happily married man. He thanks his stars for saving him from being the husband of a writer.

Shriranjini writes poems in English and people do talk about her too. Why should all these women have the urge to write? He has read Shriranjini's poem that won a prize from the British Council. It begins:

Strip me and see the real me with naked vision

And be frightened, shocked, morally decayed.

Who else but Shriranjini can writes such beautiful lines?
Strip me ... what an interesting deconstruction it would lead
to! Reghuraman's tongue passed over his lips.

Now there are three more lines in Sushama's poem. They
are:

how each rain-drop blossomed to a flower,
how fire burned in each of its petals,
how the redness and warmth spread through the body,

The incomplete poem rests on the dining table. Sushama,
all her chores over, is having her bath. As the water flows
down her body we can see that her mind is still dazed with
the half-born poem. The noon blazes hot around the house.
The plants drop their heads unable to bear the heat. But it
rains where Sushama is. It rains in the mind of Sushama. And
suddenly one more line is born in her:

how your eyes were hid by my scattered tresses,

And we see Sushama, naked, running to the dining table
to add that line to the bottom of the poem – in a hurry to
catch it before it vanishes. She scribbles it down without even
bothering to notice if the curtains are drawn or if the idle
neighbour's vulturing eyes are preying around. As she writes,
a little pool of water forms around her feet; she runs back to
the shower shaking her dripping hair. As she does so, she
catches a glimpse of herself in the bedroom-mirror.

Once again she stands under the shower, now
remembering Reghuraman's flippant remarks on her body.
He remarked to his colleagues who had come home for tea –
You see, there is only one difference between my wife and
Miss Universe. The curves are in the right places on Miss
Universe and in the wrong places on my wife. His laughed,
enjoying his own joke, while his colleagues, evidently
uncomfortable, made a pretence of smiling. Only one lady –
a Ranjini or so -expressed her dislike. She came to the kitchen

later and tried to comfort Sushama – Take it easy, Sushama. Reghuraman is really proud of you. He talks about you in the office at least one hundred times a day.

Sushama, knowing well that if at all he talked about her, it would only be in comparison with other women, did not ask for details. In fact she did not like the memory of that afternoon to intrude into her poetry-dazed mind. Go away, she told that memory. Don't stand in the way of my poem. Get lost!

Reghuraman comes from the Canteen, his hands and breath smelling of roast chicken, and asks Shriranjini – Aren't you taking any food? Are you fasting today too?

Yes, she tells him. Today's Thursday. I observe the Santana Gopala Vrata for the benefit of my children.

What a combination of contradictions you are, remarks Reghuraman. You hold such free and fearless opinions, but sometimes behave in a very conventional manner.

When Shriranjini refuses to respond, he adds: But I must tell you that your contradictory nature adds to your charm.

To lure him away from the subject Shriranjini asks – Why can't you bring lunch from home? Sushama would prepare it happily for you.

I don't like cold food, he says. I enjoy only hot or warm food. That is why I was particular about marrying an unemployed, unambitious girl. You know there is no refrigerator in my house. Sushama tried her best to make me buy one, but I was firm not to. Now do you understand, Shriranjini, the secret of my healthy body?

Shriranjini's eyes steal over his firm hands and broad chest.

She withdraws her eyes guiltily, gets up and moves away mumbling some excuse.

The poem now rests on the lap of Sushama. She has added a few more lines to it.

how our paths forked in two different ways,
how our memories were blotted out by hands unseen,

I remember all these for ever and ever.

Sushama reads the poem again and again and makes some changes. Outside the house sunlight has started losing its heat. Sushama is very happy now. There is no trace of any fatigue though she has risen with the sun and moved with the sun. There is a celestial rapture on her face as if she is an aspsara who has come to the green woods to give birth to a baby in secret. Her eyes rise from the poem and wander round the room, not seeing the snacks and the tea kept on the table or the time on the clock.

I'm leaving early, says Reghuraman to Shriranjini. I'll not come back as usual after dropping the children at home. I've to go to the workshop to see how my bike is.

Shriranjini looks up from a file and gives him a smile.

See you tomorrow. He pauses at her table to whisper in a how tone – Will you wear the red saree tomorrow? Please – it's a request.

He walks fast without waiting for a reply. Shriranjini looks after him with confused eyes and mind. His firm footsteps seem to tread on her heart.

Sushama's trembling hands are now dialling a telephone number. She cradles the poem on her lap like a baby. She hasn't added any line to it; so we can safely conclude that it is complete. After dialling the number Sushama sits back restlessly.

We can hear the faint ringing of a telephone somewhere far away. It stops. Someone has picked up the receiver. We can hear a masculine voice saying – Hello? Sushama's face tightens like a heart that is about to break. After a slight pause the masculine voice asks again –

Hello? Please say who you are. How can I know unless you tell me?

Sushama suddenly replaces the receiver. Her pulse-rate slowly comes down to normal and the face relaxes. She is now adding a few more lines to the poem.

Though you no longer hold me in your mindscape
You are still the tear-drop on my lashes.
As each rain-drop falls from the sky
You fill my thoughts like the waves of the sea.

Reghuraman and the children have arrived in the autorickshaw. Sushama, hearing the sound, jumps up from her seat and tears the poem to small pieces. She throws them out of the window and rushes to the door to open it before the doorbell rings, for she is the ideal wife and the ideal mother!

Since Sushama has destroyed the poem, the readers who want to read it in full can pick up the verses scattered in the story, put them together and read them.

Translated by the author